RAVE REVIEWS
FOR CINDY HOLBY AND
CHASE THE WIND!

◆

"Cindy Holby takes us on an incredible journey
of love, betrayal, and the will to survive.
Ms. Holby is definitely a star on the rise!"
—*The Best Reviews*

"*Chase the Wind* is like no other book you'll read,
and you owe it to yourself to experience it."
—EscapetoRomance.com

"Cindy Holby proves she is quite talented
with an enjoyable saga that fans will relish."
—*Midwest Book Review*

"A novel filled with warmth and love."
—*Old Book Barn Gazette*

"An enthralling book."
—*All About Romance*

WOLVES IN THE NIGHT

"*Jamie!*" Jenny's scream brought Chase straight up from tending the fire, causing him to bump his head on the mantel. He turned and saw stars circling around Jenny, who was sitting up in the bed with tears streaming down her face. His head was reeling from the blow and he shook it as he stumbled toward her.

"I'm here. I'm here. What's wrong?" He had her in his arms and she was sobbing against his chest. He really wasn't surprised that she was having nightmares after everything that had happened to her, but the way she had screamed her brother's name had nearly torn his heart out.

"Chase, don't ever leave me. Promise you won't ever leave me."

He smoothed her hair, which had gone wild with the dream. "I won't. You know I won't."

"I couldn't find you." Her voice was muffled against his chest.

Chase pulled the blankets over them as he settled back against the pillows with Jenny in his arms. "It's okay now. You're safe." He felt her nod, but she was still trembling against him. "I will never leave you," he whispered against her hair.

Wind
OF THE
Wolf

CINDY HOLBY

LEISURE BOOKS NEW YORK CITY

For my husband, Rob.
For your love, your support and your faith.

A LEISURE BOOK®

June 2003

Published by

Dorchester Publishing Co., Inc.
276 Fifth Avenue
New York, NY 10001

ISBN 0-8439-5208-3

Visit us on the web at www.dorchesterpub.com.

ACKNOWLEDGMENTS

Lewis Sapp and Rick Larrimore, the cowboys

Reece, for his "suggestion"

HCRW for their acceptance, their encouragement and their excitement

And, of course, my family, who has given me wings to fly with and a safe place to land

Wind
OF THE
Wolf

Chapter One

Wyoming, 1860

Jamie Duncan pulled the collar of his coat up around his neck as the bitter wind swirled over the ridge where he was waiting for his brother-in-law, Chase. His left hand brushed against the heavy ridged scar on the side of his face. He shivered when he touched it, not from the cold, but from the awful memories of the night his mother and father were murdered. *Seven years ago next spring*, he thought to himself as he fought back the terror of being burned that still haunted him when he least expected it.

Storm snorted and tossed his head against the wind. Jamie reached down and rubbed the finely arched neck of the thoroughbred stallion. He knew the cold was hard on the old gray horse, but he couldn't resist tak-

1

ing him out every now and then. "Hang on there, as soon as Chase shows up we'll go home," he assured the animal in soothing tones. The dark ears pricked back as he talked, responding to the voice that sounded so much like the man who had raised the horse from a colt. "You still miss him," Jamie murmured. The stallion had belonged to his father, had been the start of his dream of breeding fine horses. Now Storm was all that remained of Ian Duncan's dream—along with his son and daughter, who refused to let the dream die.

"Chase, where are you?" Jamie groaned into the wind. The half Kiowa was long overdue. The two of them were checking the herd for their employer, Jason Lynch. The herd had scattered for cover at the threat of the storm, and the two of them had split up to cover more ground. *I can't believe you're out here fooling around when you could be warm in your bed with Jenny.* A wide grin split Jamie's face at that thought. The man who had been like a brother to him for years was now his brother-in-law, and Jamie couldn't have been happier for his best friend and his sister.

The wind picked up, lifting Jamie's hat from his head and sending Storm into an impatient dance. Jamie shoved back the mass of hair that always fell into his eyes and slammed the hat firmly down on his head before adjusting the lanyard beneath his chin. "That's it, we're going home." He took the reins firmly in his hand and turned Storm toward the south. "He's probably already there, cuddled up with Jenny, the two of them laughing at me out here freezing my behind off."

As he headed Storm down the ridge he heard a yell, and turned to see Chase riding at him with his long dark hair flying behind him and his buckskin in a full run.

Chase was soon beside him, his horse blowing huge puffs of steam in the cold air. "Where've you been?" Jamie asked.

"I found the herd, but something else had been there first." Chase's dark eyes were snapping with anger in his regal face.

"Wolves?" Jamie asked, guessing the answer by the look on his friend's face.

"Yes, they've already had a feast and it hasn't even snowed yet. I tracked them back into the hills, but you know they'll be back again as soon as they get hungry. Once they get the taste of beef..." Chase's voice trailed off as he contemplated the job that lay before them.

"I guess it's going to be a long winter." Jamie sighed as they turned towards home.

"Yes, and I don't want to spend it out here chasing wolves."

"Why, do you have something better to do with your time?"

"As a matter of fact, I do."

"If it involves my sister, I don't want to know about it."

Chase laughed out loud as the horses settled into a trot over the rolling land that would lead them home.

* * *

3

There's something about being in the barn, Jenny thought to herself as she brushed the shaggy coat of her mare. She had always thought that Jamie used it as a place to hide his scars from the world, but she was beginning to realize that it was a very peaceful place to be. Even though the wind was howling outside, it was nice and warm inside in the company of the horses. "I bet you enjoy being inside on a day like today," she said to the mare as she came around front to brush out her forelock. The mare just sighed in contentment, and daintily nibbled at the straw. Jenny carefully worked her way around to the back of the mare and took time to rub the ears of one of the barn cats that had decided to join her in the stall. "Looks like you've got your winter coat on too," she remarked to the tabby as he tilted his head to give her better access to one of his ears. A purr came rumbling from deep within his throat as he leaned his head against Jenny's hand. Both of their heads came up when they heard voices approaching.

"Why are you so upset that Lincoln has been elected?" It was Cat, Jenny's closest friend and the feisty daughter of Jason Lynch, the man who owned the ranch.

"Because it means that we will have a war," Ty replied in exasperation, his soft southern drawl becoming more pronounced. "Don't you see? The South will never stand for it."

"But what does that have to do with us?" Cat had made her feelings for the soft-spoken Tyler Kincaid known from the first day he arrived in Wyoming to ask for a job from his grandfather's old friend. Ty, on the other hand, had been a bit slower to see the light.

Jenny ducked down below the wall of the stall and settled the tabby in her lap. Obviously Ty and Cat had come to the barn to talk and she did not want to interrupt them. Ty was very methodical in everything he did, including his courtship of Cat, which frustrated that assertive young woman no end. When she made up her mind she wanted something, she went after it, and everyone else had better stay out of the way.

Jenny recalled a brief time when Ty had courted her until they both had realized that their hearts were already claimed. Jenny smiled into the striped fur of the tabby at her own foolishness in not realizing that Chase was the only man for her. Ty had been similarly blind, holding Cat at arm's length because of his own careful nature. Even now, when he admitted that he loved the fiery daughter of his employer, he still was cautious, thinking about the future instead of the time at hand.

"Cat, there is going to be a war."

"On the other side of the country." Cat was clearly growing exasperated.

"Which happens to be my home." Ty was tall enough that Jenny could see the blond tips of his sandy brown hair over the stall door. She did not have to see his face to know that his earnest blue eyes were sad.

"I thought this was your home now."

"No, North Carolina is my home; that land has been in my family for over two hundred years." His

5

soft southern accent was thicker now, his voice despondent.

"You haven't been to North Carolina in years."

"That doesn't mean I don't think about our plantation. I just couldn't stand to be there and watch what was happening." It sounded like Ty was leaning against a barrel just outside the stall. "Do you know that if I hadn't left, I would be a lawyer right now?"

"You can still be a lawyer, Ty; you know my father would send you to school."

"That's not the point, Cat." He ran his hands through his hair in frustration, making the sandy brown curls stand up on end. "I cannot stand by and let my entire way of life be destroyed by people who don't know anything about it."

"But I thought you were against slavery."

"I never said that. I left because I could not stand to watch how my brother treated our slaves. And I couldn't let someone tell me how to live my life on my own land."

"What you are saying is that a piece of land in North Carolina is more important to you than I am." Cat's voice held the heat of anger.

"What I am saying is that I have to stand by my principles. If you love me, you will respect that."

"Even if it means you will leave me and probably get yourself killed a thousand miles away?" Cat's voice broke and Ty reached out to take her in his arms, but she shrugged him off.

"It hasn't come to that yet," Ty sighed as he ran a hand through his hair. "Maybe it won't."

"Promise you will marry me before you go."

Jenny ached for Cat when she heard the desperation in her words.

"I can't do that, Cat." There was sadness in Ty's voice and Jenny knew it must show in his serious blue eyes. There was a moment of silence and then the next sound Jenny heard was booted heels against the hard wooden floor, followed by the creak of the door. A resounding slam of the portal left no doubt about Cat's mood. The tabby looked toward the sound with round green eyes and then settled back to purring. Jenny waited until she heard Ty go out the other way before she rose from the floor of the stall.

The discussion at the dinner table in the cookhouse was a bit subdued that night. Jamie and Chase had come in stamping and rubbing the chill from their arms. Jamie grinned and stuck a cold hand down Jenny's back, bringing a howl from her as she set biscuits on the table.

"You boys get lost?" Zane asked as he reached for a platter of roasted beef. For once the cowboy's hazel eyes were not brimming with mischief. He had been the one who made the mail run that day and even his teasing nature was subdued as he realized the impact Lincoln's election would have on the country as well as on the tight-knit group that had gathered around the table. Zane liked things the way they were and hoped life at the ranch would remain the same.

"No, just a bit sidetracked." Jamie, always ready to eat, did not waste any time digging into the meal prepared by Jenny and Grace, the ranch cook.

"What's wrong?" Chase was always observant; he had noticed when he planted a kiss on her cheek that Jenny was troubled. The fact that she had not smacked Jamie when he stuck his cold hand down her back had been a dead giveaway.

"Lincoln won the election," explained another of the hands; Jake always liked to get right to the point.

"So most likely we will have a war," Ty added.

Grace, who was still at the stove, slammed a wooden spoon against a pot. "Men," she said in disgust. "Always letting their pride get in the way of their sense."

"I thought you were raised in the South," Jenny asked the elegant woman who was both cook and housekeeper for the hands on the Lynch spread.

"I was, but that doesn't mean I think slavery is right."

"The government should not tell people how to live their lives," Ty stated.

"So what makes it right for plantation owners to tell slaves how to live their lives?" Grace retorted. Caleb, another ranch hand, looked between the two, his sensitive brown eyes wide at the tension between them. Ty, Caleb, and Grace had all been raised in the South: Ty and Grace on plantations where slaves were a way of life; Caleb as the son of a merchant in a small town. Ty's brother still controlled the plantation that had been in the family for several generations. Grace's father had gambled his heritage away, leaving his teenage daughter to make her own way in the world. She had survived as best she knew how, making a living as a gambler in New Orleans until the man she had thought she loved took all her money and scarred her beautiful face with his knife. Jason Lynch had come across her working as a maid in a seedy hotel. He had brought her to Wyoming and given her a home and a job without asking anything in return. Jason was always taking in orphans; the group gathered at the table was proof of his generosity.

"Instead of trying to solve the world's problems, why don't we take care of the ones right here?" Chase suggested. He could see that Ty was troubled, and Cat's absence from the table told the reason why.

"What's going on?" Jake asked. If there was trouble, Jake wanted to be first in line to attack.

"I found wolf signs up in the north pasture. They've already taken down a calf."

"Game is that scarce in the mountains?" Zane asked.

"Apparently so or else we got us some lazy wolves," Chase replied. "We all know it's going to be a rough winter, the signs are all there, but to have wolves coming down so early is not good."

"Have you told Jason yet?" Jenny asked her husband.

"No, I thought we could walk up to the big house after dinner." Chase's dark, hawk-like eyes glowed as he looked at the perfect oval face of his bride. Her wide sapphire-blue eyes smiled in return.

"Don't you want to hear about the latest adventures of Cole Larrimore and his dog Justice?" Zane asked. He had picked up another dime novel about his hero and was anxious to have Jamie read to them about the

Cindy Holby

Texas Ranger's latest adventure. Jamie had a way of making a story come alive, and the group passed many an enjoyable evening listening to him read.

"You can fill us in tomorrow," Jenny assured him.

"Lord, you guys just aren't any fun since you got married." Zane's hazel eyes were twinkling as he leaned back in his chair. "You two act like you got something better to do than hang around here with us."

"Oh, believe me, we do." Chase grinned devilishly at the faces gathered around the table.

"You two go on," Grace said as she began to gather the dishes. "Maybe one of these guys will help me out tonight so I can listen to the story too."

"Anything for you, Grace," Zane said as he shoved his chair back from the table. He began gathering plates and made a production of placing them in the sink.

"Don't try that nonsense with me." Grace's words followed Jenny and Chase as they bundled up against the frigid wind. "You might have your way with every saloon girl in the territory . . ." The words trailed off as the couple went out into the cold night air.

Jason was not happy with the news of the wolf attack. Chase and the former lawyer turned rancher discussed options while Cat sat miserably silent in the exquisitely decorated parlor. Jenny wanted to reach out to her friend, but couldn't without letting Cat know she had overheard everything. There really wasn't anything she could say to her anyhow. Cat and Ty would just have to work out their problems on their own.

The snow had finally started when Jenny and Chase walked down the hill from the big house to the little cabin that Jason had given them as a wedding present. It was on the other side of the valley from the rest of the outbuildings, but close enough that they could still take their meals with the others.

Chase stirred the fire to life when they came in, then pulled Jenny down on his lap as he sat in one of the well-worn wingback chairs that flanked the stone fireplace. His hands worked at the loose braid she wore down her back until the golden blond hair framed her face in waves that glowed in the firelight. The sapphire blue of her eyes deepened as he brought his lips to hers.

I can't believe that she loves me, Chase thought as he always did when he had Jenny in his arms. It still seemed like a dream to him, that this beautiful woman could want him, could love him, and had actually married him.

He had loved her for so long, since the first time he saw her that day in the mission orphanage when they were setting his broken leg, and the searing pain had roused him enough to look up into the beautiful face of an angel hovering over him. He had actually thought he'd died and gone to the spirit world until he had awakened later that night and seen her peacefully sleeping in the bed across the room. The day she was stolen away from the orphanage, he felt like a piece of his heart had been taken. During all the years that they spent looking for her, even when Jamie had given her up for dead, he knew that they would find her, because she was meant to be with him.

He still marveled that she was his. And now her hands were unbuttoning his shirt, caressing the wide planes of his chest before her left palm settled over his heart. Each time she touched him there, his heart skipped a beat. It felt as if she were actually holding his heart in her hand.

"Chase," she murmured against his ear as his mouth moved down to her neck. "I hope it snows over the rooftops so you won't have to go wolf hunting tomorrow."

"That would be nice, wouldn't it?" He smiled against her neck and she arched her back. "Let's go to bed." The windows rattled with the wind as he latched the door. Jenny was spreading her mother's blue wedding-ring quilt over the bedspread for extra warmth when he turned. It was her most prized possession, along with the carved angel box and Bible that had also belonged to her mother.

Chase wondered briefly what Faith Duncan had looked like. Brother and sister both said Jamie was the image of his father, although a bit taller, but Jenny claimed she did not look like her mother, except around the mouth and chin. She always said her mother had been beautiful and she was nothing like her, but Chase thought Jenny was beautiful too.

His wife had a natural grace even when she was working alongside the men in her usual outfit of pants, shirt, and a gun strapped to her side. Chase had only seen her in a dress a few times—the elegant white one

12

with a multitude of tiny buttons she had worn on their wedding day, which was now safely stored in a trunk at the big house, and the simple blue calico that she wore to church. But there was no doubting that she was a woman. *My woman*, he thought as he watched her shed her clothing and slide under the blankets.

"What are you doing?" Jenny asked when she had pulled the blankets up under her nose. Chase was standing in front of the door with a slightly lopsided smile.

"I love you, Jenny." The windows rattled again.

"I love you, Chase. Now come here—I'm cold."

He was still laughing when he slid under the blankets and took her in his arms. She shivered against him until the press of their flesh warmed them. His hands roamed her back, pressing her hips against his own as her mouth and hands trailed across his broad chest, trailing down the ridges of his stomach, and then lower, until he was overcome with the need for her. His hand sought out her breast, his thumb rubbing across a scar marring the smoothness of its upper swell. He kissed her there, and her breath caught in her throat as his mouth trailed down. His long dark hair fell around their faces when he entered her, curtaining them from the world that began and ended for them in a small cabin in the foothills of Wyoming. The windows rattled with the wind, and the snow blew around the stout walls, but inside they were warm and safe in the comfort of each other's arms.

* * *

Jenny was back in the cabin that had been her home for the first part of her life. Even as she dreamed, she remembered that she'd had this dream before. She was running from room to room, looking for her mother, her father, her brother. There was no one inside, just empty rooms that seemed to stretch on forever. She ran to the window and saw wolves approaching, so she went to the door to make sure it was locked. The wolves turned into men—men with faces she recognized. They kept rattling the door and howling at her. When she'd had the dream before, Chase had come and rescued her. She remembered how he had fought the wolves with his knife, how his eyes had flashed silver with each strike of the blade, but he did not come now. There was no one coming. In her dream she reached out for Chase, but he was not in the bed where she could touch him. All she could see were wolves with the faces of men who hated her.

"Jamie!" Jenny's scream brought Chase straight up from tending the fire, causing him to bump his head on the mantel piece. He turned and saw stars circling around Jenny, who was sitting up in the bed with tears streaming down her face. His head was reeling from the blow and he shook it as he stumbled toward her.

"I'm here, I'm here, what's wrong?" He had her in his arms and she was sobbing against his chest. He really wasn't surprised that she was having nightmares after everything that had happened to her, but the way she had screamed her brother's name had nearly torn his heart out.

"Chase, don't ever leave me, promise me you won't ever leave me."

He smoothed her hair, which had gone wild with the dream. "I won't, you know I won't."

"I couldn't find you." Her voice was muffled against his chest.

Chase pulled the blankets over them as he settled back against the pillows with Jenny in his arms. "It's okay now. You're safe." He felt her nod, but she was still trembling against him. "I will never leave you," he whispered against her hair.

Chapter Two

Jamie had decided to settle into a good long pout. While the rest of the hands were resting up from the never-ending search for the pack of wolves that continued to harass the herd, he had drawn the short straw and been sent to town on a cold, wet day to pick up the mail and do some shopping for Grace before the weather turned bad again. And of course, Zane had reminded him a hundred times to pick up the latest installment about Cole Larrimore and his dog Justice. If Zane had not proven his prowess with the ladies a hundred times over, Jamie would have sworn he was in love with the Texas Ranger in the dime novels. Luckily he had found the book, so he wouldn't have to listen to Zane whine for another week. The drizzle that had made the trip into town miserable had turned into a downpour on the way back. Sleet mixing with rain was turning the road into mush. Jamie pulled his hat down over his eyes and promised himself he would sulk tremendously when he got back. Maybe Grace would feel sorry enough to make him something special to eat. It had turned into such an awful day that he was a bit surprised when he came over a rise on the road out of town and saw a wagon stuck in the mud.

An older man with a slight frame was working at the wheel, trying to free it from the muck that had risen over the spokes. He was yelling instructions to a petite young woman who was standing with the team, trying to urge them forward. Animals and humans were soaking wet and the man looked up gratefully at Jamie when he dismounted and threw his shoulder against the wheel.

"Would you like come with us and dry off?" the man asked when the wagon was free. "We live just about a half mile from here in the old Jordan place."

Jamie agreed. A half mile was a lot shorter than the ten he still had to go, and it would do Grace good to have to worry about him after sending him out in this weather. They reached the small homestead in no time and Jamie left his horse steaming in the barn along with the team from the wagon before he went inside the house.

"I'm Roger Nelson and this is my daughter Sarah," the man said when Jamie came stomping into the house. Jamie took off his coat and hat, slicked back his damp hair and shook Roger's hand. He turned to flash his grin at Sarah and in the space of a heartbeat fell head over heels in love. She was standing at the stove setting a pot of coffee to boil, and he thought she was the most beautiful girl he had ever seen. She was smaller than Cat, but still curvy, with long strawberry blond curls and huge green eyes. Then he realized that she was blind. She held her hand over the flame to make sure it was hot enough before she set the coffeepot down. When she turned to greet him, her eyes stared past his face, seeing nothing but darkness.

"I'm James Duncan," he finally managed when he had regained his composure. "I work for Jason Lynch."

"Must not be much of a job if he sends you out in this weather," Roger commented from the scarred table.

"No, he's great; it was just my turn to make the run into town."

"I hear he's got quite a spread."

"It's pretty big."

Roger seemed anxious for some manly conversation and Jamie was willing to oblige, just so he could watch Sarah, who quietly fixed lunch for the three of them while they talked. Roger explained that he and his daughter had just come north from Denver. Roger was hoping the town could use another blacksmith. Jamie promised to ask Jason to throw some business his way, and his mind began to race as he wondered what he could scrounge up at the ranch to bring to Roger to repair.

The rain showed no sign of letting up and they lin-

18

gered around the table, laughing at the outrageous
stories that Jamie shared about life on the ranch and
the characters he worked with. Sarah seemed especially interested in hearing about Storm and the mares
Jason planned to mate with him, and he offered to take
her out to see them before he realized what he was
saying. When she turned a sweet smile on him and
said she'd love to, his heart did a flip-flop in his chest
and he knew he was lost. Roger did not seem to mind
and was actually encouraging, so Jamie promised to
come for her on the first sunny day.

His ride home was much better than his ride into
town, even with the freezing rain that was now falling.
He was in such a good mood that he forgot to pout
for Grace. Jenny kept giving him strange looks as he
shoveled in his food but he just grinned at her until
she shook her head at his foolishness. Unfortunately,
Jamie's high spirits did not reach the rest of the group
at dinner. Ty had received a letter from his mother
that was full of news of the reaction to Lincoln's election. Cat listened to the report in subdued silence. She
had been keeping Ty at arm's length since the day of
their conversation in the barn, a move that was totally
out of character for the usually impetuous young
woman. For once Zane wisely held his tongue, one
look at the misery in their eyes enough to convince
him to keep his witty observations to himself.

The freezing rain finally turned to snow with the coming of darkness. Jason made an appearance at the end
of dinner and the men began planning another search

for the wolves, which had struck again that very day. Jenny noticed that Cat had taken advantage of her father's appearance to silently leave the cabin, so she quickly grabbed her coat and went after her friend.

The trail of boot prints led to the barn and Jenny stepped carefully on the slick ground as she followed, smiling to herself when she noticed skid marks in the fresh snow and deduced that Cat had nearly lost her footing herself. By morning the ground would have a fresh coating of snow that would make it easy for Chase to track the wolves harassing the herd. Jenny wished the men luck; she knew they were tired of the hunt and anxious to settle into the quiet routine of winter in Wyoming territory. She certainly had her own plans for the winter with her handsome husband, and most of them revolved around the huge bed that took up one wall of the small, cozy cabin.

Jenny found Cat in a stall with one of the breeding mares. She had her arms around the finely arched neck of the animal, her mass of soft brown curls blending in with the mane in the soft light of the lantern. "It's peaceful in here," Jenny said when Cat looked up at the sound of her footsteps.

Cat smiled ruefully at the comment. "From what we've been hearing, it might be the only peaceful place left in the country."

"It does seem like we're heading for war, but I don't think it will come this far west."

"It doesn't have to; Ty will go east to meet it." Cat laughed bitterly.

"Maybe he won't," Jenny said hopefully.

"Oh, he will." Cat dashed at the tears that had started to well up in her eyes. "He can't wait; he's just dying for an excuse to go so he can prove to his brother that he's the righteous one." The mare sensed Cat's agitation and shuffled away from her. Cat observed the mare's actions and left the stall to join Jenny on the same barrel that Ty had leaned against the day they had their argument. "Why are men like that?" She sighed when she sat down.

"Like what?"

"You know . . ." Cat circled the air with her hands, searching for the right words.

"Proud? Stubborn? Foolish?" Jenny suggested.

"Yes."

"I don't know, I guess for the same reason that we're the way we are—so we'll fit together."

"Ty and I fit together, don't we?"

"Yes." Jenny saw the hopeful look on the sweet face of her friend. Cat must resemble her mother, Jenny thought, for there was nothing of her father's distinguished features in her face. Her steely resolve, however, was all Jason's. It had taken determination to carve an empire out of the wilderness and Cat had settled on Ty with the same tenacity that Jason had used to win his land. "Ty loves you, Cat, there's no doubt about that."

"But why . . ."

Jenny interrupted her. "But men have to answer their call; it's what makes them men. Would you keep Ty here against his will when he knows in his heart that he should be at home, defending his land?"

"Wouldn't you keep Chase here if you knew it would save his life?" Cat challenged.

Jenny sighed and examined the toes of her boots. "Not if keeping him here would destroy him. Not if every time I looked into his eyes I knew that I was keeping him from following his true self." Jenny swallowed hard and looked up at the rafters where the tabby had taken up residence; his great green eyes glowed in the lantern light. "There are parts of Chase I'll never really understand."

Their eyes met as each remembered a night of awful retribution and bloodshed.

"It was savage and brutal but that is a part of Chase, just like the loyalty and patience and independence; all pieces that make up the whole that make him the man that I love. I wouldn't change any part of him."

"Just like Ty loving his home and feeling the way he does is a part of him."

"Yes."

"Well then—" Cat's eyes took on the same determined look that she'd had when she had been pursuing Ty. "I will just have to make sure that he has a reason to come back."

"What do you mean?"

"I mean that whether he wants to or not, Mr. Tyler Kincaid of North Carolina is going to get married before he goes to war."

Jenny watched as the young woman walked out into the snow. "I don't doubt it for a minute," she said to the tabby, who was watching Cat's departure with his great green eyes.

Chapter Three

Even though it had only been a few weeks, Chase decided that he enjoyed being married and sleeping in the big bed with Jenny much better than he had liked being single and sleeping in the bunkhouse with the boys. Marriage definitely had its advantages, last night being one of them.

But right now, being married was a disadvantage. After all, he had to get out of a nice warm bed where at this very moment his beautiful wife was lying across his chest, her golden blond hair tickling his nose as she slumbered, oblivious to the bombardment that was about to begin. Chase winced when he heard the crunching of the snow outside and the hushed whispers of his friends. Luckily he had barred the door the night before; he would not put it past Jamie to come in and pitch him headfirst into a snowbank if he found him still lying in bed. Chase groaned when a barrage of snow balls hit the wall of the cabin, only to be followed by several hoots and hollers, most of them referring to the benefits of the marriage bed. Jenny raised her head and blinked sleepily at the window where most of the noise was coming from. A fist began to pound on the door and Chase groaned again when Jenny leaned in for a kiss.

"Are you sure you want to go hunt wolves today?" Her teeth nibbled at his lower lip.

"Let's go, Chase. Time's awasting," Jamie yelled through the door as he continued his pounding.

"I'm coming!" Chase hollered back as he reluctantly left the warmth of the blankets and his wife.

"I bet you are!" Zane was never one to miss a chance for innuendo and the rest of the gang joined his raucous laughter.

Chase flung the front door open and stood with legs spread and arms crossed as he looked down his nose at the group in the yard, who were still punching each other with the joke.

"Geez, Chase, don't you think you ought to get dressed first?"

Chase scowled at Zane as the frigid air blew across his bare chest. Jenny came up behind him with the quilt thrown around her shoulders and grinned mischievously at the guys.

"He'll be out in a minute." She wrapped her arms around her husband and pulled him back, then kicked the door shut.

"I heard it doesn't even take that long," Jake said

24

dryly from the back of his horse, surprising everyone with his teasing. Caleb couldn't help it; he had to sit down on the stoop, his body shaking with laughter, and even Ty, who had been rather morose lately, joined in.

Chase reappeared moments later, fully dressed but looking a bit irritable and startling Caleb, who scrambled for his horse. Chase started off the stoop but then turned and grabbed Jenny, who was standing in the door still wrapped in the quilt. He bent her backwards into a ravishing kiss and the gang started whooping and hollering again as he dragged his hand through her hair. They both came up panting, but Chase was grinning now and so was Jenny.

Jamie shook his head as Chase swung up in his saddle. "Can we get some work done now?"

"You're just jealous."

"Of my sister?"

"Of the situation." Chase surveyed the grinning faces around him but his words were meant for Ty. "You ought to try it, you might like it."

Jake snorted at his words and took off, the rest following with their horses' hooves flinging snow behind them in the frigid air.

Jenny was still straightening up around the cabin when Cat appeared at her door, dressed in a stylish coat with a matching hat set at a jaunty angle on her artfully arranged curls. "Let's go to town." Her golden green eyes were glowing and Jenny, who had learned to be wary of Cat in this mood, looked at her skeptically.

"Why would I want to go to town in this weather?"

"The weather is fine, the sun is shining, and we both need new dresses."

"For what?"

"The Christmas dance, silly." Cat held out Jenny's coat. "It's next week and you can't wear the blue dress again."

"I don't even know if Chase wants to go."

"He'll go. He's gone before."

"He has?" Chase and Jamie had been at the Lynch ranch nearly three years before she had arrived, so she was unaware of his social habits. They had danced together at their wedding, but the idea of him reeling around a room full of people, his long dark hair flying out behind him, gave her pause. "Did Chase ever . . ."

"Have a sweetheart?" Cat's eyes were positively merry as she considered Jenny's confusion. "No, we always teased him because he never stopped mooning over you."

"He didn't?" Jenny was close to being dumbfounded.

"Jenny." Cat looked at her in exasperation. "Let's go to town."

The idea of dressing up for the dance was actually beginning to appeal to Jenny. There was a new dressmaker in town and though she could never afford dresses like Cat's creations from New York, it would be nice to have something new and attractive. Jenny imagined her mother's disappointment if she could see her daughter now. Faith had always wanted Jenny to dress like a lady when she was a small girl. But only a stern look from her father would get her in a dress when it was called for. It had been worth it, however, when Ian had looked on her proudly with his sapphire blue eyes and called her his darling daughter.

Cat and Jenny took the buggy into Laramie and were amazed at how busy the place was. There were soldiers from the nearby fort everywhere and they all were friendly and admiring of the two women as they drove down the busy street. Jenny ignored them. She had spent years hiding in men's clothing and though she could no longer hide her womanly curves, she could protect herself if the need arose. She imagined people noticed her because of the way she dressed and the gun she wore slung low and tied on her hip. Cat smiled and batted her eyes and actually flirted with some of the better-looking soldiers, even letting one help her down from the buggy when Jenny pulled to a stop in front of the dressmaker's shop.

"I hope to be seeing you at the dance, miss," the soldier said as Cat accepted his hand.

"Oh, you will," she assured him. "I'll save you a waltz." The man's companions nudged each other as Cat sauntered into the dress shop and then tipped their hats to Jenny, who could not believe what she had just heard.

"What was that all about?" she asked Cat.

"I told you, I'm going to marry Ty."

"I don't think Ty would want his wife-to-be dancing waltzes with the local cavalry."

"Exactly." Cat rubbed her gloved hand down the skirt of a dark red velvet dress that was on a form in the shop window. "Jenny, you should try this on. It would be perfect for you."

"I can't wear that, Cat; look at the way it's cut in the front."

"It would look lovely on you," chimed in the woman who owned the shop.

"No." Jenny shook her head.

"Try it on, Jenny. Maybe she could add some lace." Cat saw the stubborn set of Jenny's mouth. "Please, for me?" Jenny sighed; she knew her friend well enough to know that Cat would win, so she let the two of them fuss over her and the dress. The scar on her left breast showed, as she'd known it would, but the seamstress soon had a piece of lace artfully arranged and Cat was holding Jenny's hair up on top of her head as she positioned her in front of a mirror. "See?" Cat said in satisfaction as Jenny's wide blue eyes looked in amazement at the woman in the glass.

"I can't believe that it's me," Jenny whispered to the reflection. An image flashed through her mind of a skinny, frightened girl being examined by the flashy madam of a tawdry whorehouse in Austin, Texas.

"You were right, Wade. She has a lovely face and great hair, but I can't tell anything else until we get her clothes off."

"It's not me." Jenny shook her head at the reflection.

"What do you mean? It's perfect," Cat exclaimed as she dropped Jenny's hair and arranged a fold of the skirt.

"You really have a lovely, elegant figure," the seamstress added in agreement.

"Imagine the look on Chase's face when he sees you in this." Cat was closing in on her.

"I don't know." The memory had disturbed her. "I probably can't afford it."

"That's not a problem, I'm buying." It was clear that Cat really wanted Jenny to have the dress.

"What are you going to wear?" Jenny ran her hands down the soft fabric and turned to see her reflection from the back.

"Oh, I have something in mind." The seamstress had disappeared into the back and came back with a bundle of shiny gold satin.

"I've almost got it finished if you want to try it on."

"Cat!" Jenny exclaimed when she realized that Cat had tricked her into shopping for herself.

"Jenny, it's not any fun having a friend if we can't shop together," Cat declared innocently. Jenny had to laugh, and the chill from the memory of Wade Bishop and the time that she had spent as his captive disappeared.

The seamstress promised to have the dresses ready in the next few days and Cat decided that they should eat lunch at the hotel. Jenny agreed, realizing that she no longer needed to hide. She could now lead a normal life and do the things typical young women did. After the long years of loneliness and searching for her brother, she was safe. She always felt protected when she was in the confines of the Lynch property, but she still felt defensive around town. They strolled down the boardwalk side by side, Cat in her elegant coat and hat, Jenny dressed as usual like a cowhand with her gun at her side. They stopped at the mercantile to see what kinds of gifts they could find, and Jenny was thrilled to find a new book for Jamie, *A Tale of Two Cities*. Cat said it looked depressing, but Jenny was taken with the newness of it. The books they'd had in the orphanage had been well used before they had been passed on. She found a nice pair of gloves for Chase and then helped Cat pick out some small gifts for the rest of the hands, including the latest Cole Larrimore story for Zane.

"Don't tell Zane I told you this, but Daddy knows Cole Larrimore," Cat informed Jenny as they dropped their packages in the buggy, and began to cross the muddy street toward the hotel.

"Really?"

"Daddy was a federal judge. That's where he met him. He doesn't mention it because Zane would pester him about it. Of course, that was before Larrimore got his dog if he really even has one. It's kind of hard to believe some of those stories." Cat was trying to save her skirts from the slush in the busy main street while carrying on the conversation, and Jenny laughed, until some activity in front of the saloon caught her eye. A young woman was sitting on a wagon that was hitched to the post outside the saloon. A few of the local whores were leaning over the balcony in their scanty attire, encouraging a drunk who was trying to get the young woman to come down. Jenny squared her shoulders and turned towards the saloon. Cat was hard pressed to keep up without sloshing her fine coat and dress.

"Think you need t' come in wi' me and have a drink." The drunk was trying hard to enunciate but was too far gone to notice he was slurring his words.

"I *know* that you need to go on your way and leave me alone." The words were firm, but Jenny noticed that the young woman's hands had a solid grip on the wagon bench beneath her.

"Ah honey, go on and have a drink with Bud. He won't hurt ya none," one of the whores hollered. The strawberry blond curls of the young woman tossed with an emphatic no.

"I don't think the lady wants to go with you." Jenny had felt the fear that she knew the young woman was feeling and she would not wish that fear on anyone. She caught a glimpse of deep green eyes staring straight ahead as she stepped between Bud and the wagon.

"Eww, Bud, I think this one is jealous," one of the whores yelled.

"Don't you have something better to do with your time?" Cat yelled back.

"Ooohhhh." The whores swooned in mock horror.

"Go on now, leave this girl alone." Jenny's tone was firm, but gentle, her stance wary.

The drunk stood weaving before her, looking at her with bloodshot eyes. "I know you; you're the girl that married that half-breed out at the Lynch place." He laughed as he came up with what he considered a witty remark. "Half-breeds ain't nothin' but half a man.

31

Why doncha' come with old Bud and let him show you what a whole man's like."

"Yeah honey, let him show you." The whores were laughing.

Cat grabbed Jenny's arm just as her hand twitched towards her holster. "Do you know what happened to the last man who messed with her?" Cat pushed Jenny's rigid body back towards the wagon, gave her a firm look, and then stepped up to the drunk. She leaned in close, wrinkling her nose at the smell, and whispered in his ear. The man's eyebrows flew up and the bleary eyes grew wide with fear as he looked at Jenny. She grinned at him and nodded, casting her eyes down towards his crotch. Bud stumbled back away from Cat and crashed through the saloon doors.

"What happened?" the young woman on the wagon asked.

"He left." Jenny had realized that the young woman was blind.

"No, what happened to the last man who messed with you?" Jenny and Cat exchanged looks and Cat started laughing. Jenny tried to shush her but the giggles poured out from behind her gloved hand.

"Let's just say that my husband didn't like it and made sure it would never happen again," Jenny explained sheepishly as Cat continued her merriment. "My name is Jenny, and this braying idiot is Cat."

"Sarah Nelson. Thank you for your help. My father loses all track of time when he goes in . . . um . . . there." It was obvious that Sarah was unhappy with the situation.

"Would you like me to find him for you?" Jenny asked.

"No, I'm sure he'll be along any minute." Sarah pulled her coat up tighter around her shoulders. Jenny knew it must be cold sitting on the wagon just waiting, but she saw that the girl was proud also. Luckily, a man came out of the saloon just then, and it turned out to be her father. Sarah introduced them but Roger was embarrassed that he had left his daughter alone for so long and hastily took to the wagon.

"She's a pretty thing," Cat observed as the wagon pulled away. "Makes that bunch upstairs look like a herd of cows," she said loudly enough for the lingering whores to hear her. Jenny pulled Cat out of the way just as an empty whiskey bottle hit the ground behind them. Cat tossed her head, laughed, and picked up her skirts again as they made their way to the hotel for lunch.

Even though the sun was high in the sky, Chase felt a chill running down his spine and it was not because of the crisp winter air. It was a beautiful day: Much of the ground was frozen solid so they had good footing; there was just enough snow to cover the long grass and it sparkled in the sunlight. The sky was a pale blue, not as bright as Jenny's eyes, but pretty, with just a few lingering clouds hanging about. Everyone was in a good mood, joking with each other, still ribbing Chase for his tardiness. So why did he feel this sense of foreboding?

They were making their way up one of the canyons

that led deep into the mountains. The last carcass they had found had been close to the mouth of several small fissures, so they were checking them one by one. This would be the last one they could check if they were going to make it home by dark. No one was anxious to spend a night out camping in the snow when they could be at home sleeping in a warm bed, so they spread out to cover more ground. The only tracks that Chase had seen had belonged to elk, deer, or rabbit, though once he had seen the huge paw print of a mountain lion. As long as the great cat did not bother him, he would leave it alone; there was no reason why they couldn't live in harmony together. But the wolves had decided to invade the world of men. Why was still a mystery, since there seemed to be an abundance of game in the area. Everyone knew it was going to be a hard winter, but the bad weather had just begun and had yet to take its toll on the creatures of the mountains. So why were the wolves attacking the herd?

He stopped his horse on a rocky outcropping close to the canyon wall. He was up high enough on a rise that he could see Jamie and Ty picking their way along a small stream that wandered the floor of the canyon. His sharp ears could hear Zane and his horse crashing though the underbrush close to the other wall of the canyon. Jake and Caleb were behind them. There was a stand of evergreens below him, the branches much too thick to allow his horse to pass. He left the animal on the outcropping and proceeded on foot. As he made his way, his hand brushed the handle of his gun to make sure it was still there. It was a habit born of long years of caution, something he did without even thinking about it.

Chase stepped into the shelter of the trees, quietly pushing the branches away from his face as he took each step, his dark eyes scanning as the chill in his spine made its way around into his stomach. Something was out there watching him, he was sure of it, but there was no sound, no movement, just the restless stamping of the buckskin behind him. The branches closed in around him, sheltering him, as he cautiously made his way a step at a time. The feeling in the pit of his stomach grew until he could feel it close in on his heart like a fist squeezing the life out of him.

The trees gave way to a clearing, a small cove of soft winter grass against the wall of the canyon where there was a shallow cave. The stream curved around, its banks coming up against the grass before it moved back to the center of the canyon. Chase counted six wolves, three young males lying with their tongues out, their ears pricked towards the stream. Under the shelter was a female with two young pups. Her back leg lay at a strange angle and had an abscess of some kind that she kept licking. The pups had come late in the season and their arrival, along with her injury, had made life hard on the pack.

Chase looked at the three males, who were now standing up and staring down the stream in the direction that Jamie and Ty would be coming from. There must be another male some place, the dominant wolf, the leader. The female stopped licking her leg and pricked her ears towards the stream. Chase felt the soft hairs on the back of his neck stand up and he drew in his breath, not daring to exhale. His eyes slowly shifted up, drawn by something, and he found himself staring into a set of golden eyes. *Strange color for a wolf*, he thought as the fangs bared and a low rumble began in the wolf's throat. The wolf leapt at the same instant that Chase's hand went for the knife at his belt. *Wolves mate for life*, Chase said to himself as the wolf hit him and they went rolling back into the trees.

The sound of gunfire came to him above the snarls of the wolf. Luckily the coat he wore was thick. He could feel his arm bruising with the force of the jaws but the sharp fangs had yet to penetrate the fabric. The heavy body of the wolf had him pinned on the ground while its strong hind legs scrambled for a purchase in the soft mud beneath the trees. Chase tried to dislodge the wolf with his legs, but he could not get a footing either, his feet sliding out beneath him in the mud. He managed to keep the wolf from his throat with his forearm, but he could feel the hot breath on his face and see death in the golden glow of its eyes. So far he had not been able to land a solid blow with his knife. Chase knew he couldn't last much longer. He heard the horses screaming in fury as shots were fired. He heard a howl and a yelp, probably from the female. At the sound of her death cry the wolf released his hold, his head going up with a great whooshing sound as if the breath had been knocked from his body. Chase buried his knife in its side, pulling it out for another blow, but the wolf took off, the hind legs propelling its body from Chase's chest in a mighty effort. Chase was left gasping for breath in the mire beneath the trees.

"*Chase!*" He could hear Jamie and Ty yelling, but he could not draw a breath to answer. He just lay there with his arms spread out, gasping for air. Jamie and Ty came in from the clearing, Jake and Caleb from the other side.

"Did you see him?" Chase finally managed to say. He struggled to turn over and get to his knees. "He went that way." He swung his head towards Jake and Caleb, who looked at each other in apprehension.

"We didn't see anything," Jake answered for both of them.

"Are you all right?" Jamie hauled Chase to his feet by the lapels of his coat as if he were weightless. Chase nodded but had to lean over with his hands on his knees, still trying to fill his lungs with air.

"Looks like you got him," Ty said. Chase still held the bloody knife in his hand.

"Not enough to do any real damage." He could stand up now; his breathing was normal again.

They heard Zane calling out, so they returned to the clearing where the bodies of the wolves were scattered. "Dang, I missed it!" Zane exclaimed when he came splashing across the stream on horseback.

"Do you think these are the ones who were getting the herd?" Caleb asked as he toed one of the carcasses.

"Yes, the female was injured, and she was nursing." Chase waved in the direction of the shelter. "They needed prey, and the cows were easy."

"You mean stupid." Zane added.

"Well, yeah." Chase had to sit down.

"Are you sure you're not hurt?" Ty asked.

Chase rubbed his hand across his chest. "Just bruised, and glad to be alive." He examined the sleeve of his coat. "Glad it was wintertime." The gang all looked at the churned up mud under the trees.

"You'll be stiff as a board by the time we get home with all that mud on you." Zane observed.

"Inside and out." Chase could already feel his body tightening.

They cleaned up the mess in the cove, dropped the bodies between some boulders and piled more rocks on top of them, and started for home. Jamie and Ty told their part of the story: They had hit the clearing at the same time that the wolf had jumped on Chase. They had seen it leap, but had thought it was running from them. The two of them argued over who had killed the most, neither wanting credit for the pups. By the time they hit the pasture, the sun was beginning to set and the sky over the mountains had turned into a soft whirl of pink, lavender, and orange.

"Going to be a pretty day tomorrow," Ty commented when they pulled their horses up to watch the show.

"Yep, and I got me a date with an angel." Jamie grinned mischievously at the group. He kicked his heels into his horse's sides and the animal took off at a full run, the snow churning up behind him. Jamie whooped and hollered as he rode bent over the horse's neck, his voice encouraging the animal in the race against the sunset.

"Now what was that all about?" Zane asked as they watched his wild ride.

"Beats me," Chase answered.

"Just look at him go." Caleb was painting the picture in his head. His portraits were remarkable, and they all knew the scene would be down on paper before the night was over, the man and horse as one, the snow flying and the beauty of the sunset. Even though it would be drawn in charcoal, they would all see the colors.

"You know he's going to beat us to the supper table," Zane observed. They all groaned and took off after Jamie.

Chapter Four

Jenny was brushing Storm the next morning when Jamie appeared in the barn with Sarah on his arm. He had left early that morning with several extra blankets piled on the seat of the buggy but no explanation. They had all put their heads together, trying to figure out who the "angel" could be, but no one had a clue. Jenny gave Jamie a look that spoke volumes when he introduced Sarah to her. Then it was his turn to be confused when the two women explained that they had already met, but left out most of the circumstances. Jamie whistled "Good King Wenceslas." At the familiar tune, Storm came over and politely put his head down to Sarah's level when he was introduced. She held her hand out under his nose and he sniffed at it before nudging her fingers. Sarah laughed and Jenny watched in amazement as her giant brother melted next to the petite young woman. She barely came up to his shoulder, yet Jenny felt that Jamie would have crawled on the floor of the barn for Sarah. Jenny and Storm both stuck their heads over the door of the stall to watch quizzically as Jamie took Sarah down the line of mares, describing them all in great detail to Sarah, who talked to each one as if they were old friends. Storm snorted as they watched Jamie gush over each mare, and Jenny felt herself agreeing with him.

There was a lot of kicking going on under the table when they all sat down for lunch. Zane was beside himself with joy at having Jamie vulnerable to his sharp wit, but Jamie gave him a look that said he would pay dearly if he opened his mouth. Zane wisely kept quiet, knowing well the pain that would come to him if he embarrassed Jamie in front of his girl. When the couple left, everyone gathered at the two windows on either side of the door to watch them go, each one asking the other for information, but no one having any answers.

"He hasn't mentioned a thing to me," Jenny said when Cat asked her how Jamie had met Sarah.

"Me either," Chase added as he dropped the blue-checkered curtain back into place.

"I guess he was afraid of the competition," Zane said confidently.

"From who, you?" Jake asked. Caleb already had his sketch book out. He couldn't resist it when someone new came around, and Sarah was definitely worth drawing.

"Hey Caleb, how about using your imagination.

You know, like you did before." Caleb looked at Zane in confusion. "You know," Zane whispered loudly as he looked at Jenny.

"That's right, I forgot about that." Chase turned around, placed his palms down on the table in front of Caleb and glared. Caleb stopped his drawing with a heavy sigh and flipped back through the pages of his sketch book to a drawing of Jenny he had done early that summer. He had drawn Jenny bathing in a spring before they knew she was Jamie's sister. Chase ripped the sketch out and stuck it in his shirt. "Thanks for reminding me, Zane." Zane gave him a cheeky grin as he bent over Caleb, who was already moving his pencil across the page.

When they were back in the cabin, Chase opened the wardrobe and slid the drawing behind the mirror so that it hung inside the door. "For my eyes only," he explained to Jenny, who just laughed at him. He came up behind her, put his arms around her and began to nuzzle her ear. "Just be glad I didn't have to fight him for it." His chest and arms had turned black and blue from the wolf attack. Jenny could hardly stand to look at the bruises, and the thought that he could have been killed was more than she could bear.

"Well, I'm pretty sure I could handle Zane if I had to," Jenny assured him as she tilted her neck to give him better access. Chase laughed, remembering an occasion when Jenny's "handling" of Zane had left the cowboy limping for hours.

"Now where do you suppose Jamie found Sarah?"

"I don't know." Jenny leaned back against the solid

strength of her husband and stroked his arms. "He's been walking around here all week with a big goofy grin on his face and then he just shows up with her out of the blue. When he gets back we are going to have a long talk."

"If you rope him, I'll tie him down." Jenny gave way to a fit of giggles as Chase attacked her neck with his mouth, but she grew serious when she turned in his arms.

"These lazy winter days are going to spoil me." She sighed against him.

"I know, and winter's not even really here yet. Wait until January; the snow will be piled up higher than the barn."

"Snowed in with you, that doesn't sound so bad."

"If you're planning on getting snowed in here, then you'd better learn how to cook in that fireplace." Chase nodded at the chimney as he pulled her shirt open.

"Don't worry. I'll keep you so busy that you won't even have time to think about eating."

"That's what I'm afraid of." Chase kissed the top of her breast. "How am I going to keep my strength up?" Jenny playfully punched him, and then was horrified when she realized that she had struck a bruise. Chase winced and placed his arm across his chest to protect himself. "See, you're taking advantage of my weakened state already." Jenny flung her arms around his neck and realized, when his hands settled beneath her backside and he pressed her hips against his, that he wasn't as bad off as he had led her to believe. She wrapped her legs around his waist and he carried her to the bed, pretending to drop her a few times as if he were too weak to hold her. He became serious, however, when he lowered her to the mattress, his eyes smoldering like glowing coals as he leaned over to kiss her.

"If only we could stay like this forever," Jenny murmured against his chest as his hands began to trace a now familiar pattern over her body.

"We can," he whispered against her ear.

"Can we?"

"Yes." Her worries were driven away by his kiss.

Jamie realized on the ride home that Sarah was noticing things about the countryside that he had never seen before. She had asked him to describe what he saw as the buggy covered the miles back to her house on the outskirts of town. He talked about the rolling terrain rising up to meet the mountains in the west, the scattering of trees, a rabbit foraging for food, and heavy clouds that were beginning to gather in the sky.

"It feels like snow," Sarah commented as he described the clouds to her and he looked again. Yes, they would get snow again soon.

"How can you tell?" he asked as she pulled the blanket up tighter around her shoulders.

"When you lose one sense, the others take over. Hearing, smell, feeling. It feels like snow."

"Have you always been blind?"

"No, I could see until I was seven. Then I got the measles and a high fever and it took my sight."

"Do you remember what things look like?"

"Oh yes, I remember my mother's face. She died last year—that's why we moved. Poppa was just too sad to stay in our house."

"Our parents died six years ago."

"Your sister is nice. Does she look like you?"

"No, except for our eyes. She has blond hair, but mine is red."

"Red like mine?"

"No, dark, more like copper. That's what my mother used to say anyway. Jenny's hair is gold and mine is copper, and my mother's was silvery blond. I look like my father, or so the people who knew him tell me."

"I guess he was tall then."

"I'm taller—hey, how could you tell I was tall?"

"Your voice is up here." Sarah raised her hand to his mouth level and Jamie grinned. "What are you doing?"

"Smiling, I guess."

"Are you making fun of me?" Sarah playfully landed a punch on his arm.

"Owww, are you sure you can't see?" She laughed at his teasing. "Tell me what else you remember."

"Clouds, I remember lying in the grass and watching them dance across the sky, all the different shapes. And leaves, the way leaves looked when a storm was coming and the wind turned them inside out."

"I never thought of that, leaves turned inside out, but you're right, they are."

"We're close to home now, aren't we?"

Jamie looked around the road and saw her turn up

ahead. "Yes, we are, how could you tell?"

"It just feels like it." Jamie looked at her in amazement. "Are you smiling again?"

"Chase calls it grinning like a fox."

"Now that's something I wish I could see."

Jamie pulled on the reins, bringing the buggy to a stop in the road. He picked up her hand and pulled off the knitted red glove that covered it, then held it up to his face. "This is me grinning." She ran her hand down the side of his face, her fingers slipping into the groove that his cheek made when he smiled. She moved her hand up and felt the lines around his eye and the flutter of his long dark lashes.

"Blue eyes?" she guessed.

"Yes."

Her hand went up to his forehead and bumped into his hat and then pushed it back off his head, which made his hair flop over on top of her hand. "Does it always do that?"

"Yes, it does."

"You're grinning again." She shoved his hair back and laughed when it came back down. Then she moved her hand to the left. He brought his up suddenly and stopped her, taking her hand in his, marveling at how small it looked in his own.

"There's something you should know before you go any further." Jamie felt himself tense up as he searched for the words to begin.

"You have a scar," Sarah stated simply. "Poppa told me."

"What did he say?"

Sarah smiled sweetly at him. "He said you were a handsome young man and it was a shame about the scar."

"Handsome young man?"

"That's what he said. You're grinning again, I can tell."

"How do you do that?" Jamie laughed. He was still holding her hand in his and noticed that it was getting chilled. "I should get you home. It's freezing out here."

"Tell me about your scar first. What happened?"

Jamie sighed and looked at her sweet heart-shaped face turned towards his; she was waiting and willing to listen. He raised her hand up to the left side of his face and pulled her fingers down the length of the scar, ending at the collar of his coat. "I caught on fire; oil from a lantern burned me. It happened the night our parents were murdered. There's more on my chest, back, and shoulder, but this is the worst."

"How old were you?"

"Fourteen. We were sent to an orphanage after that. Those were bad times for us. The man who ran the place hated Jenny. And there were a couple of bullies who did everything they could to make our lives miserable."

"I'm sorry." Jamie looked at her and saw that she was genuinely sorry. She was totally blind and she was sorry that *he* had suffered so much in his lifetime.

"Sarah?"

47

"Yes?"

"Will you go to the dance with me?"

"I was hoping you would ask."

"In case you don't know, I'm grinning again."

Chapter Five

The women had taken shelter at the big house early in the afternoon before the dance. Jenny had left her new dress in Cat's room, wanting to surprise Chase, anxious to see the look in his eyes when he saw her in the deep red velvet. Grace had decided to go also, so the three women spent the afternoon pampering themselves and each other. Cat's new dress was stunning, a soft gold that shimmered like a glowing candle with every move she made. She wasn't a bit surprised when her father knocked on the door of her room and announced that there was a gentleman downstairs to take her to the dance.

"What's Ty doing here so early?" Grace asked as she pulled on her stockings. "I thought we were all going to ride in together."

"It's not Ty." Cat took one last look in the mirror

and picked up her cloak. Jenny and Grace exchanged looks and followed Cat out of the room. Jason was waiting for her, a look of pure aggravation on his face.

"There's a Captain Myers downstairs waiting to escort you to the dance."

Cat brushed a kiss on her father's cheek as she went to the stairs. "Thanks, Daddy, I'll see you there."

"Catherine," Jason said sternly. "What is going on?"

"It's very simple. Captain Myers asked me to the dance. Ty didn't."

"He probably felt he didn't have to." Jason was clearly distressed by his daughter's behavior.

"Ty has been taking a lot of things for granted lately." Cat adjusted the cloak around her dress and hurried down the stairs.

Jenny and Grace peered over the railing as Cat greeted the smartly dressed captain from the fort. Jason smacked his fist in his hand as the door closed behind them. "There's going to be trouble tonight. I can feel it."

"Hope it's not anything like the last time," Jenny commented wryly, remembering her own past experience of standing between Cat and what she wanted.

"Do you suppose that Ty knows about any of this?" Grace asked.

"I'd bet the ranch he doesn't." Jason went into his room.

"Well, at least Zane will have a good time," Grace mused. There wasn't anything left for the two women to do but finish getting ready, and worry about the coming reaction from Ty.

Jamie had already departed with the buggy to get Sarah, which left the rest of them to ride in the wagon. The men had loaded the back of it with straw and blankets and brought it around to the front of the big house to pick up the women. Chase and Ty went in the house while the rest waited outside with their horses. Grace came down with Jason, anxious to see Chase's reaction to Jenny.

Chase had been stunned before when he looked at Jenny, but this time his appreciation of her beauty was mixed with a sudden jealous rage. His first thought was to take her to the cabin, make mad passionate love to her and most of all, not ever let another man lay eyes on her, because he knew that any man who saw her would want her. He didn't even want Ty to look upon her, not the way she looked now, with the deep red velvet dress enhancing the curves that were usually hidden under the men's clothing she always wore. Her golden hair was artfully arranged on top of her head, a few tendrils hanging around her ears, brushing against the graceful curve of her neck, showing the ticklish place that only he knew about. Her face glowed in the soft light of the late winter afternoon and her sapphire-blue eyes were sparkling beneath dark lashes, looking at him expectantly, waiting to hear what he would say.

Why me? he thought. *Why did she pick me?* She could have had any man in the world. If the circumstances had been different, if her parents had not been killed when she was so young, she would have had countless suitors and he never would have met her. If given a chance, would she take back her old life? And if she did would she notice him if their paths crossed? Was it a twist of fate that had brought them together or was it something that was meant to be? It was too much to comprehend, especially now when she was coming toward him and the rising heat in his loins was scattering every intelligent thought from his head.

"Jenny . . ." Chase didn't know where to begin. Her wide blues eyes were waiting.

"He's speechless, Jenny." Grace helped him with his predicament.

Chase looked at her gratefully and reached his hands out to his wife. "You amaze me."

"Thank you." Jenny suddenly didn't know what to do.

"You look very beautiful, Jenny," Ty complimented. "Are we making our entrances one at a time tonight?"

"Cat's already left." Jason prepared himself for the explosion.

"What?"

"She went to the dance with some captain from the fort. We didn't . . ." Ty was out the door before Jason could finish explaining.

"Caleb, give me your horse." One look at Ty's face and Caleb dismounted. Ty swung up and had the horse at a full gallop before he hit the saddle.

"What the heck is going on?"

"Cat went to the dance with someone else," Grace explained. Zane and Jake looked at each other and took off after Ty, the sound of their hoofbeats echoing from the frozen ground. Caleb climbed up on the bench with Jason and Grace, leaving Chase and Jenny alone in the back of the wagon, a situation that wasn't entirely bad as far as Chase was concerned. They snuggled under the blankets with their backs against the bench, and watched the sun set in the pale winter sky. The snow had melted a few days earlier when the weather had turned mild, leaving nothing but a few frozen clumps in the shady spots. They all knew it was just a small break, however, a little Christmas gift from Mother Nature before she returned with a vengeance.

Sarah was alone when Jamie came for her. Her father had gone on into town, anxious for the camaraderie of the saloon since he was relieved of the burden of his daughter. Jamie was more than happy to take care of her. He marveled at how light she was when he lifted her into the buggy. Both of his hands could span her waist with room to spare, yet his knees were shaking when he joined her. She tilted her head to one side as he took up the reins.

"What are you doing?" he asked, curious.

"Listening for your grin." She gave him one of her own.

He picked up her hand and placed it on his cheek. "It's right here."

"Just so you know I don't dance very well," she confessed.

"I don't either. I'm just too big to be a good dancer."

"Then whatever shall we do?"

"We'll just be together."

"I like that plan." Jamie turned the small hand that he was still holding and gently kissed the palm. Then he tucked it under his arm and picked up the reins.

When he came to the road he had to pull up for another buggy that was approaching at a quick trot. Jamie watched in amazement as Cat went by, elegantly caped, riding on the bench with a cavalry officer. "Uh oh."

"What is it?"

"Looks like we might have some trouble tonight." As they rode along, Jamie explained the Cat and Ty situation to Sarah, going all the way back to the last dance when Cat had pretended that Jenny spilled punch all over her because she was jealous of Ty's attention to her. Sarah did not seem to be surprised at the story, which led her to explain the circumstances under which she had met Jenny and Cat.

"What happened to Jenny?" she asked after she had explained the details of their first encounter.

"What makes you think something happened?"

"Cat said that her husband did something to the last man that messed with her. They wouldn't tell me what it was so I knew it had to be something awful."

"The years after our parents' deaths were a lot harder on Jenny than they were on me. I had Chase—we'd met him in the orphanage—but Jenny had no one. She was completely on her own. Even when we were together, I didn't do a very good job of protecting her."

"How could you? You were just a boy."

"I could have listened to her when she told me the priest at the mission was dangerous. She knew something was wrong, but I was scared to leave, scared of what people would see when they looked at me." Sarah squeezed his arm. "One day, when I was out, the priest sold Jenny to a man who was going to California. Chase tried to stop them, but he was all busted up from the renegade attack that killed his mother. They were too much for him, and Jenny just disappeared. She was gone for five years. We searched for her, wound up on the Lynch ranch after we saved Cat from a stagecoach robbery, and then Jenny found us. A lot of men had tried to use her, so she disguised herself as a boy. When that didn't work anymore, she started carrying a gun. She still does. A lot of times she just doesn't feel safe."

"But you're all together again, and she has Chase."

Jamie had to choke back the fear that threatened him every time he thought about the happenings of last summer. Sarah felt the tensing of his body on the seat beside her and moved her hand to his. "We thought the worst was behind us, so we went back, just Jenny and me, to our old place in Council Bluffs. Our mother had this quilt and we were hoping that it would still be there. Jenny wanted it because it symbolized our family, and she was about to marry Chase and start her own family."

"But something happened?"

"Yes, something happened, something terrible hap . . ." Jamie felt the old terror rising within as he pulled the buggy over to the side of the road and took off his hat. His hair fell over his forehead and for once he left it there. "The man who murdered our parents was living at our place. He recognized me because I look just like our father. He knew he had hurt me that night because he heard me screaming." Sarah wrapped her other arm through Jamie's. "He wanted to burn me again . . . he wanted to burn me alive and Jenny stopped him." His voice broke. "She stopped him by offering herself to Randolph Mason—" he spat out the name—"as a substitute for our mother. He was obsessed with our mother because she chose our father over him. There was nothing I could do . . . there were too many of them for me to fight . . . they would have killed me and had Jenny anyway."

"It wasn't your fault."

Jamie didn't hear her. "Four days, that animal had her four days, and when we found her . . ." He took a minute to compose himself. "Chase had this look of death about him. I know him better than anyone in this world and he scared me, but I didn't want him to stop. He killed Mason, but before he did it, he carved on him with the knife that I gave him. It was the knife that belonged to our father."

"Jamie, she's okay now, she's happy. I can hear it in her voice, especially when she's with Chase."

"Yes, she's happy; she's strong, and stubborn." Jamie had to laugh even though there were tears forming in his eyes. "One time I got so mad at her, I just about drowned her in the trough—it was after the last dance as a matter of fact."

Sarah laughed then, a soft musical laugh that lifted Jamie's heart back up from the misery of his memories. "Now that's something I would like to see." Jamie laughed with her, and then turned as they heard the sound of pounding hooves coming up on them.

"Well, there goes Ty." He looked back down the road. "And here comes Zane and Jake. There is no way Zane would miss this. If there's trouble, he wants to be right there in the middle of it, cheering."

"I don't want to miss it either." Sarah had a look of pure delight on her face.

Jamie grinned and shoved his hair back. "Me too." She looked so sweet he couldn't help himself; he leaned over and kissed her. He felt her eyebrows go up in surprise, but then her hand made its way to the back of his neck, so he took his time, enjoying the soft play of her lips against his. "We'd better get a move on. The next people we see on this road will probably be Grace and my sister, and I don't want to get them started on me tonight." Sarah laughed again, and then settled in against him for the ride to town.

The hand that Chase placed on the small of Jenny's back as they entered the dance hall felt strangely possessive. When they were at the ranch he would often touch her, gently stroking her arm or smoothing back a lock of hair that had managed to escape the braid she usually wore, but this time was different. Jenny could feel the tension in his hand as they entered the brightly lit building. By the time they had hung up their coats and whirled onto the dance floor, Chase was scowling at everyone who looked their way and Jenny was grateful that the men had checked their guns at the door.

"What is wrong with you?" Jenny was puzzled by the way he was acting.

"Everyone is looking at you." Chase's dark eyes flashed dangerously as he looked around the dance floor.

"Is there something wrong with my dress?" Jenny was looking over her shoulder to make sure that she hadn't damaged the soft fabric.

Chase was tempted to laugh but his eyes were still narrowed at the crowd. "They are looking at you because you are so beautiful." Her sapphire-blue eyes glowed up at him. "And I want to kill all of them." Chase glared at a group of soldiers who were watching the half-breed with the graceful blonde. His perfect white teeth flashed a smile that didn't reach his eyes, threatening any that were thinking of cutting in on him and his bride.

"I only care that you think I'm beautiful." Jenny captured his attention with her words, and his dark eyes glowed.

"I think we should leave now." Chase's hand caressed her back as they moved around the dance floor.

"Leave, why?" His mouth brushed her ear as he whispered his plans for the two of them. Jenny blushed, then flashed a Duncan grin. "Later," she promised. "Right now I want to dance." Chase raised an eyebrow in disapproval, but relaxed. She was with him and the rest could look all they wanted. He caught Jamie's eye. His friend was sitting in a corner with Sarah, a plate balanced on one knee and a cup of punch on the other. Their heads were together and they seemed almost oblivious to the crowd of people around them. Jamie grinned at Chase as they whirled by. Jenny caught the exchange and stuck her tongue out over Chase's shoulder.

"I guess Ty decided not to come," Chase observed when the music stopped playing. Cat was busy flirting with her escort and had not paid any attention to her friends or father when they arrived.

"Do you honestly think Zane would let him get away with that?"

"You're right; Zane probably has him over at the saloon right now, pumping him up for a showdown." Chase surveyed the room again, taking note of the number of uniforms in evidence. "And when it comes, it will probably get ugly."

"Do you really think it will come to that tonight?" Jenny was enjoying herself and did not want this dance to end like the last one.

"If Cat has her way, it will." They made their way through the crowd to where Jamie and Sarah were sitting.

"What's going on with Cat and Ty?" Jamie asked as soon as they were in earshot. "We saw Cat go by with some cavalry officer, then Ty came charging after them on Caleb's horse."

Jenny filled them in, and Sarah covered her mouth to suppress a burst of laughter as Jamie exclaimed over their stupidity. "Some people just can't see what's right in front of them." He shook his head and squeezed Sarah's hand, then turned to his sister. "Hey, is that a new dress? I thought there was something different about you." Jenny smacked his arm and he grinned at her, his hair flopping over in his eyes again.

"Sarah, I hope you have the patience to deal with this big oaf."

"I'm a lot stronger than I look," Sarah assured them all. The band began to play a waltz and Chase spun Jenny out onto the dance floor again. He had never imagined when he was a young boy that the dance lessons his mother had given him in the privacy of their tent would be so useful, but here he was doing the steps with the most beautiful woman in the room. They fit together perfectly: The top of her head came right against his cheek; the length of her stride matched his; she was as graceful as a swan; and they moved together in such perfect unison that he hardly felt the floor beneath his booted feet. How could the sister be such a good dancer and the brother look totally lost on the dance floor? Chase wondered as he watched his friend make an attempt at the steps with Sarah, who was trying to show Jamie what to do.

"He'd better stick to dancing with the horses." Chase turned Jenny so she could watch her brother's poor attempts at the waltz, his head bobbing as he counted the steps.

"Poor Sarah, I hope he doesn't step on her, he'll squash her." Jenny laughed. "It's not because he never tried. Momma and Daddy used to dance with us, but Jamie just got too big to be anyone's partner." The top of Sarah's head barely came up to Jamie's chest but neither one seemed to care. It was obvious to any and all who cared to look his way that Jamie had fallen head over heels in love. Cat whirled by, a flash of bright gold that reflected the light of the lanterns strung around the hall. "I wonder what she'll do if Ty doesn't show up."

"I don't think that's going to be a problem."

At that moment Ty made an appearance in the doorway with Jake and Zane right behind him. Caleb came over to meet them but Ty stepped right past him, his intense blue eyes searching for the source of his frustration.

"Do you think you should say something to him?" Jenny didn't like the look of things.

"I don't think it would make any difference." They made their way off the dance floor trying to intercept Ty, who was heading for Cat and her partner with a grim look of determination on his handsome face. Ty went straight for the couple and tapped the captain harshly on the shoulder to indicate that he was cutting in. The captain gave Ty a strained look, but his West Point manners dictated that he should give in gracefully, so he turned Cat over, knowing he would return in a moment to claim her.

"What do you think you're doing?" Cat hissed at Ty as soon as they were in motion.

"Dancing with my girl. What are you doing?"

"You've been drinking." Cat turned her head away in disgust.

"And you've been going out on me behind my back."

"I have not." Cat was indignant.

"Oh yeah, well what do you call this?"

Cindy Holby

"I call this accepting a polite invitation." Cat smiled at the captain, who was making his way back to claim her. "If I recall, you didn't ask." She turned defiantly and held her arms up for the captain, who waltzed her away. Ty watched in shocked silence for a moment, then caught up and tapped Myers on the shoulder. The captain shrugged him off and Cat gave her partner a long-suffering look. Ty tapped again.

"We're in trouble now," Chase sighed to Jenny.

"Think there's gonna be a fight?" Jamie had come up behind them with Sarah on his arm. Jenny stood on her tiptoes to see if she could find Jason in the crowd, but he was nowhere to be seen. Grace was standing with the rest of the hands, but Jenny knew she couldn't stop them if they got it in their heads to fight.

"I'm cutting in," Ty said to the officer.

"I'm escorting the lady tonight."

"The lady is my fiancée." Ty stood with his legs spread and fists ready, belligerently anxious for what was coming.

"I don't recall your ever asking me." Cat was determined to make Ty suffer.

"We're going home, Cat, now."

"She's not leaving." The music had stopped and a group of soldiers were beginning to gather on the dance floor. Five sets of shoulders lined up behind Ty and the crowd of dancers stepped back to clear the floor. "But maybe you should go. I hear your mammy calling you." The officer had picked up on Ty's soft southern drawl, which was a contrast to his own sharply clipped northern tones. Cat had chosen well and there was no doubt in Jenny's mind that she knew what she was doing.

"Well, as usual, Cat, you've gotten what you wanted," Ty said grimly. Cat's gold-flecked eyes grew wide as she realized what was about to happen. The soldiers present outnumbered the cowboys three to one, but that didn't matter to any of them. The tension was thick in the air as bodies tensed, nostrils flared, and eyes darted, waiting for someone to make the first move. The captain raised his head a notch, looking down his nose at Ty, and that did it. Ty swung his fist, all of his frustration coming to a boil with just that one look of superiority. After that it was a toss-up as to who struck next. The two groups waded into the melee together, melding into one large swirling, snarling mass of bodies. Jenny pulled Sarah back as Jake and a man in blue rolled at her feet. Grace had grabbed Cat, who had tried to stop Ty and Myers, only to be met by a stray fist. Jamie looked absolutely gleeful as he tossed bodies away, his great size not hindering him at all in this dance. Ty and Myers were rolling on the floor, first one on top and then the other. Caleb went flying by, and then dove back in, taking two men down with his shoulders. Chase seemed to be everywhere, his long hair flying out behind him as he punched and ducked, sending several bodies reeling towards Jamie, who had begun to pitch them in the corner like firewood.

"Who's winning?" Sarah asked Jenny, almost screaming above the noise.

"It looks about even now," Jenny screamed back as she pulled Sarah out of harm's way.

A gunshot stopped some of the commotion; a few well-placed kicks by the sheriff and his deputy stopped the rest. Jason came to the front of the crowd and looked down at his ranch hands, who suddenly were feeling rather contrite when they saw the look on his face.

"Who started this?" the sheriff asked as they all began to pick themselves up and brush themselves off.

"I did." Ty stepped up.

"We did," the rest chimed in.

"Idiots," Jenny said in disgust as Chase and Jamie joined Ty.

"Let's go." The sheriff went out the door and the cowboys followed, the deputy bringing up the rear with his gun on the group. The commanding officer from the fort started in on his own men, focusing most of his tirade at Captain Myers, who should have known better.

"Daddy?" Cat was tearful but it was hard to tell if it was because of the fight, or the black eye she was nursing.

"No more dances for you, young lady." Jason clearly did not know what to do with his impetuous daughter. "Now get your coat. We're going home."

Jason, Cat, and Grace went home in the buggy. Jenny decided to stay with Sarah, but first felt the need to punish the boys for spoiling her evening. Her sapphire-blue eyes were snapping when she entered the jail. Jamie and Chase both came to the bars when she appeared with Sarah on her arm. Jamie called out to Sarah and she immediately went to him, taking his hands through the bars. He pulled her as close as he could and whispered his apologies.

"Are you mad at me?" Chase asked Jenny.

"I'm mad at all of you." She raised her voice so that they all heard her. "I was having a wonderful time until you showed up." She jerked her head towards Ty. "And the rest of you egging him on." That was directed at Zane, Jake, and Caleb. "I bought a new dress and everything."

"You do look nice tonight, Jenny."

"Shut up, Zane. Do you know how cold it is out there? I have to drive the wagon in this dress and the wind is blowing right up my legs and it's freezing. I should be snuggled up in the back of the wagon under some blankets with my husband." She was shouting at them all now, stalking the bars in her righteous anger, her eyes throwing sparks. "But no, he had to go and help his friends fight a bunch of soldiers."

"Jenny." Chase tried to grab her hands, but she stayed out of his reach.

"When you get back to the ranch tomorrow, I'm going to take a whip to all of you—first you, then you, then you . . ." She tossed her head at each of them in turn.

"Okay, Jenny, we're sorry," Ty apologized.

"Yeah, but it was fun, wasn't it boys?" Jake was grinning from ear to ear, which had to be painful with a split lip. They all started laughing then and began talking about how well they had done, and arguing about how sorry their opponents were, leaving Jenny to stand with her hands on her hips, looking at them with contempt.

"Come here." Chase stuck his hands through the bars.

"No."

"Jenny." She stuck her lower lip out and slowly approached until he could touch her and pull her against the cell. "This isn't exactly what I had planned either." He ducked his head so he could look into her eyes. "Are you coming back for us in the morning?"

"Well, I'll come back for *you*." She looked up at the gang behind him. "But the rest of you can walk for all I care." Chase managed to plant a kiss on her forehead through the bars. "Do you realize this is our first night apart since we were married?" She sighed against him.

"Yes, I do. I don't plan on making it a habit."

"Better not."

Ty came up beside Chase. "Where's Cat?"

"Jason and Grace took her home." Jenny flashed her grin. "I think she's got a black eye." Zane let out a great whoop at that news and the rest fell in laughing beside him. Ty even had to grin as he thought about Cat getting punched. Jenny joined in the laughter and turned toward her brother, who was grinning at her over the top of Sarah's head. Her heart swelled when she saw the happiness in his eyes and a great feeling of contentment washed over her. Life was good for them now; they had found a home and a future. All she needed was to get her husband out of his cell.

* * *

Jenny decided to make the guys suffer a little longer the next morning, since she had endured a long restless night at Sarah's. The two women had come home to a cold dark house and hastily sought the warmth of Sarah's narrow bed after Jenny had stabled the horses. Sarah and Jenny had talked for a while, Jenny sharing stories of Jamie's childhood. As the excitement of the evening wore off they fell asleep, only to be awakened by the drunken sounds of Roger Nelson arriving home after a night at the saloon. He had appeared at the door of Sarah's room with a lamp in his hand, demanding to know who was sharing his daughter's bed. Sarah introduced Jenny, explained who she was, and her father had gone stumbling off to his own bed after mumbling an apology.

"He's been that way ever since Momma died," Sarah explained.

"Our parents died together," Jenny answered in the darkness. "I don't think they could have survived without each other."

"I hope to have that kind of love someday." Sarah's voice was strong beside her, but Jenny barely heard her, her thoughts now focused on Chase.

Whatever would I do if I were to lose him? she wondered, already feeling the loneliness of his absence washing over her. She missed being able to reach out and touch him, feeling his solid presence in the bed beside her, placing her hand on his chest right over his heart. The rest of the night had been lost to a restless longing. She dreamed of Chase's dark eyes and dark hair hanging around her face as he made love to her, only to be woken by the lonely howling of a wolf. The noise disturbed her sleep a few times, making her wonder what a wolf was doing so close to town, but she soon drifted off into a half sleep that left her feeling exhausted the next morning.

Since it was Sunday, Jenny decided to go to church before picking up the men; it wouldn't hurt them to have a few hours to ponder their transgressions. Sarah went with her, and the two women enjoyed the hour of worship, which seemed especially meaningful with the coming of Christmas.

The men were grumpy went she arrived; Jamie immediately began complaining about being hungry and what a sorry breakfast they had been served. The sheriff seemed anxious to be rid of the lot of them and threatened to hang them all if they ever caused any more trouble. They gathered their weapons and went stomping out into the bright winter day, all of them nursing cuts and bruises except for Chase and Jamie, who had come through the whole thing unscathed. Jamie decided to spend the day with Sarah, so Zane lent him his horse and stretched out in the back of the wagon for the ride home, enjoying the comfort of the straw and blankets. He was soon snoring away, making so much noise that Ty climbed up on the seat to ride with Chase and Jenny.

"I definitely don't miss that sound." Chase commented as they listened to the sawing noise coming from the back.

"Oh, so there are some benefits to being married?" Jenny slipped her arm through his.

"Yes, there are." Chase arched a brow, then looked over at Ty. "Some great benefits."

"Did Cat put you up to this?" Ty sighed, preparing himself.

"No, but you did refer to her as your fiancée last night."

Ty laughed. "You're right, I did."

"She loves you, Ty, and I know you love her, so what is the problem?" Jenny asked.

"I just don't think our marrying would be fair to her. What if we have a war and I don't come back, or worse, I lose an arm or a leg . . ."

"I think she is fully aware of those possibilities." Chase deliberately guided the wagon towards a rut in the road which brought a curse from Zane as his head banged against the floor of the wagon bed. The three of them laughed silently when the snores resumed.

"I just think it would be better if we wait until this is all behind us," Ty said, resuming the conversation.

"It sounds to me like you two are a world apart in your thinking." Jenny placed a comforting hand on Ty's arm.

"You're right about that," Ty sighed. "But we've got to work it out. We can't continue like this."

"Amen to that!" Zane hollered from the back. "She might wind up getting us all killed next time."

"Yeah, your love life is hard on us," Jake added from his horse.

"Well, why don't you all go get your own and stay out of mine."

"How can we when you keep dragging us into the middle of it."

"Hey, I didn't hear any of you complaining last night. If I remember, Zane, you were the one who said we needed to go fight those bluecoats and show them that they couldn't mess around with our women."

"Ty, I was just trying to help out, you know, keep you focused on the task at hand."

"Which was?"

"Keeping Jamie off the dance floor. Did you see him last night?" They all dissolved into fits of laughter as Zane began throwing out comparisons between Jamie and assorted animals lumbering around in the waltz.

They arrived at the ranch and Ty headed for the bathhouse to clean up before confronting Cat. The rest of them scattered, knowing that they would have only a few minutes of peace before the next storm erupted.

Jason answered the door, a bemused expression on his face when he saw Ty. Usually Ty and the rest of the hands would just walk in the back door and wait in the hallway until Jason or Cat came down. "She's been locked in her room since last night; she hasn't even come down to eat yet." Jason was determined to let the two young people work it out, however, after the happenings of the evening before, he was seriously considering sending Cat back east for a visit with her mother's sister in New York City. Ty combed his fingers through his still damp sandy blond hair and gathered himself before he knocked on the door of Cat's room.

"Go away." Cat's voice was muffled on the other side of the door.

"Cat, we need to talk."

"I'm through talking to you."

Ty tried the door, but of course it was locked. "Unlock the door, Cat." Something crashed against the door with a solid thud. "Catherine Lynch, unlock this door!"

"No!" Ty looked around in exasperation. Jason was standing at the foot of the stairs and the look he gave Ty was encouraging. Ty sighed; then he leaned back and kicked the door. His boot landed next to the knob and the lock gave way, the door crashing open and bouncing against the wall behind it. Cat scrambled out of the bed and dove behind her dressing screen as Ty came into the room. He strode around the bed and ducked as a hair brush flew at him. "Don't come any closer, Ty!" He shoved a chair out of his way and rounded the screen. Cat screamed and ducked under his arm, leaving him with nothing but a handful of air as he tried to grab the tail of her robe. Cat scrambled onto the bed and dove under the blanket and pillows, holding the edge of the bedspread firmly in place over her head.

"Cat, quit acting like a child and talk to me."

"I can't. Now go away."

Ty sat down on the edge of the bed and placed his hand on her back. She tried to jerk away but there was no place for her to go; she was trapped under the covers. "Cat, we can't go on like this," Ty said gently.

"I know." It was a wail followed by a sniff. "Please go away." Her body shook with a sob.

"I can't leave you like this." Ty pulled on the blankets. "Please come out." Cat sniffed again and pulled her head out from under the pillows. She emerged from her shelter, her golden brown curls wild around her face. Ty reached up to push them back and couldn't help laughing when he saw the shiner she was wearing.

"I hate you," she wailed and began to pummel his chest with her fists.

Ty gathered Cat up against him to stop her barrage and tried to smooth the wild abandon of her hair, which was tickling his nose. "Shh, it's okay now." He calmed her like he would a wild colt and he finally felt her relax, the tears subsiding. "Now let me get a look at the shiner." He placed his hand under her chin and brought her face up so he could get a good look at her eye. "Who did this?"

"It was either you or Captain Myers,"

Ty started to laugh again. "Cat, what am I going to do with you?"

She wrapped her arms around his waist. "Just love me."

Chapter Six

Christmas was coming and Cat was determined to make it the best ever. She knew there was nothing she could do to keep Ty from going, if and when a war happened. She planned a wonderful Christmas dinner for everyone at the big house, where Jason would hand out gifts. Jamie asked politely if Sarah and her father could join them, and they were made to feel welcome.

They enjoyed the bountiful feast, opened the gifts that they had carefully selected for one another and then gathered around the fireplace in the study. Jason handed Jamie a Bible and asked him to read the Christmas story. Jenny squeezed Chase's hand as Sarah sat on the arm of Jamie's chair, her face enraptured by the sound of his voice. Their eyes met in agreement: Sarah was the one for her brother. Jenny's heart was full of joy when he closed the Bible and took Sarah's hand in his.

Jamie knew she was the one also, and hoped desperately that she felt the same way. He rode back to the house with Sarah and her father in their wagon, his horse tied to the back for his trip home. Sarah's father was feeling melancholy and decided to go into town for a drink at the saloon, saying he wasn't quite ready to face the night alone. When they came to the turn to their house, Jamie took Sarah up in the saddle in front of him and they paused in the cold night air and watched as Roger drove off towards the town. Jamie marveled at how well she fit against him, the top of her head coming up right under his chin as she made herself comfortable in his lap.

"He'll be gone most of the night," Sarah said as Jamie turned the horse down the road towards her home.

"Will you be all right?"

"I'm used to it. He does all right for a while and then he gets to thinking about Momma and he drinks, then he feels bad about it and he sobers up. I thought that moving up here would help him not think about her so much, but it's hard around the holidays and her birthday. He just misses her so much."

"I guess it was better that my parents died together. I couldn't imagine one of them without the other, especially my father; he was so devoted to her."

"I think that's what we all want, someone to love us more than anything else in the world, like your father

74

loved your mother, and like Jenny and Chase love each other."

"How do you know that about Jenny and Chase?"

"I can feel it. If you listen, you can hear it when they talk to one another, or when they say each other's names. I can always tell when one comes in or leaves; it's like their hearts skip a beat."

"That's amazing." Jamie wrapped his arm tighter around her waist as they came up to her house. "What else do you notice?"

"I notice that your friends treat me very politely, like they're almost afraid to talk to me."

"That's because I threatened to kill them if they said anything at all." He swung from the saddle and reached his hands up to take her down, amazed to feel how light she was, almost like a doll. It scared him sometimes when he held her like this. He was almost afraid of breaking her.

"I won't break, you know." He couldn't believe it, she was reading his mind. "You act like I'm made of porcelain or something." Her hands were braced on his shoulders as he continued to hold her in midair, and he brought her closer so that when he lowered her to the ground, her body skimmed along his. She turned her head up as if to look at him and he noticed that she had a mischievous smile on her face.

"Sarah?" His voice was as soft as the fog that came out with his breath. He had to bend down; she felt his intention and rose up on her toes, falling against his chest as he kissed her. He wrapped his arms around her and pulled her up to his level, never taking his lips from hers and was amazed once again at how she responded to him. "Do you think you love me, Sarah?"

"I have since the first day you took me to the ranch."

"Really?"

"Maybe I'm not the only one around here who can't see." Jamie laughed and scooped her up in his arms. They fumbled around with the key at the door and finally made it into the cold dark house. Sarah went directly to the lantern when Jamie put her down and he knelt to bring the fire back to life. He pulled her into his lap when the flames flared up and they sat with their heads together, soaking in the warmth.

"I hate to leave you here alone all night. Are you sure your father will make it home?"

"It will be the wee hours of the morning before he makes his way back, if at all. I'm not sure if the team can find their way on their own; he might wind up back in Denver."

"Do you want me to go find him?"

"No, stay with me." It was said so quietly, so sweetly, that he had to dip his head to hear her. She turned her face up towards his and he brought his mouth down on hers, timidly, tenderly. She turned to him, her arms crept around his neck and he moaned at the fire that was lit in his loins. He kissed her harder and she answered him, her lips parting slightly beneath his. His hand found the back of her head, encompassed it, and she sighed against him. "Stay with me, Jamie. I am so tired of being alone." He drew away, searching her face, and she pulled his face down again, giving him her answer with her kiss.

"Sarah, do you know what you're saying?"

"Yes, I do. I love you, Jamie, and I know you love me. That's all that matters."

"I do love you, Sarah. I never knew what love was until you."

"Then stay with me."

Jamie groaned and dropped his forehead against the top of her head. "I can either hate myself in the morning or hate myself now." She began to rain kisses on his neck and he felt a burning urgency coil up inside him. His hand found her breast and she pressed it against his palm and he was lost. He didn't know how he found her room, except maybe he had seen her come out of it at one time or another. He just knew that he was on the bed with her, that they were undressing each other in the darkness, which became difficult because they couldn't stop kissing, and then she was cradled in his arms, their bare skin pressed against each other.

"I'm afraid I'll hurt you," he murmured.

"The only way you can hurt me is to stop loving me."

"I'll never stop." He found her mouth again in the darkness of the room.

Sarah's hands became her eyes as she explored his body. Jamie realized he had never guessed that someone so petite could hold such power over him; he was helpless beneath her hands. He wanted to look at her, but there was no lamp in her room—she did not need one. Somehow, the darkness accentuated the feel of her, the softness of her skin, and the sound of her sighs. Each touch sent shivers down his spine. He thought he would die of pleasure, but knew he would die without it. Her fingers found the soft furring at his navel and trailed down, bringing a groan to his lips as they brushed against her cheek. He felt her mouth move up in a smile as he moved against her. Jamie raised himself over her, his hair flopping over in his eyes as he braced his arms so he would not crush her. He felt her sheath stretching; then she rose up and buried her cry in his shoulder, her small white teeth nipping his skin. Now he was inside and she was moving against him. He heard her calling his name, then felt his own world explode. His arms trembled as he pulled her over to him on her side. She felt so small against him, but she had amazed him with the size of her passion.

Sarah fell asleep in his arms, her body curled against him with her head on his shoulder. Jamie felt spent; he knew he should move and he dreaded to think about what would happen if her father arrived home in a drunken state and found them together. He kissed her as he slid his arm out from under her and dressed quietly in the darkness. He searched with his hands for his socks and his boots and sat down on the bed to pull them on. Sarah scooted up against him, missing his warmth in her sleep, and then sat up when she realized he was leaving.

"I'll be back tomorrow to talk to your father," he assured her.

"About what?"

"About our wedding." His grin flashed in the darkness. "Or were you just using me?" Her arms wrapped around his waist from behind and she laid her head against his shoulder.

"Better make it in the afternoon so he'll have time to sober up." He kissed her and made her get back under the blankets, tucking them in around her chin before he left. He built the fire up for her so she would stay warm, and locked the door behind him. Instead of turning towards the ranch, though, he made the turn into town to bring her father home.

Jamie found Roger at the saloon, leaning against the bar with a whiskey in his hand, solemnly singing Christmas carols to the tinkle of the piano. There were a few other patrons around, most of them lonely men who had nowhere else to go. Each sat at his own table, lost in his own memories, except for one, who looked up in surprise when Jamie entered the saloon. That one watched in open-mouthed amazement as Jamie gathered Roger up and led him out to the buckboard. When they were gone, he picked up his drink and held it up in an imaginary toast.

"Well, Merry Christmas to me!" he said and drank the whiskey down.

Jamie noticed a light shining in the window of Jenny's cabin when he got home late that night. He felt weary and spent after getting Roger into his cabin and helping Sarah put him to bed. She had begged him to stay, but he'd decided to go home. He wanted to return the next day and formally ask for her hand in marriage.

He put his horse up and walked across the valley to Jenny's. She was sitting in front of the fire wrapped up in her quilt. Occasionally she would lift up the silver, heart-shaped locket that Chase had given her for Christmas and examine its delicate beauty in the firelight. It was the most beautiful gift she had ever received, made still more precious because of the words that he had said when he'd placed it around her neck.

"My heart is yours," he had whispered in her ear as he gave her the gift. Jenny's own heart had swelled with the love she felt for him and the happiness that surrounded her. They had made tender and passionate love and now Chase was asleep, sprawled on his back with the sheets tossed down around his waist, one arm thrown over his head as if to block the glow of the fire. Jenny had turned the chairs around so that they faced the fire and she had her feet propped up on the wood box. Jamie slid into the empty chair beside her and stretched his long legs out so his toes would thaw.

"I was hoping you would come by."

"I saw the light and figured you were up."

"I was waiting for you."

"Okay, you got me here, now what do you want to know?" He grinned at her, knowing full well what her answer would be.

"Tell me about Sarah."

"What about Sarah?" he teased.

"If I weren't so comfortable right now, I'd get out of this chair and smack you."

"Ooh, I am so scared."

"Jamie." Jenny sighed in exasperation.

"Okay, okay, Sarah, well . . . I guess you should be the first to know that we're going to get married."

Jenny smiled in approval. "When?"

"As soon as possible."

"What's the rush?" Jamie had the decency to blush. "You didn't," Jenny exclaimed and Jamie nodded. "You did, just now, didn't you?" Jamie rolled his eyes and Jenny reached over and smacked his arm. "Right under her father's nose? He is going to kill you."

"Like Daddy always said, only the good die young, and besides, he was in town at the saloon. Sarah said he gets melancholy sometimes. I went and got him and brought him back home."

"That might become a habit."

"I know, but it's okay. I'm going back to talk to him tomorrow."

"To ask for Sarah's hand in marriage?"

"Something like that." He leaned over and tossed another log on the fire, then sat back contentedly. "So tell me, do you like her?"

"Yes, I do. She's sweet and funny and doesn't seem to feel sorry for herself, but most important, she loves you."

"Yes, she does." He had been saying it over and over to himself and it felt good to say it out loud.

"I think she's perfect for you."

"So do I." They sat in companionable silence, listening to the pop and hiss of the logs and the soft sound of Chase's breathing behind them. "So when are you going to tell him?"

"Tell who what?"

"Tell Chase that he's going to be a father."

Jenny's mouth dropped open in amazement. "How did you know? I haven't told anyone."

"Your eyes." Jamie leaned over the arm of the chair and met her sapphire-blue eyes with his own. "They are looking inward like the mares'. There's a glow right there." He pointed a long lean finger at her eye. "In my opinion I will make a very good uncle." Jenny raised a finger to her mouth to quiet him and looked back over her shoulder to make sure Chase was still asleep. "What are you waiting for?"

"I just want to make sure everything is all right. It's only been a few weeks."

"It must have happened on your wedding night."

"I think you are right about that."

Jamie reached over and locked his fingers through Jenny's. "Are you happy?"

"Oh yes, Jamie, I never knew I could be this happy." Their hands dangled together between the chairs. "How about you, are you happy?"

"Yes." He looked into the fire, then turned to Jenny. "Yes, I am." The hypnotic blaze became too much for Jenny and she yawned widely. "Go to bed." Jamie motioned behind him with his head and Jenny nodded sleepily. "Mind if I stay here for a while?"

"Go ahead." Jenny shoved his hair back from his forehead as she passed by his chair. She handed him the quilt and he pulled it under his chin, leaving his legs exposed from the knees down. Jenny rolled her eyes at him and crawled into the big bed next to Chase, who promptly rolled over and pulled her against him, his arm wrapped securely around her waist. When she finally closed her eyes, the sight of Jamie's hair glowing copper from the flames lingered in her dreams.

Chapter Seven

Jenny woke with a start, automatically reaching for Chase.

"I'm here." His mouth was against her ear, his breath warm against her cheek.

"I had the dream again." It was almost a nightly event now.

"The one about the wolves?" Chase asked.

"Yes, and I've realized who the wolves are—Logan and Joe," she whispered, almost afraid to speak the names of the two men who'd hated her so much. Jenny turned into his bare chest, seeking comfort in the heat of his body beneath the blankets. "Why do I keep having the same dream over and over again?"

"Are you sure it was the same dream?"

Jenny took a moment to recapture the threads that had drifted off like smoke when she had awakened.

"Yes, I was in the cabin, and Logan and Joe were at the door, but they were howling like wolves, and it was like they were one and the same. I don't know how to explain it . . . I knew they were wolves, but they were Logan and Joe, too. And I could feel their hatred tearing at me, just like when they used to torment me at the mission. Just like when they shot me . . ."

Chase smoothed the tousled blond hair back away from her face. "Why don't you tell me what happened when they shot you. You've never really talked about it."

Jenny didn't like to think about the time when she had been apart from Jamie and Chase. She had tried to put those years behind her like a bad dream, but like a bad dream they kept coming back to haunt her. It had taken her more than a year after she was stolen from the orphanage before she could make her way back to St. Jo. She remembered sitting on her horse and looking at the ruins in front of her.

The mission was gone, the outbuildings burned to the ground, the stone walls that once held the orphanage nothing but an empty shell.

She had spent the time since escaping from Wade Bishop working odd jobs on her route north from Texas, earning just enough to get her to the next town. The entire time she was trying to maintain her disguise, afraid of what would happen to her if anyone found out she was a girl. It had not been easy; many a night she had cried herself to sleep in whatever loft or shed she happened to be sleeping in, if she was lucky enough to have shelter. She was thin, her hair cropped as short as she could get it, and her face was constantly smeared with dirt to hide her delicate features. She had learned how to survive in the wild, learned how to survive on the edge of society, and she was tired. The sight of the burned-out mission was enough to send her screaming across the plains, but that wouldn't solve anything, so she had turned her horse to St. Jo.

The sheriff's office had been easy to find and the most logical place for answers. She had started there, disturbing the napping man by the slamming of the door behind her.

"What do you want, boy?" he asked as his feet hit the floor.

"I was wondering what happened to the mission." She spoke with a raspy voice to disguise her identity.

"Smallpox, swept through it like wildfire. Had to burn the place down last spring."

"What happened to the children and the sisters?"

"What's it to ya?" The sheriff looked at her face, trying to see beneath the dirt and the hat that was pulled low over her eyes.

"I used to live there; I came back looking for someone."

"Who?"

"Jamie Duncan."

"Jamie Duncan, yeah I remember him, big boy with reddish hair?"

"Yeah, that's him."

"He's long gone; he lit out of here right after I let him out of jail."

"What was he in jail for?" Jenny's stomach lurched at the thought of Jamie being in jail.

"He tried to kill that priest that was out at the mission, choked him right there with me watching him. He said he *had sold his sister away, turned out he was right too—that priest was crazy. They sent a replacement for him a few weeks after that but it was too late, the girl was done gone."* Jenny shook her head as the man told the story. *"He took off to find her and that half-breed went with him. Ain't seen hide nor hair of them since."*

"What about Sister Mary Frances?"

"She went east, took what was left of them orphans with her. Some of them had died, some of them older boys took off, and we burned out the buildings to keep the pox from spreading."

"Do you have any idea how to find her?"

"No, sure don't, you might check out the post office to see if she left them an address or something. That's all I know to tell you."

"Thanks."

"Say, are you related to that Duncan boy?"

"No. Why?"

"Something about you reminds me of him." The sheriff scratched his chin as he considered the boy before him. *"He was like a caged grizzly when I had him in here, got plum loco at times."* Jenny left the office as the sheriff went on about Jamie. She remembered him well enough without the man's recollections. The post office was down the street and she went in to inquire about Sister Mary Frances.

"She's back in Boston, that's all I know. She got one letter after I left and I sent it on to her."

"Do you remember who it was from; was it from a James Duncan?"

The postmaster looked at the ceiling and scratched his neck. *"Nope, can't say that I remember, but I'll be happy to send one on for you if you want to ask her."*

"How long will it take?"

"I don't know. Winter's fixin' to set in—three months, maybe four."

Jenny hung her head in despair. "You got a piece of paper I can use?" she finally asked. She quickly wrote out that she was alive and looking for Jamie, and if sister Mary Frances knew of his whereabouts to please let her know care of the St. Jo post office. She handed the letter to the postman and went back out on the street. She mounted her horse and headed north out of St. Jo towards Council Bluffs.

Jenny rode through the town that had been her home for most of her life and did not recognize a soul; nor did she attract more than a glance. It had been two and a half years since she had last been there and she could not believe how much the town had changed. She took the road that led to their ranch and set the horse that she had stolen back in Texas toward what had once been home. She stopped on a vantage point above the ranch instead of riding directly to the house, and crept up the ridge on her belly to survey the grounds below. Someone was living there, that much was apparent at first glance. She scanned the group of cowboys who were hanging around the corral, hoping to catch a flash of copper, or see one head that towered above the rest, but they all looked pretty much the same. There was a horse being broken; it stood saddled, hobbled, and tied to a post that was now stationed in the middle of the corral. A large man dressed in black and silver was mounted on a huge black horse and seemed to be overseeing the activities. Jenny watched as a man cautiously approached the horse staked in the corral. The horse became agitated, the whites of his eyes visible even from her place on the ridge. The poor beast couldn't move with his head tied and his feet hobbled. The first man grabbed one of the horse's ears and loosened the tie under the bridle. Another man carrying a huge crop and wearing huge silver spurs mounted the horse. Jenny watched as the man dropped the hobble, dug his spurs in, and smacked the horse between the ears with his crop, breaking the skin with the impact of the blow. The horse sprang up in surprise and then began shaking his head vigorously as blood trailed into his eyes. The horse was trembling and the men around the corral seemed to be disappointed that he did not put up a fight. Jenny slid back down to her horse. She did not know who was now living in her home, but she was sure Jamie wasn't there; he would never tolerate the abuse she had just witnessed.

Jenny mounted, skirted around the main part of the ranch and headed north, following the stream that ran through their property. After she had ridden for a while she noticed that she was being followed by two riders. She urged her horse into a canter and the riders kept pace. She remembered a place ahead where the stream widened into a pool with a spit of sand on the side. It was a favorite watering hole for the horses that ran wild over the plains, but it also offered good cover, so she decided to make her stand there. She sent her horse into a run, bending low over his neck, and looked back to see the two riders break out after her. Her horse splashed through the stream and she jumped off, slapping him on as she took shelter behind a rock.

Jenny pulled her gun out and aimed it at the place the riders would be appearing. When they came barreling through, she pulled the trigger and the bullet landed right in front of the first horse, causing the animal to rear and its rider to tumble into the sand. "That's far enough!" she shouted, hoping her fear was not audible in her voice.

"You're trespassing," the bigger rider yelled at her.

"This is open range and I'm passing through. Now throw down your guns."

"Nah," the bigger one said. He dismounted and pulled his gun. "You ain't gonna shoot me."

Jenny shot at his feet and the smaller one crawled after his friend, seeking cover. The bigger one fired, hitting the rock she was hiding behind and then the smaller one fired. Jenny dropped the smaller one with her first shot and hit the bigger one in the shoulder as they returned fire. The big one lost his gun when his shoulder was hit, and stood clutching the wound as Jenny came out from behind the rock.

"You killed him," the big guy cried out.

"He's not dead; I just saw his foot move. Now you two get out of here and leave me be. I'll be moving on just as soon as you go."

"No, Mr. Randolph ain't gonna like that." The bigger one moved in front of the one on the ground and Jenny felt a start as she recognized him. It was Logan from the mission, which meant the one on the ground had to be Joe. The next thing she knew, a pain shot through her stomach and she saw blood beginning to pool up on her shirt. Joe was grinning at her from his place on the ground. Logan looked at her, too, and his eyes hardened in recognition. "It's you." He started for Jenny, his face filled with the same hatred for her that he had shown at the orphanage. Jenny

*shot again, using her last bullet. It grazed Logan's forehead
and he fell over on top of Joe.*

*Jenny placed one hand over her stomach to stop the tide
of blood that was pumping out of her body. She heard her
horse come up behind her and she grabbed the reins and
used the rock to mount him. She knew she had to move on
before someone else came, so she kicked him into a gallop
while trying to stem the flow of blood. She rode on, desperate
to leave the place behind, eventually becoming dizzy as she
rode. Each step of the horse sent a jarring pain through her
body until she thought she couldn't stand it anymore. She
bent low over the animal's neck, wrapping her fingers in
his mane because she did not trust herself with the reins.
The saddle became sticky, the blood running down and
blending with the horse's red hide until it all became a blur.
He finally stopped, his natural laziness taking over when
Jenny was no longer urging him on. She slid from the
saddle and fell into a heap on the plain. The horse snorted
at her motionless form and set himself to grazing, moving
away from the scent of blood to the more tender grass that
lay beyond.*

*Jenny tried to call out as she watched the horse wander
away, but she could not make the sounds that formed in
her throat. She knew she had lost a lot of blood but she was
powerless to stop the flow. She watched as the horse grew
smaller and smaller, until there was nothing before her but
a haze and then blackness.*

"That's when I had the dream for the first time." As
Jenny told the story, Chase found the scar on her abdomen, knew there was one that matched it on her

back where the bullet had passed through her body. He had known she had been shot, but had not realized how close to dying she had come. It was a miracle she had survived.

"Why does the dream keep coming back? Do I feel guilty for shooting them?"

"It was you or them, Jenny, you did what you had to in order to survive."

"I know that, so why do I keep dreaming about them? Joe was killed when Randolph Mason captured Jamie and me, and only God knows where Logan is."

"Dead, too, I hope. I should have killed him along with the rest of them."

Jenny laid her hand on Chase's cheek. "Don't say that."

"Are you sorry that I killed Mason?" Chase found himself fearing her answer.

"No." She didn't hesitate. "I am sorry that I was the cause of your doing it."

"He wasn't the first man that I killed, Jenny."

"I know that." She did not want to hurt him. "It was different with Mason."

"I will kill again if it means your survival." His arms tightened around her. "I would die to save you."

Jenny blinked back tears as she felt the intensity of his words and the strength of the arms around her. "Chase, we're okay now. Nothing is going to hurt us."

"I know." His voice was trembling. "It's just when I think about what happened, and what could have happened . . ." Jenny smoothed back his dark hair and searched for his lips in the darkness. "I love you,

Jenny. You are my life." His hand caught the back of her head and pressed her against him as he poured his feelings into a kiss that left her breathlessly clinging to him as his passion stormed over her like the winter wind that howled out of the canyons to the west.

A rustle of fabric followed by a snore brought them up, blinking at the fire. Jamie was sound asleep in the chair and the realization of his presence washed over Chase like a bucket of cold water. He dropped his head on the pillow and groaned.

"I didn't even think about him being here," Jenny whispered as she snuggled back into Chase's arms.

Chase had to take a minute to calm down, his body still wanting what his mind said was impossible at the present time. "So tell me what happened next," he said when he had himself under control.

Jenny remembered that she had been dreaming, hallucinating really. The delerium of fever had made the wolves in her dream terrifying. But gradually their howling turned into pounding, the pounding of hooves. In her dream, she looked out the window again and saw her father's stallion, Storm, bearing down on the cabin, his mane and tail flying and his eyes flashing fire. On his back was a rider with long dark hair and piercing dark eyes, and the look on his face was murderous.

The vibration of the ground beneath her had stirred Jenny to consciousness and she slowly opened her eyes. She could still hear the pounding and she realized that it was the sound of horses running close by. She groaned as she tried to move and pulled her hand out from underneath her body. Her entire arm was bright red, but the blood was sticky instead of fresh, so she realized that the bleeding had stopped for the moment. She slowly sat up while putting pressure against the wound. Right before her was a herd of racing horses and the sound was deafening. In the midst of them was the horse she'd stolen, running for his life with his reins flying behind his white-rimmed eyes.

"I wish you'd move that fast when I need you to," Jenny had said to his vanishing back. A cloud of dust arose as the herd passed, making Jenny cough and sputter. She heard several high-pitched whinnies as they flew by. A flash of light against the dark caught her attention, and then suddenly rearing before her was Storm.

"Whoa!" she cried out as he danced on his hind legs with his forelegs pawing the air. Jenny's mouth was dry from the dust but she puckered her lips to whistle the song her father had used to calm the stallion. Nothing came out, so she wet her lips and tried again, hoping he would hear her above the pounding of the herd. She whistled "Good King Wenceslas" over and over until she thought she would pass out from blowing so hard. Finally Storm pricked his ears at her and took a tentative step towards her.

"Hey, Storm," she cooed. "Remember me? Dad used to ride me in front of him on your back before I could even walk." The horse took another step, his nose to the ground, drawing in great whooshes of air as he sniffed around her. He nuzzled her leg and then shook his head, almost knocking her over when he got the scent of blood. Jenny kept talking and whistling until he had his nose at her neck and the heat from his breath was blowing down her back. Jenny softly touched the finely arched neck while she talked to him, gently rubbing him until she was able to wrap her fingers in his mane. She moved to stand and he started, pulling her up and dragging her until she was on her feet. "I know it's been a while, but you're going to let me ride you," she said into his ear. He stood patiently while she decided how to mount. Ordinarily she would have just swung up as she had done hundreds of times, but she knew she didn't have the strength for that. Storm took a few steps with Jenny along-side, desperately hanging on, and then he stopped. Jenny was gasping for air, her wound throbbing, when to her amazement she saw a boulder sticking out of the ground. "Remind me to give you some extra oats when I get some." She managed to turn him around, and used the boulder to mount while wrapping both hands into his mane. "Okay, can you find me a doctor now?" Storm bobbed his head up and down and whinnied deep in his throat. Then he started walking north.

"The next thing I remember was the dream again." Jenny hoped Chase wouldn't be too tired to work after being up so late listening to her story. "It was the same as before except this time you"—Jenny had not realized who the mysterious rider was until she had discovered her love for Chase—"made it through the wolves."

Jenny remembered how Chase had ridden on Storm, his long dark hair flowing out behind him and his dark eyes flashing silver with murderous rage. Storm's hooves lashed out as the wolves attacked, and Chase dismounted and began throwing them aside with his bare hands or slicing them with the huge knife that had been strapped to his waist. He came onto the porch as the subdued wolves slunk *away, their tails between their legs, licking their wounds as they went. Jenny looked through the window to see him standing there dressed in nothing but a loin cloth and leggings, with his chest bleeding where a wolf had ripped at him.*

Now she ran her hand over the wide expanse of undamaged skin, but she saw him in her mind as he had looked in her dream with his hair flowing down around his shoulders, his face regal and his eyes dark and deep, showing her the depths of his soul.

"That's when I woke up and realized that Gray Horse had found me. I will never forget what he said."

"What was that?" Chase's mouth moved against the top of her head.

"Hello, Duncan's daughter. I almost did not know you without your hair."

"Maybe your dreams are a premonition," Chase suggested.

"What do you mean?" Some of the things he said amazed her. Chase had been raised in a Kiowa village, but since his time in the white world, he had read everything he could get his hands on, including some of Jason's law books.

"You dreamed about me, without knowing it was me, and we're together." His arms tightened around her. "You dreamed about me fighting wolves, and I fought a wolf. The dreams Jamie and I had with Gray Horse came true, so why can't yours?"

"But that still doesn't explain why Logan and Joe keep showing up."

The howl of a wolf broke the stillness of the night.

"That's it, Jenny. The wolf, I hear him almost every night. The sound must trigger your dream."

Jenny could feel the tension draining out of her body as Chase made the connection. His explanation made sense; there was nothing to worry about. She hadn't even realized she was worried until the sense of relief washed over her.

Chase held her until she fell asleep again, but for him slumber was a long time coming. He could not believe how close he and Jamie had been to her that fall. They had missed her by only a week. His mind wandered back to the time when the two of them had made their way to St. Jo in their fruitless search for Jenny.

Jamie had gone into the post office while Chase waited with the horses.

"Anything?" Chase asked his friend.

"Nope, the postmaster said the same thing as the sheriff—a young guy with short, light-colored hair came in asking about the mission, Sister Mary Frances, and me, and he sent a letter off to Boston. The only one I can think of who fits that description is Marcus and he's supposed to be in Denver."

"Why don't we try Council Bluffs?"

"There is no one there for her to go to and I think she would stay as close to the mission as possible." Jamie kicked at a stone. "It seems like she's disappeared into thin air."

"I can't believe that."

"I know you believe in the visions we had. We both dreamed that we found her; we both dreamed she was in the water. I dreamed about a fox, you dreamed about

wolves. So where is she? Should we go look in all the lakes and ponds between here and California? Who knows, maybe we should just go look in the Pacific Ocean. It couldn't be any harder than trying to find her around here. Why don't you just go to sleep and have another vision about her, only this time try to narrow it down some."

"The vision will happen Jamie, you just have to believe in it."

Jamie had rolled his eyes as he mounted his horse. "Let's go to Council Bluffs. Hey, maybe she even went home to the ranch." The horses were moving before he hit the saddle.

How much they had changed in those eighteen months! When they had left the mission they had been mere boys, but now they were noticed as men. Jamie was so tall, people looked twice at him, and his build was such that no man dared to challenge him with his fists. There was something about him, despite his youth, that spoke of danger and experience. The men they'd been forced to kill on the trail had changed Jamie. He still had a pleasant manner and was usually smiling or flashing his dazzling grin, his deep blue eyes shining at some secret joke, but he could become serious in an instant and lethal when he needed to be.

Jamie had tried to grow his russet hair long, thinking it would hide his scar, but he soon became tired of the added nuisance and kept it neatly cropped in much the same manner as his father. His skin was bronzed from endless days in the saddle, his chest broad, his waist narrow, and his legs long and muscular. He always drew an admiring glance from the ladies, even with the horrible scar on his face. He *had charmed many a meal from homesteaders' and ranchers' wives that they had met along the way.*

Chase had teased Jamie about being better at getting women to feel sorry for him and feed him than he was at hunting. Jamie had retorted that at least the food he provided tasted good, and he had yet to see Chase run down an apple pie in the wild.

Chase had grown up during the years since his own father and mother had died when he was seventeen years of age. He'd ended up in a white man's orphanage, been cut off from the Kiowa people he'd grown up with. Once again he felt grateful for the twist of fate that had brought him to Jenny and Jamie.

The time on the trail had matured him until he was tall and lean like his father, with a bearing that seemed to issue an unspoken challenge to men less confident. He had learned to quietly analyze before speaking, always studying the people around him to learn their weaknesses and strengths.

He had been a steadying influence on Jamie, keeping the other boy's spirits up, never abandoning the search, confident that they would some day find Jenny. Jamie had taught him how to use the gun that he now wore, and Chase had soon matched his teacher's prowess. They'd wasted countless bullets trying to outdo each other. They had become brothers on the trail, complementing each other's strengths and weaknesses until they became a team, deadly to those who crossed them.

They had ridden easily to Council Bluffs, being accustomed to long hours in the saddle. The trip had been silent, both of them contemplating what they would do next if there was no trace of Jenny.

The minister in Council Bluffs could tell them nothing of Jenny, only imparting the news that someone was now living at the Duncan ranch. They had left, Jamie realizing after they did so that he hadn't even stopped to see his parents' graves.

They had wandered then, mostly heading west, without purpose, neither of them wanting to admit that it was time to stop, that there was no place else to look, that maybe, just possibly, Jenny was dead.

Once again Chase squeezed the sleeping form of his wife, and once again he sent a prayer of thanksgiving up to God for bringing Jenny back to him and to her oaf of a brother who was now snoring loudly in the chair. He considered throwing a pillow at him to shut him up, but thought better of it when he realized that he might miss and throw it in the fire. Chase rolled from his side to his back, bringing Jenny's head up onto his chest. He stuck an arm behind his head as he listened to her soft breathing.

Luckily fate had brought him and Jamie to a place where they had stayed long enough for Jenny to find them. He still had to laugh when he remembered the day they had met Cat Lynch.

"Winter will be here soon," Jamie had pointed out as they rode.

"Yeah, I know."

"We need to find a place to stay, some jobs, something."

"We could always go back to the Kiowa," Chase had teased his friend, reminding Jamie of the previous winter, and long nights he had spent in the arms of a young Kiowa widow who had introduced him to the wonders of being a

man. Jamie had grinned mischievously at his friend and waggled his eyebrows.

"That would be nice, but I thought the reason you dragged me out of there was because Deer in the Meadow was getting married again."

"She was and I didn't want her new husband to bump into you under her blankets," Chase had laughed. "At least Deer in the Meadow would have been able to keep that part of you she liked the most, because I'm sure her husband would have hung it on the lodge pole."

"What, my scalp?"

"That too."

Jamie had flinched, and couldn't resist checking to make sure everything was still attached. "And here I thought she loved me because of my good looks and outstanding personality."

"It had to be your looks, because she didn't understand a word you said."

"She understood me well enough when we were under the blankets." Jamie grinned again and Chase doubled over his saddle horn in laughter.

The sounds of gunfire interrupted their laughter and they took off towards the sound. They crested a ridge and saw a stagecoach turned on its side, one of the wheels still spinning around as if it were going somewhere. A group of men on horseback circled the grounded stage, exchanging gunfire with someone within. Moments later Chase and Jamie were barreling down the ridge with their guns drawn, both of them easily picking off the surprised bandits.

One of the outlaws dove from the back of his horse to the shelter of the stage and managed to wrestle the door open.

He pulled out what appeared to be a wildcat but turned out to be a young woman, and held his gun to her head.

"Drop 'em or I'll kill her" he threatened.

The wildcat started screaming obscenities and began clawing at his eyes until they both tumbled off the stage to the ground. When she gathered her skirts to take off, Jamie dropped the man with a single shot. The girl turned and kicked the bandit to make sure he was dead then picked up the revolver.

"Thanks, I would have been dead for sure if you two hadn't shown up." Chase remembered the beautiful smile Cat had turned on them, and the way her stylish hat was set upon her golden brown curls. *"My name is Catherine Lynch, but everyone calls me Cat."*

That had been the beginning of an association that had soon become a fast friendship. Chase and Jamie had both been offered jobs on the Lynch ranch. Now Jason had also given Jenny and Chase the cabin where they lived. With a smile on his face, Chase settled himself beside Jenny, grateful they had both found their way home.

Chapter Eight

Jamie announced his engagement the next evening at the dinner table. He had talked to Jason that morning, and then gone into town to ask Roger for his daughter's hand in marriage. The boys all saw it as a reason to go into town and celebrate and Jamie let them carry him off. He even talked his brother-in-law into tagging along, though Chase would have rather stayed at home with Jenny. Grace, Jenny, and Cat all gathered around the table after the crew had taken off with a series of whoops and hollers.

"I swear everyone in Wyoming territory is going to get married before I do." Since the dance, Cat and Ty had come to an impasse in their relationship. He didn't talk about leaving and she didn't talk about marriage.

"The last thing you want to do is force Ty to marry

you." Grace usually kept her peace but knew that the motherless Cat needed some advice.

"I'm just so afraid that something will happen to him."

"I think he's afraid of the same thing, Cat." Jenny spoke from her own experiences. "But I agree with you—you shouldn't waste the time you have together. Life is fragile. You have to reach out for happiness when you find it."

Grace couldn't have been more proud of Jenny if she had been her own mother. She had come a long way from the skittish girl who had shown up at the ranch last spring. The trials she had faced had given her a quiet maturity and had made her much more observant of the pain other people were going through.

"So how do I make Ty come to the same conclusion?"

"You can't, honey." Grace placed her work-worn hand over Cat's. "He's going to have to find his way on his own."

"Just be there, like Chase was for me." Jenny shook her head at her own foolishness. She had almost missed out on the love she and Chase had for each other.

Jamie and Ty were having close to the same conversation on the way to town.

"You're planning on getting married right away?" Ty asked again. His cautious nature could not comprehend Jamie's haste.

"Why wait? We love each other." Jamie had thought it through and made his decision.

"Where are you going to live? What about work? Who's going to watch out for Sarah during the day?" Ty had a hundred questions, more of them having to do with his own life than Jamie's.

"We'll just take it as it comes." Jamie said confidently.

Chase nodded his agreement from the other side of Jamie. "All you have to do is love each other, Ty, the rest of it will fall into place."

"The only thing you should be worrying about right now is who's buying," Zane added, drifting back into the conversation.

"Hey, not me, I'm the guest of honor."

"And I'm the best man," Chase added.

"So you should be buying," Zane decided.

"You were the one who suggested this," Chase argued.

"Zane just wanted an excuse to check out the new girl at Maybelle's," Caleb interjected.

"There's a new girl at Maybelle's?" Jake's head came up.

"I'll let you know all about her tomorrow."

"No, you won't. You know we have to get on that fence first thing in the morning," Ty said.

"Damn, why don't you go on and get married, Ty. Maybe you'd quit being so grumpy all the time," Zane retorted.

"Maybe we should just let him have the new girl tonight," Jake offered.

"Yeah, you need to get laid, Ty," Zane agreed. Jamie and Chase grinned at each other. "Either that or switch hands." Zane reached over and squeezed Ty's bicep. "Have you guys noticed how much bigger this arm is than the other one?"

"Have you guys noticed how big Zane's mouth is? I bet you'll notice when I shut it up for him," Ty shot back.

Jake shook his head. "I don't know, Ty; I think I have to go with Zane on this one. You need to do something to put us out of your misery."

"How 'bout if I shoot all of you? Then I won't have any misery at all."

"Best start with Cat then." Zane shook his head in mock seriousness. "That's the source of the misery right there."

Ty sighed in exasperation, which brought chuckles from the rest of them. The horses picked up the pace as they went on into town.

Jamie and Sarah's wedding was held on the morning of New Year's Eve in the small church in town. Jason officiated and the ceremony was attended by just family, which included everyone at the ranch. Sarah was radiant and Jamie strangely nervous as they exchanged their vows before the small group. He recovered however when it was time for the kiss, literally swinging Sarah off her feet with his joy. They all laughed and Jason offered to treat everyone to lunch at the hotel dining room so Grace, Cat, and the boys went on while the wedding party stayed to sign the license.

The day was sunny and cold, December having been a dry month after all the snows in November. Everyone knew it was just a matter of time before the blizzards set in again, so they all were eager to make the most of the good weather. They walked briskly down the sidewalk towards the hotel, Chase and Jenny hand in hand, Sarah's arm through Jamie's, and Jason and Roger with their heads together as Jason assured Roger that he was getting a fine son-in-law. They were just stepping off the boardwalk to cross the street when a voice from the past rang out.

"I knew where the brother was, the sister couldn't be far behind." Logan sneered at Jenny, who turned white with the sudden realization that her nightmare was coming true. Logan was standing across the street with his gun drawn and aimed directly at them. His hair was wild and unkempt, his clothes filthy, and his eyes narrowed at them in contempt. He looked as if he had just come out of the saloon, where Jenny was sure he had been drinking to find some courage. It was odd to see him without Joe at his side, snickering at everything he said. Chase stepped in front of her and Jamie came up on the other side after leaving Sarah in the safe company of her father and Jason. A silent communication passed between Chase and Jamie. Chase was wearing his gun—the years of being unwanted in the white world had taught him well, and he never went out without it. Jamie had left his at home; it was his wedding day and the last thing he was looking for was trouble. Whatever was about to happen, Chase would handle it and Jamie would keep Jenny out of harm's way.

"What do you want, Logan?" Chase's voice was low and dangerous.

Logan laughed and looked around, but no one laughed with him. He pointed a finger at Jenny. "She has caused me nothing but misery, her and her brother. She killed Joe and she is gonna pay for it."

"Go away, Logan, and be grateful that I didn't kill you when I had the chance." Jenny showed no fear.

"She's gonna pay and I know how she's gonna do it."

"You won't get away with it, Logan. Now just get on your horse and leave town." Chase's dark eyes flashed dangerously in the morning sun.

"No, I think she should have to choose." Logan looked as if he was enjoying himself. "Which one should it be? One of you is going to die." He began to move the gun between them. "Choose, Jenny, will it be your brother?" The gun moved to Jamie. "Or your lover?" The gun barrel pointed to Chase. "Or maybe even you?" The gun raised a notch and settled on her forehead.

"Don't do this, son, or you will hang for sure," Jason said from the sidewalk.

"This isn't any of your business, old man." The gun kept moving from target to target while Chase stood poised and ready, waiting for the instant when he could make his move. "Hey, I think I'm enjoying this." Logan laughed, but his eyes remained fixed on them, enjoying the fear that was beginning to show in Jenny's sapphire-blue eyes.

"Poppa?" Sarah could only imagine what was going on in front of her. Chase saw Logan's eyes flicker towards Sarah and went for his gun. Logan fired at his movement, just as Jamie threw himself against Jenny and Chase, knocking all three of them to the ground. Chase fired again as he fought his way back to his feet and his shot splintered the post that Logan had dashed behind. Jake and Ty came running down the street, followed by Zane, Caleb, Cat, and Grace. Logan began firing in earnest when he saw the reinforcements coming. He used the corner of the building for shelter as he mounted his horse and took off, all the while firing over his shoulder. Jake ran out in the middle of the street with his gun drawn but could not get a clean shot with all the people who had poured out to watch the gunplay. He watched in helpless frustration as Logan galloped away.

"What happened?" he asked as he turned to the group behind him.

"Oh my God, Jamie." Jenny turned Jamie on his back in the street, leaving a puddle of blood exposed to the sun. "Jamie?" Chase was at her side, the others surrounding them speechlessly as they saw the blood spreading out on the front of his shirt.

"Poppa?" Sarah was desperate to know what had happened.

"He's been shot."

"Jamie? Where is Jamie?"

Jenny choked back a sob as Chase knelt over Jamie.

"He's still alive," he said. Jenny gathered up the skirts of her red velvet gown and pressed them against the wound in his chest.

"Hold on, Jamie, hold on." Zane had already run for the doctor and was soon back, making his way through the crowd that had gathered. Grace and Cat were both holding on to Sarah as the boys lifted Jamie to carry him to the doctor's office. Jenny walked beside him, her skirts still pressed against the wound to stop the blood that kept coming, blending into the red of her gown.

He was awake finally. The doctor came out of his surgery into the office where they had all gathered. "You can go in now," he said to Jenny, who was holding tightly onto Sarah's hand. Jenny bolted through the door, nearly dragging Sarah into the room where Jamie was lying on a table with his chest tightly bandaged. Despite the wrappings and padding, the blood was still seeping through. In the other room the doctor shook his head at Jason's questioning look. "The bullet nicked his heart," was all the explanation he gave to the shocked silence of the room.

Chase felt a wave of grief wash over him but he willed it into submission, his dark eyes narrowing as he imprinted a vision of Logan and his coming death into his mind. He went into the room where Jenny and Sarah stood, one on either side of the table. Grace was at the window; she had helped the doctor all she could and was now dealing with her own grief, her face in her hands as she willed herself to be strong for the others who would soon need her.

"Hey," Jamie said weakly as Chase approached the table. Sarah was on the other side holding tightly to his hands, the tears flowing freely down her face. Jenny reached down and pushed back the hair that had fallen over his eyes. "Thanks," Jamie whispered as he looked up at Jenny with eyes of deepest blue.

"Don't go." Her voice squeaked on the words. Jamie tried to shake his head as if she were being foolish and then his eyes moved to Chase, who took his outstretched hand and held it tightly clasped in his own.

"I think I believe in your visions now." Jamie was struggling to talk and Chase bent lower to hear him. "Remember, you were with Jenny and I moved on."

"I remember, but the best part was you found her."

Jamie weakly grasped Chase's head and pulled him closer. "You still have to watch out for the wolves." Chase nodded as Jamie's arm fell away. "Take care of her." Jamie looked at his sister. "She's a handful."

"*No!*" Jenny cried out in anger.

"I will," Chase assured him, his voice gentle but strong.

Jamie turned his head to Sarah, who was clinging tightly to his arm. "You'll be all right, Sarah. You're strong. Remember that I love you."

"Not without you, Jamie." She couldn't stop the tears.

"Jamie, you are not going to die. I won't let you." Jenny's anger fought with her disbelief that this could actually happen.

"Jenny. Like Dad always said, only the good die young." He tried to grin and almost succeeded. It flashed across his face, chased by a look of desperation, then resolve. "This is another argument you are not going to win. It's not that bad, really. It's warm, and bright." His voice grew softer. "Jenny, look, Momma is an angel." Chase turned and left the room. "And Dad . . ." The long dark lashes fell against the bronze skin of his cheeks. The light was gone from the sapphire-blue eyes and the russet hair finally stayed where it belonged.

The room began to swirl around Jenny in a multitude of colors and light. She heard Sarah's cries, heard Grace call her name, then saw her mother in front of her on a sidewalk, a young Jamie beside her as their mother fell to the ground. Faith Duncan had given birth later that day to a baby girl who was too small to breathe. *Please God, don't take my baby too,* Jenny prayed silently as she slid to the floor.

Jenny stood in the cemetery staring down at the coffin that held the earthly remains of her brother. Her gloved hand was still tightly clenched around a handful of dirt that she was expected to throw on top of the box, but her hand refused to let go. She felt the presence of her friends—they were waiting to catch her if she fell or hold her if she cried—but she chose to do nothing, because anything else required feeling and that was something she was incapable of right now. It was better to be this way than to be like Sarah, who had been too grief-stricken to come.

The service had been brief. Jason's voice had broken over the words as he tried to speak of Jamie, who had touched his heart in a way none of the others ever had. He had loved the boy like a son, feeling a kinship with him. They had all stood huddled together in the cemetery on New Year's Day, no one saying a word because there were no words to say. Zane had been the first to walk away with his head in his hands, his grief as silent as the others'. Ty had scooped up the first handful of dirt from the pile that was waiting to cover the coffin and dropped it in with Cat at his side, her own fears for him evident in her eyes. The rest had followed suit until only Jenny remained, a lone figure at the graveside.

Jenny brought her clenched fistful of dirt up to her heart and held it there, her arm trembling with the effort. She looked up at the dark heavy clouds that were gathering above, making the heavens seem so close. They gave her no answer and there was no peace to be found. She knew everyone else was cold but she did not feel it; she couldn't feel anything. She held her hand out over the hole and let the dirt fall, the clumps hitting like hail against the wood of the coffin. Tender hands helped her up into the buggy. Jason sat on one side, Grace on the other, holding her hand the entire way home.

Jenny did not want to eat and she did not want to talk. They finally left her alone in her cabin. When they were gone, she wrapped herself up in her quilt and sat in her chair before the fire. She had not been there long when she got up and took from the mantle the framed drawing that Caleb had given them as a wedding present. Her fingers traced the faces—hers, Chase's, Jamie's—and then she put it back, this time turning the lifelike image towards the chimney. Huge wet flakes began to come down outside, clinging to everything, but Jenny did not see them; all she could see was the fire.

Chapter Nine

Chase looked at the sky and cursed as the snow began
to pile up on the trail before him. Logan had at least
an eight-hour start on him. His panicked escape from
town had taken him north and across the Lynch ranch.
When Chase had left his dying friend yesterday afternoon, his only thoughts had been of revenge, and the
difficult task of finding Logan in the wild country surrounding them. He had swung by the alleyway where
Logan's flight had begun and identified the distinctive
print left by his horse's shoes. A grim smile had come
over his face as he followed the trail back toward
home. Chase took time to go back to the cabin for
warm clothes and to pack some supplies. He had
looked around the cozy room that he'd shared with
Jenny as if he were saying goodbye to it one last time.
The picture on the mantle had caught his eye, the

three of them together, laughing, their personalities captured by Caleb's talented hand. Tears welled up in his eyes, but he denied them. Later he would grieve and ask Jenny for forgiveness for leaving her, for letting her brother die, for not keeping her safe as he had promised. Or maybe he wouldn't come back, just move on into the wilderness and hope that she would make a better life for herself without him. He couldn't think that far ahead right now; the only thing he could think about was killing Logan, of feeling him beneath his knife. Then Jenny would be safe, and that was all that really mattered.

Chase kept going until the buckskin could no longer plow his way through the heavy snow that was drifting about them. They found shelter against some boulders and as Chase shivered beneath his blanket, his mind went once again to Jenny. He knew their friends would take care of her and he prayed that she would understand. Logan had to pay for what he had done to all of them. He had to suffer as they were suffering now; he had murdered Jamie, who was closer to him than a brother. Chase stared at the small fire before him and the memories began to overtake him.

"It's like she's disappeared off the face of the earth," Jamie had exclaimed as he came out of the general store in one of the small towns along the trail west. Chase had handed him his reins as he came stomping off the porch. It had been weeks since Jenny was taken from the orphanage and they'd been following the wagon trail, stopping in the towns along the way to ask if anyone had seen her. They

knew the folks who'd bought her would stop somewhere for supplies, so they checked everywhere. The first thing they had learned was that Chase was not welcome in most of the small mercantiles along the way. To make things easier for Jamie, he waited outside with the horses. As for Jamie, he was having a hard enough time dealing with the stares that his scars got every time they rode into a new town. When they were on the trail, he almost forgot about them but then they would catch up with a wagon train, or stop at a farm along the way for information, and he would attract stares.

Chase had been having much the same problem as Jamie, except people were not as polite. There were several times he was told to move on because he was a half-breed, and he began to wonder if there would ever be any place where he would fit in. Neither whites nor Kiowa seemed to want him, and he saw a long, lonely future stretching out before him.

Now, Chase poked at the small fire with a stout stick and shook his head. How fortunate he'd been to find a home at the Lynch ranch with Jenny. Where would he be right now if not for Jamie and the time they'd spent together on the trail?

"She's bound to turn up somewhere," Chase had said as they rode out of town. "We'll catch up with them eventually; I know we have to be covering more miles in a day than they are."

"Yeah, but we lose ground every time we stop in one of these towns."

"So don't stop."

"Suits me, I don't like towns." Jamie had kicked his horse into a trot just to prove his point.

"I know what you need," Jamie said after the town was well behind them.

"What's that?"

"A last name." Jamie seemed pleased with his conclusion.

"A last name—why do I need a last name?"

"You're in the white man's world now, where everybody has a last name. For instance, my name is James Duncan and yours is Chase . . ."

"Chase the Wind."

"Exactly. See what I mean? 'The Wind' does not qualify as a last name."

"Oh, do you have something else in mind?"

"Well, it's got to be something that means something to you, I guess. I don't know, what's something that's important to you?"

"My horse is important. I'd be walking right now if it wasn't for him, so how about Chase Horse?" Chase grinned innocently at Jamie from the back of his buckskin.

"That's not going to work."

"Why not, it works for Gray Horse, doesn't it?"

"That's different."

"Oh, I see. How about . . ." Chase looked around to see if something inspired him. "Sky, Chase Sky."

"Nope."

"Bird?'

"Nope."

"Tree?"

"Nope."

"Saddle? Knife? Boot? Gun?"

Jamie grinned and shook his head at Chase's foolishness. "I'm trying to be serious now and you're just messing around. When we come into contact with people, we need to have a name for you besides Chase the Wind. Then maybe people wouldn't get so, I don't know . . ."

"Stupid?"

"Yeah, stupid, when we're around. It would make you sound more like a regular person."

"I am a regular person."

"Don't get all mad on me. It's just that after we find Jenny, we're going to have to get jobs and it would just be easier on you if you could walk up and say 'Hi, I'm Chase So-and-so and I would like a job,' instead of 'I'm Chase the Wind,' like 'I'm the king of England.' Do you understand?"

"Yes, I do." They rode on in silence for a while, Jamie constantly checking to see if Chase was mad or just thinking.

"Well?" he finally asked after a while.

"Well what?"

"What's your last name going to be?"

"I don't know. I would take my mother's if I knew it. She never mentioned it. She said it was from her old life and she didn't want any part of it."

"I thought you were going back to her old life when she was killed."

"No, we were running away from her new life when she was killed. The Kiowa people wouldn't accept her after my father died."

"What was your father's name?"

"I'd rather not mention it, and I wouldn't use it even if I could. That would go against Kiowa tradition."

"Where do your names come from, anyway? I mean, how do you get your names?"

"*My father had a vision right before I was born. He saw me, as a grown man, and I was riding across the plains on a mighty horse from one end of the world to the other, following the wind. He said my destiny was in the wind and to find it I had to chase it, so that became my name.*"

"*I guess his vision was right—you've already been back and forth once.*"

"*Yes, I guess I have, and who knows how far we'll have to go before we find Jenny. The Kiowa have a lot of faith in their dreams. Maybe I need to start paying more attention to mine.*"

"*But that still doesn't solve the problem.*"

"*I know what name I want,*" Chase announced.

"*What is it?*"

"*Duncan.*"

"*But that's my name.*"

"*And your sister's.*"

"*Yes. So?*"

"*Well, you said it should mean something and it does. You're the closest thing to family I have now, so it makes sense to me.*"

"*Since you put it that way, it makes sense to me, too. So from now on you will be known as Chase Duncan.*"

"*I can't wait to see people's faces when they try to figure out how we're related,*" Chase laughed.

"*That's easy; we'll tell them we're brothers.*"

"*Blood brothers?*" Chase pulled his horse to a stop. "*I would like you to be my blood brother.*"

"*What do you mean?*" Jamie asked, stopping alongside.

Chase dismounted and pulled his knife from its sheath. The blade caught the reflection of the sun as he held it up to the sky as if in offering. Jamie dismounted and came to stand beside him.

"What are you doing?"

"I'm asking the spirits to bless our friendship." Chase then slid the point of the knife across the palm of his hand, slicing the skin until blood welled forth and began to drip. He handed the knife to Jamie and held his bleeding palm up to show him. Jamie grimaced, then sliced his own palm and extended it to Chase. They clasped hands tightly in a handshake, each one bleeding into the other. "Now we are one spirit," Chase announced.

"If you say so, but I knew that without slicing my hand open," Jamie replied as he wrapped a kerchief around his hand.

"You have no respect for ceremony," Chase retorted as he wrapped up his own hand.

"And you take things way too seriously."

"You need to be taught a lesson."

"Oh, and who's going to do that?" Jamie looked around as if Chase were hiding someone behind him. "Did you bring anyone with you?"

"I don't need any help," Chase said as he plowed into Jamie, taking him to the ground. They rolled around in the dirt, playfully punching at each other, crashing into the horses who danced around as they continued their wrestling. Jamie was bigger than Chase; but Chase was quicker than Jamie, so neither one gained an advantage. They just rolled around, each one threatening the other with bodily harm until they were exhausted by it all and lay panting and laughing in the dirt.

When they heard the creak of a wagon, they both scrambled to their feet, creating a great cloud of dust as they stamped and brushed at the dirt they had picked up along the way. A buckboard went by with an older couple on the bench and a pair of young girls sitting in the back.

"Chase Duncan, at your service," Chase yelled after the wagon, and gave the girls a courtly bow in the middle of the dirt track. They dissolved into giggles at his play and their mother turned to shush them. The words 'crazy Indian' drifted back to Chase and Jamie.

"I don't think the name's going to help," Chase said as they remounted.

"I guess you're just not man enough to pull it off." Jamie grinned and then rubbed his arm where Chase punched it. "I'm hungry. What are you going to catch for dinner?"

"You're always hungry."

"No wonder, with your cooking."

"You're right, we need a good meal."

"Well then, lead on, great scout. Find us a good meal," Jamie had suggested with a grin.

Chase chewed on some dried jerky as his memories of that day drifted like the smoke of his fire. "I don't even know Logan's last name," he murmured to the swirling flakes of snow.

Chapter Ten

Jenny was overwhelmed by loneliness; it surrounded her now as it had in the past, closing in on her and encasing her in its coldness, just as the blizzard had enclosed her cabin within the drifting snow. The first time, however, there had been hope: the hope of returning to the orphanage, the hope of Jamie coming after her, the hope of escape. Now there was nothing, just a big empty hole shaped like Jamie that could never be filled. She wondered briefly if having Chase there to share her grief would make a difference, would give her hope, but there was no use thinking about it because he was not. Her husband had walked out of the doctor's office as her brother took his last breath, and disappeared into the swirling snow. She knew why he had gone; she also knew his hunt would not make a difference. Jamie was gone, the beautiful spirit that had filled his huge body taken before its time, his remains now lying in the cold earth. Killing Logan wouldn't bring Jamie back, just as killing Jamie had not brought Joe back.

Caleb and Zane had been checking on her, braving the drifts to bring her food that sat uneaten on the table. She knew it was just a matter of time before Grace or Jason showed up to drag her back to the world of the living. She wasn't even aware of how much time had passed or what day it was. She was content to sit, huddled in her quilt and staring at the fire that Caleb and Zane kept going without her even noticing their efforts.

Jenny's mind drifted as it had since the funeral. She let it go where it would; the memories it summoned were poor substitutes for the love her soul craved, but she didn't have the strength to do anything else. She soon found herself going back to the time when she was first taken from the orphanage, carried over the shoulder of Thad Miller and thrown like of sack of potatoes into the back of a covered wagon.

She had risen out of the back like a wild cat, only to be greeted with a swift backhand that left her unconscious as she was carried away from Jamie and Chase, and the kind-hearted nun who had been so good to her in her time of need.

The first thing Jenny was conscious of was movement. She felt herself lurching and swaying as she lay with something gouging her in her side and her back. Her back hurt worse, so she reached her hand underneath and pulled out an iron skillet, holding it in front of her as if it held a clue as to where she was. She sat up and immediately saw that she was not alone.

"I've been waiting on ya to wake up," said a voice behind her. Jenny turned her head to find a small, mousy young woman sitting near the front of the wagon. She was around six months pregnant, her belly protruding under her dress like a small round melon. "I thought I'd have to wait on this one to be born to be a mum, but Thad says we adopted ya, so I guess that makes me one now."

Jenny looked down at the skillet in her hands and wondered if it had ever been used on the woman's head; she seemed utterly senseless. Better yet, perhaps if Jenny used it on her, it would knock some sense into the woman. She tightened her grip on the handle and decided it would make a good weapon in any case.

"What's yer name?" the woman asked. She smiled at Jenny, revealing the loss of a few teeth.

"Jenny." She looked out the back of the wagon as she answered and saw nothing but endless rolling plains stretching out behind them. "How long have I been out?"

"Most of the day. I tried to rouse you at lunchtime, but Thad said to let you be."

Jenny grimaced at Thad's generosity, and then began calculating in her head. She was a day's ride by wagon from the mission. It would probably take her three days to walk back, and she might meet Jamie halfway there. There was no doubt in her mind that he would set out after her as soon as he found out what had happened.

"You don't have to call me Momma, you can call me Millie." The woman giggled.

"Millie Miller?" Jenny looked at her as if she was the

stupidest creature on earth, which might be true. Mille giggled again and nodded. Jenny remembered the calculating eyes of Thad Miller and wondered why he had married Millie. *She probably thinks he hung the moon,* Jenny thought and then decided there was no accounting for taste. Jenny felt a twinge of sympathy for the woman, who obviously didn't know any better.

"We're going to California," Millie offered.

"I heard something about that," Jenny replied.

"We're going to open a saloon in one of the mining camps and you're going to work for us." Millie seemed very excited at the prospect.

"Work doing what?"

"You know," she giggled. "We need a pretty girl to bring the men in. I used to be pretty before I lost my teeth; that's what Thad always says anyhow."

Jenny pulled the skillet closer and began to look around to see if there was a gun in the back of the wagon. She was being held captive by an idiot and by a weasel who wanted to open a saloon and use her as his top whore. It was almost funny, and she had to fight against the insane laughter that threatened to spill out as she considered her predicament. No guns where she could see, and if she remembered correctly, Miller hadn't been wearing one, but that didn't mean he didn't have a rifle up on the bench with him. She measured the distance between her and Millie and decided she could whack Miller on the head and be out of the wagon and gone before Millie could stop her. She knew she could easily handle the small woman, but she hoped she wouldn't have to. Jenny didn't want to be responsible for hurting the baby. She eased the skillet up under the fold of her skirt *and tried to make herself more comfortable in the lurching wagon.*

"So how long have you been an orphan?" Millie asked.

Jenny realized Millie was trying to make conversation so she decided to go along with her, hoping to lure the woman into thinking that she would not be any trouble.

"A year."

"How'd it happen?"

"My parents were murdered."

"Oh." The woman contemplated for a minute. "I guess I'm an orphan too, though I was married to Thad at the time it happened. My parents just up and died in their sleep one night. They left us 'nuff money to go to California and get started, so I guess that's all right."

Jenny wondered briefly if everyone else where Thad and Millie had come from was as stupid as Millie. Her parents had obviously been murdered by Thad, and the sheriff had apparently let him go without question. Well, at least she knew now why Thad had married Millie, and that he was capable of murder. She also realized she would be of no use to him dead, so she had that much going for her. She would just have to make sure she hit him extra hard when she had the chance. Jenny tried to look interested as Millie chatted on about California, but inside she was preparing herself to launch her attack.

Dusk had settled before the wagon finally lurched to a stop in a clearing close to the trail. Jenny was glad of the darkness; it would make it easier for her to disappear. She listened to the crunch of footsteps come around the wagon. Millie had stuck her head out the front, which made it easier for Jenny to bring the skillet up. A head poked in *and she swung down with all her might, the skillet making a resounding clang as it hit. Jenny dropped the weapon and jumped over the limp body that was hanging over the back-board of the wagon. She took off at a full run, pulling her skirt up around her waist. She hoped to disappear into the tall grass before Millie had a chance to react. The sudden sound of hoofbeats behind her sent a chill through her body. She felt the horse breathing down her neck and suddenly she was off her feet, her body suspended in air by the waist-band of her skirt. She felt the worn fabric start to give as she pushed against the horse with her arms. An arm as solid as an oak branch came around her waist and she found herself deposited across the front of the saddle with the horn planted solidly in her stomach. Struggling to catch her breath, Jenny endured the trot back to the wagon and looked up to see Millie administering first aid to Thad's bleeding head.*

"She cracked you a good 'un, Thad," Millie said by way of comfort to the man lying on the ground.

Jenny was flipped off the saddle, landing with a grunt on her bottom. She looked up at the horse to find a huge stocky man with the same mousy hair as Millie looking down on her.

"That's my brother Earl," Millie said as an introduction. "He's going to be our bouncer."

"I can see why," Jenny answered as she considered the bouncing he had just given her. Earl smiled at her, re-vealing the same problem teeth that Millie had. Jenny promised herself that no matter what the situation, she would make sure she took care of her teeth from that time on.

"*Tie her up, Earl,*" *Thad said from the ground. He looked a bit out of sorts and Jenny wondered if she would be able to stand up to the beating he was sure to give her for knocking him on the head. Earl quickly obeyed Thad's orders and hauled Jenny to her feet and tied her hands together. Jenny tried to make eye contact with the big man, hoping she could charm him, but he ignored her, shoving her back to the ground when he was done. Thad staggered to his feet and felt the side of his head where she had hit him. "I ought to beat you good for what you've done."*

"*But you don't want to mess up my pretty face?*" *Jenny finished for him. Thad looked at her, stunned by her impudence, and then kicked her in the stomach.*

"*I can hit you other places. Don't you worry your pretty head about that.*" *He said as he bent over her doubled-up body. He grabbed her by the hair, dragged her over to the wagon and left her there, gasping and gagging.*

When the stars quit exploding in her head and she could draw breath again, Jenny began to reconsider her situation. The first thing was not to be so quick to talk; she had learned that lesson well. The second was that Thad was not as dumb as Millie, who gave the rocks on the ground some serious competition. The third thing she needed to consider was Earl, who had come as a complete surprise. He must have joined up with them after they left the orphanage. Since he had yet to utter a word that she could hear, she couldn't tell if he was in Millie's camp or Thad's. Jenny was betting on Millie since he had been so quick to obey the much smaller Thad.

Just now, her most pressing concern was finding a way to relieve herself.

"Excuse me," she said from her place by the wagon. "I need to go."

"You can't go. You're staying with us," Millie said.

Thad shook his head at his wife's stupidity. "She means use the outhouse," he explained. "Go with her and don't untie her hands."

Millie led Jenny off into a tall clump of grass and crouched down to go herself while Jenny struggled with her clothing. Jenny wondered if she could loosen the knots binding her hands while the others were sleeping. She wouldn't know unless she tried, and she was definitely going to try.

The grumble of her stomach reminded her that she hadn't eaten since breakfast, and as the two walked back to camp, she wondered if Millie could cook. She was surprised when they returned to see Earl working over the fire with the same skillet that she had used on Thad. Her mouth began to water as a wonderful aroma filled the air. A few minutes later Mille set a plate filled with a concoction of beef, potatoes, and peppers in her lap and after one bite, made all the more difficult by her tied hands, Jenny decided Earl should be the cook in the saloon instead of the bouncer. Earl was watching to see her reaction, so she smiled at him as she took another bite, closing her eyes as if it were heavenly. Earl smiled back and even blushed, leaving Jenny to think that maybe she could get him on her side.

Suddenly Thad jumped up from his place, stormed over to Earl, and knocked his plate out of his hand. "Don't you be getting sweet on her now. Do you know how much them miners will pay just to be the first with her? She's not for you, so you just stay away from her before she sweet-talks you into doing something stupid. Do you hear me?"

"Yeah, I hear ya, Thad."

Jenny watched the exchange from her place against the wagon. Thad was brighter than she had thought. On the other hand, Earl was pretty stupid. He looked as if he could flatten Thad with one punch, but he let himself be bullied anyway. She would have to be cautious from now on where Thad was concerned; she knew she could use Earl if she was careful. All she had to do was be nice to him, and Millie too; the woman was harmless enough and could be fooled easily.

Thad finished his meal and then walked over to where Jenny was sitting with her back against the wagon wheel. "Don't you be trying none of your tricks on Earl. I'm going to be watching you like a hawk." He pulled some rope from the wagon and looped it around her shoulders and then tied it behind the wheel.

"How am I supposed to sleep like this?" Jenny asked.

"I don't care if you sleep or not. You can stay up all night for all I care and sleep all day tomorrow. I just want to make sure you don't go nowhere so I can sleep. You understand me, girl?" He threw a blanket at her and she pulled it up with her bound hands. "Now keep quiet and don't go talking to no one." Thad stalked back to the fire and lay down on the bed Millie had made for him. Earl curled up on the other side of the fire.

Jenny laid her head back against the wheel and looked up at the stars that were beginning to appear in the midnight-blue sky. She heard the horses browsing where they were hobbled, their gentle blowing and snuffling reminding her of home and the stable full of beautiful animals that had been her father's pride and joy. Close to the fire, *someone passed gas and she looked over at the trio with disgust, wondering who the guilty party was and then deciding she really didn't want to know.*

Now, Jenny pulled her quilt up around her nose and remembered how the loneliness had washed over her that night. She had wondered about Jamie, whether he was on his way to rescue her. She had known without a doubt that Chase would help. Chase had always been there for her. He had become a part of her life so quickly that she hadn't even realized how much she depended on him, and now he was gone. Just like Jamie was gone. Jenny swallowed hard to keep the tears from coming. She was determined to keep them at bay, because she knew if she started she would never stop. The incessant wind rattled the windows of her cabin and whirled down the chimney, causing the fire to flicker and then burn brighter. Jenny closed her eyes.

Chapter Eleven

Caleb blew into Grace's cabin with the wind, his hands carrying a tray of dishes so that he couldn't grab the door when it was thrown back against the inside wall. "That wind will cut right through you," he observed as Grace took the tray and he wrestled the door shut behind him.

"She's still not eating," Grace declared as she looked at the now-cold food on the tray.

"I don't think she's moved since . . ." Caleb started. The subject of Jamie had yet to be raised in Grace's cozy cabin. Each one of them had gone about the motions of life, taking care of chores, gathering there as usual for meals, except for Jason and Cat, who had stayed in the big house instead of braving the hip-deep snow that was still falling. Ty had trudged up the hill a few times to see Cat, but all she could do was cling to him in desperation and weep, her fear for his life overcoming all logic.

"If only Chase would come back." Zane threw his dime novel down, finding even the adventures of Cole Larrimore could not hold his interest.

"I just hope Chase is hunkered down somewhere and waiting out this storm," Ty said. "It's up to us to take care of Jenny."

"He never should have left her," Grace snapped. The snow and the sadness were wearing on her.

"He's just doing what he has to do," Ty said in defense of his friend.

"Men and their foolish pride," Grace hissed. "It's going to wind up getting all of you killed." She flung her towel at the sink and stalked into her bedroom, slamming the door behind her.

The four men looked at each other in shocked astonishment. Grace had always been a steady foundation for all of them. But then they remembered that Grace was grieving for Jamie too.

"Maybe one of us should go out after Chase when the weather breaks," Caleb suggested.

"How would we even know where to look?" Ty asked. "This blizzard is going to cover any tracks. All we know is that he went north from the ranch, but once he reached the mountains he could have gone in any direction."

"I hope he kills the bastard," Zane said quietly.

"I'm sure that's his plan," Ty answered.

"No, I hope he kills him like he killed Mason. I

hope he makes him suffer. I hope Logan begs for his life for days."

Caleb's dark eyes looked on Zane with pained shock. He had not been with his friends when they'd rescued Jenny from Randolph Mason. He had heard the story, but he had not seen what Chase was capable of. Most of all, he could not believe the hatred he heard in Zane's voice.

"All I know is that, nobody is going anywhere in this weather," Ty finally said to break the painful silence.

The barking of the ranch dog brought their heads up and an answering bark brought the three of them to their feet. They heard a stomping on the porch and then the door swung open. A tall man—nearly as tall as Jamie had been—filled the doorway. He held a rifle in one hand and saddlebags in the other. A huge black dog stood at his heels and surveyed the room with intelligent dark eyes.

"Mr. Lynch sent me down. I guess I'm looking for the foreman." The deep voice had a pronounced Texas drawl.

Zane, Jake, and Caleb looked at Ty. "I guess that would be me." Ty rounded the table just as Grace came out of her room.

The man set his rifle down and took the time to dust most of the snow off himself before he entered the cabin. "Ma'am, would it be all right if my dog came in out of the weather?"

Grace nodded, still too shocked to speak.

"Justice, come." The dog padded into the room, his

eyes alert, and took a seat close to the door, his body poised as his master began to shed snow-covered layers of clothing.

"Did you say Jason sent you down here?" Ty asked.

"Yes sir, he said you were a few hands short and I'd find a bed and a meal down here." The Texan took off his hat to reveal a handsome, weathered face, intense gray eyes beneath graying, curly dark hair, and a thick mustache along with several days' growth of beard. "I've known Jason for several years. He said if I ever needed a job to look him up, so here I am." The man extended his hand. "Name's Cole Larrimore."

Zane snatched his dime novel up from the table and quickly examined the sketch on the cover. "Dang, it *is* Cole Larrimore."

"Don't believe half that stuff, son."

"What the heck are you doing in Wyoming?" Zane asked as he pumped Cole's hand with a big grin on his face.

The gray eyes narrowed, taking in the entire room in a second's time. "I figured I needed a break from rangering." He waved at the newsprint on the table as Zane continued to pump his hand. "It got so I couldn't do a decent job what with everyone asking for my autograph all the time and such."

"Zane, let go of his arm. He's not a pump, for goodness sake." Grace pulled her shawl up around her shoulders. "My name is Grace. I'm the cook around here." She extended a graceful hand and Cole gently took it in his own large palm. "You must be starved."

Grace's other hand fluttered up and smoothed her already perfect chignon.

"Yes ma'am. And if you got any scraps around for Justice, I'd be grateful."

"Of course." Grace went to the stove and began rattling pots and pans as Caleb introduced himself and bent down to make friends with Justice. The dog sniffed his hand and allowed Caleb to rub his ears. Grace set Jenny's untouched plate down in front of the dog, who wagged his tail in gratitude as he ate.

"Looks like Justice likes your cooking even if no one else does," Cole commented, noticing the untouched food.

"Shoot, Grace is a good cook," Jake said quickly, coming to her defense.

"Didn't mean no harm, ma'am, everyone here looks healthy and well fed."

"No offense taken." Grace set a plate down in front of the ranger.

"None of us have felt much like eating lately," Caleb explained.

"Jason told me that one of your hands had been killed?"

"Yes, Jamie was killed, four days ago. Chase went after his killer," Ty explained briefly.

"Then they were close?"

"Yes, best friends. And Chase is married to Jamie's sister."

"And that's her food that Justice just had." The dog looked up at the mention of his name, then swirled his tongue over the plate again to make sure he hadn't missed anything.

"Jenny lives in the cabin on the other side of the valley," Caleb added.

Cole nodded; he had the facts and that was all he needed to figure out the rest. Jason had been gracious when he'd showed up at the main house, appearing like a ghost out of the blizzard. He had given his old friend no warning that he was coming; he hadn't even known himself until his aimless riding had brought him to Colorado and he decided to press on to Wyoming. He needed to do something with his time now, and ranching was as good as anything when a man had failed his sister and his niece. He couldn't fail to notice the feeling of desolation in the big house or the sorrow that filled this small cozy cabin. Whoever this Jamie had been, he must have been special.

Cole was grateful for the welcome he'd received despite the unhappy circumstances. The food placed before him was excellent, and the woman who had fixed it was beautiful, despite the scars that marred her classical features.

Grace knelt in front of the huge dog and let him politely sniff her hand before she moved the plate away from him. She felt Cole's intense gray eyes on her but she resisted the urge to check her hair again. She had felt as nervous as a school girl since he had walked into her cabin. Whatever was Cole Larrimore doing in Wyoming, she wondered, and why had he braved a blizzard to come here? Zane had sat down across from the ranger and was politely waiting for him to finish his meal before he launched a barrage of questions. Grace had a feeling they wouldn't be hearing any straight answers. But Jason wouldn't have sent the man down here if he didn't trust him.

"I'm going up to check on Cat," Ty said as he pulled his coat on. "Zane will show you where to bunk." He nodded at Cole, then caught Grace's eye as he went out. Ty had felt the mystery, too, and wanted to know what they were getting into with the former Texas Ranger.

"How'd you ever manage to get through in this weather?" Grace asked.

"The snow isn't so bad south of here; it really didn't get deep until I got to Laramie." Cole laid down his fork. "That was fine, ma'am. It's been a while since I've had a good meal."

"Since Mr. Larrimore made it in, you boys should be able to make it out to check on Sarah in the morning."

"Sure, one of us will go." Caleb, Jake, and Zane nodded.

"Just call me Cole, ma'am."

Grace bestowed a lovely smile on their guest. "Only if you'll call me Grace."

Chapter Twelve

Chase was grateful for the buckskin. The horse had been steady since the day Jamie had handed him the reins almost six years earlier. One of Ian Duncan's stock, born and bred for strength and stamina, and luckily, a big heart. Chase walked ahead of the animal now, breaking the snow for him, giving the buckskin a chance to rest. He seemed grateful for it too. He followed along after Chase, delicately stepping in the narrow trench that Chase left, his nose down against the warmth of the back before him.

They were in a valley now, making their way through a forest of cottonwood whose lower branches had all been nibbled off by mule deer, moose, and elk. The swirling blizzard of the past few days had calmed to a gentle snow, and the going was easier now, no longer a fight for each mile. Chase had lost all sign of

Logan's trail; he was just hoping that the man had continued in the same direction he'd been going. He wasn't worried; he would find him; it was just a matter of time. Logan needed to be in the company of others like himself. He would leave a trail, Chase was sure of it.

The valley was a peaceful place. The only sounds were the crunching of the snow, the creak of his saddle, the steady breathing of the buckskin. The fresh blanket of snow that covered the valley was blindingly white and the huge snowflakes clung to the tree branches like the beautiful glass ornaments Cat had used on the Christmas tree just a few weeks past. It was funny how much things had changed since then, how one split second in time had destroyed so many lives.

How could one person do so much good, and another so much evil? Chase pondered the question again. Logan and Jamie had both been orphaned, although Logan earlier than Jamie. Had those extra years with loving parents made that much of a difference? Or maybe Logan had not had loving parents; maybe he had been spawned by the devil himself. What had made him the way he was? He had been causing trouble since the first time he'd laid eyes on Jenny and Jamie. Was it jealousy, spite, or just plain evilness? Jenny had said at one time that sometimes bad things happened to good people. There was no reason for it; life was just that way. Unfortunately, she'd had more than her share of bad things happening. "No more," Chase said into the snow. But he had said that before, on their wedding night. He had promised to keep her safe and he had already failed her.

A dark spot up ahead caught his attention. He needed to rest, and the buckskin needed some shelter. Luckily, it was a cabin, or what was left of one. Part of the roof had caved in and the door was missing, but it would provide protection from the weather and a place to spend the night. Chase checked out the structure for inhabitants, two-footed or four. Finding it empty, he led the buckskin in. He unsaddled his horse, gave him a good rubdown, and a portion of the oats that he had loaded in his saddlebags. The buckskin sighed gratefully at the attention. Chase placed his hands on either side of the animal's head and stared into his deep brown eyes. "So much was lost when Jamie and his father died," he murmured. The horse gazed at him intelligently as if to say, *I remember, I knew them.* Chase ran a finger down the white streak that split the buckskin's face. He picked up his rifle and went out to find some fresh game for dinner.

He soon found the tracks of a rabbit and carefully followed the meanderings of the creature through the trees. He came upon a tree fall and took shelter behind it, peering over the top with his hawklike eyes before following with the barrel of the rifle. The rabbit was browsing at the tips of some long grass that stuck through the top of the snow, and then it began to dig down to the roots. *"I've yet to see you run down an apple pie in the wild."* Jamie's words echoed in his mind as he took careful aim.

"*I'll settle for roasted rabbit right now,*" Chase answered silently as his finger caressed the trigger. The rabbit stopped his burrowing and tested the air, his nose twitching in the twilight. Suddenly, he took off in an explosion of snow, his body twisting and jumping as the startled creature sought to throw off his attacker. Chase dropped him with a single shot before he had gone ten feet, and rose from his hiding place with a big grin on his face. His mouth was already watering at the thought of a hot meal. A prickling at the back of his neck gave him pause, however, and he turned, his dark eyes scanning the scarred trunks of the trees.

A wolf was watching him, his tongue lolling, his gold eyes remarkably bright in the dimming light. *It's the same wolf,* Chase thought to himself as he remembered the gray body hurling through the air at him. He cocked the rifle, sliding another bullet into the chamber. The wolf tilted his head at the sound and snapped his mouth shut. Two sets of eyes met for a moment, and then the wolf turned and faded into the darkness.

After a moment had passed, Chase realized that he had been holding his breath. He let it out with a whoosh. His eyes scanned the area again and he cautiously retrieved the body of the rabbit. He walked backward from the fallen tree, his eyes alert, moving from side to side, and his mind now wondering if the wolf had been a figment of his imagination. He soon made it back to the cabin, where the buckskin greeted him with a soft nicker. A quarter of an hour later he had the rabbit roasting in the fireplace and it was not full dark before he rolled himself in his blanket next to the fire with his rifle handy. He awoke sometime in the predawn hours to see a set of golden eyes glowing in the darkness beyond the door, but when he rose from his bed with a flaming torch in his hand, they were gone.

Suffocating, Jenny was suffocating. The snow, the fire, the incessant wind, all of it conspired to suffocate her. The weight on her chest was unbearable, so she flung the blankets off and stumbled to the door, flinging it open to let in the fresh cold air. She stood in the doorway wearing nothing but a nightgown, her chest heaving in great gulps of the frigid night air. She had dreamed again of the Millers, of another botched escape attempt, of being tossed in the back of the wagon, and the oppressive heat that followed them in their trek across the plains.

She had felt as if she were going to suffocate if she did not get out of that wagon soon, but she knew the alternative of plodding alongside it in the blazing sun would be worse. Jenny had pulled her skirt up higher as her legs dangled from the back of the wagon, not caring how much leg she was showing, just seeking some relief from the heat that never let up. Even at night it pressed heavily down on them, making them all grumpy and snappish. Her clothes were sticking to her and she had tried to pluck her shirt away, but the dirt that was encrusted upon it made it stiff where it had repeatedly dried with her sweat. Jenny longed for a bath, to wash her hair, to wash her clothes, to find some relief from the trip that never seemed to end. Millie, who was sleeping beside her, wasn't doing much better; the woman's stomach was so big that it almost swallowed her, making her back hurt so much that she couldn't find a comfortable position. She seemed in so much misery that she couldn't sleep at night; she just tossed and turned until exhaustion overtook her and she got a few hours' rest before they had to get up and start on the road again. Jenny doubted that Millie would have the strength to birth the baby when her time came. From the size of her stomach, they had decided that the baby would favor Earl, whom Jenny had learned was Millie's brother.

Thad had promised them that relief was in sight in the form of the mountains beginning to rise up before them. He had also promised a trip into Denver for all of them. Jenny had to have shoes and a coat before they ventured into the mountains; since Thad wanted to protect his investment, he said he would get them for her in exchange for her good behavior. Jenny had agreed to cooperate, mostly so she would have an opportunity to escape while they were in the city.

They camped that night next to a small pond and Jenny begged Thad to let her and Millie take a bath. Millie had come over to Jenny's side in most things since Jenny had taught her to sew, and the two of them had made several gowns for the baby. Millie had never had another woman around her besides her mother, and she had enjoyed Jenny's company, sharing her secrets and dreams as if Jenny were a partner in the business instead of a prisoner. Jenny had encouraged her to talk, figuring the more she knew, the more it would help her to escape when the opportunity pre-

sented itself, and besides, conversation helped to pass the long hot afternoons. Thad agreed to let them bathe and sent Earl to guard Jenny.

Earl sat on the bank of the pond with his back turned, his rifle cradled in his lap to discourage anyone who might sneak up on them as the women stripped down and eased into the tepid water. Millie miraculously produced a bar of soap and Jenny felt close to heaven as she lathered her hair and rinsed it. When she had scrubbed every inch of her body, she started on her clothes, her worn undergarments turning transparent as she soaked them in the water. She hung the clean ragged garments over a bush to dry and then started in on her shirt and skirt.

"Yer just wastin' yer time. Yer just gonna get 'em dirty agin," Millie commented as she watched the efforts.

"That's okay, Millie; they will feel good in the meantime." Millie shrugged her shoulders, her round belly bobbing under the surface of the water. When Jenny was done, Millie took up the soap and started on her own clothes.

"Earl, you need us to wash yer clothes?" she asked her brother, who was still politely keeping watch with his back to the pond.

"That would be real nice," he replied. Earl had been trying very hard to conduct himself as a gentleman since Jenny had been with them, much to Thad's amusement. He had never been around anyone like Jenny before and he seemed conscious of his family's inadequacies in her presence. Ever since the day Thad had stolen her away from the mission, Earl had watched her from afar. He also watched her to learn, and listened carefully when she spoke in hopes of improving himself. Jenny had noticed his efforts and *helped him when she could, trying not to draw any attention from Thad.*

Millie was scrubbing away at her dress, singing along with the motion, which drew a scowl from Thad, who was setting up camp. He put his rifle over his shoulder and disappeared into the brush with the hope of scaring up some game for dinner. Jenny took advantage of his absence and got out of the pond, then wrung the water out of her hair. She donned her undergarments and was just buttoning up her camisole when she saw Earl freeze at his post.

Jenny looked up to see a finely dressed man on horseback in the middle of the clearing. Earl had his rifle drawn on him, but it did not seem to bother the man, who was looking directly at Jenny with a smile on his handsome face. She suddenly became conscious that her undergarments offered no protection from his leering gaze. The soft muslin was so worn that it was practically transparent, so she turned away, knowing that her hip-length hair would cover her better. She looked over her shoulder and saw the man tip his hat at her, his smile flashing under a dark mustache. Millie kept on scrubbing her clothes and singing off-key as Earl slowly stood.

"These women need some privacy to finish their baths, so I'd appreciate it if you'd just move along," Earl said slowly, clearly enunciating each word.

"I did not mean to intrude," came the reply in a soft Southern drawl. The man slowly backed his horse away, his smile still visible though one hand rested casually on his thigh close to a gun that was strapped to his hip. He finally disappeared back up the trail, and Earl took a few cautious steps in that direction to make sure he was gone. Jenny

hastily grabbed her shirt as Earl came back with relief writ-ten on his face. Millie looked up from her washing, having missed the whole exchange.

"Earl, what are you doing? You just need to sit down and wait yer turn." Earl rolled his eyes at his sister and Jenny stifled a giggle as she pulled her damp clothes on.

"Earl, you would have made some girl a good hus-band," Jenny said now to the swirling snow as she remembered the big sweet guy. Earl was dead now; Jamie and Chase had found the charred bodies of the Millers sometime after she had escaped from them. Earl was dead, Thad was dead, Millie was dead, and the baby had disappeared. Jamie was dead and Chase had disappeared. Her mother and father were dead. It was funny how history kept repeating itself. Jenny shut the door against the darkness and climbed back into the big lonely bed.

The night after their bath in the pond, a thunderstorm had rolled across the mountains, bringing with it a long steady rain and welcome cooler temperatures. Jenny and Millie had tried to sleep in the back of the wagon, but the booming thunder had kept them awake the first part of the night, Millie's extreme discomfort the rest. The excitement of going to town outweighed any tiredness, however, and it was a cheerful group that rode into Denver even though Thad hissed threats at Jenny the entire way. Jenny just smiled at him as she sat up on the bench of the wagon soaking up the sights and sounds of the first city she had been to since leaving St. Jo. She wasn't making any prom-ises; if an opportunity presented itself, she would run off.

Her main desire was to make it back to Jamie before winter set in.

They stopped in front of a mercantile and went inside, Earl and Thad stationed on both sides of Jenny while Millie went fluttering up and down the aisles squealing in delight at all the fancy things she saw. They soon had Jenny outfitted in a sturdy pair of shoes and a warm coat. Thad sent Earl to escort her back to the wagon while he finished shopping for supplies.

Earl kept a firm grip on her arm, but let her stop to run her hand over a fine calico that caught her eye. A look from Thad made him pull her along, causing her to stumble in her new shoes. Jenny fell against a display of canned goods and the tower teetered precariously. Earl threw out his hands to stop the descent and Jenny bolted out the door as the cans came crashing down.

She tore up the sidewalk, pushing people out of her way in her mad flight. With Thad and Earl hot on her heels, she flew around a corner and came up short against a solid chest covered with a dark suit, white shirt and string tie. Jenny looked up into the handsome face of the mustached stranger who had interrupted her bath.

"Well now, what do we have here?" he said in his soft Southern drawl.

"Jenny, you come back here," Thad yelled behind her. Jenny took off again and the stranger put his hands back in submission as Earl rounded the corner. Thad threw a shoulder into him, knocking the man into a pile of crates as he took off after Jenny's flying skirt tails.

Jenny found herself trapped in a dead end as Earl caught up with her. She put her hands up in surrender as Thad *cornered her, the look on his face making a shiver run down her spine. He backhanded her across her cheek, knocking her into the wall of the building, and she slid to the ground as stars exploded in her head. "I'll get the wagon; you get her into it without nobody seeing her," he hissed at Earl and stomped off. The dark suited stranger was gone when they came out of the alley.*

Earl bent over Jenny's dazed body and wiped away the trickle of blood that had formed at the corner of her mouth. "Jenny, you got to quit runnin' off like that. All it does is make Thad mad at ya."

"I know." Jenny rubbed her jaw. "Does he have to hit me so hard every time?"

"It's the only way you'll ever learn." Earl sighed. He pulled Jenny to her feet and grabbed her arm in a firm grip. "Let's go get in the wagon." The wagon was waiting as they came out of the alley and Earl handed her up into the back where Millie was waiting with a rope to tie her wrists together.

"Thad's fit to skin yer hide," Millie whispered as she hastily tied the knots. Jenny flopped down on a box and watched the buildings go by from the back. As they went by the saloon, a man dressed in a dark suit stepped out into the street and watched the wagon. Jenny raised herself a bit and saw that it was the same man she had crashed into in her flight. He stood with his arms crossed, watching the wagon go down the street until she could no longer spy him in the distance.

"Out of the frying pan and into the fire." Jenny sighed into the emptiness of her cabin. The logs in the fireplace answered with a resounding pop.

Chapter Thirteen

The rest had done the buckskin good, Chase mused to himself as they set out the next day. The snow had finally stopped and the day promised to be clear and bright. Now if only he knew which direction to go in, he might put an end to Logan's reign of terror over Jenny. But he was guessing now; there were no signs. The fresh blanket of snow that covered northern Montana made it seem as if Logan had disappeared off the face of the earth.

It had been the same when Jenny was missing. They had searched for weeks and found no trace of her, and then suddenly, in Denver, someone had seen her. Chase hoped he would have the same luck now.

Jamie had walked out of the mercantile with an incredulous look on his face. The storekeeper had just described a girl who could only have been Jenny. He had said that a tall slim girl with blue eyes and long blond hair had come in with a couple of men and a very pregnant woman. The girl had been dressed in a ragged skirt and blouse, and the man had purchased her a pair of shoes and a coat before hustling her out the door. She had knocked over a display of canned goods, causing a lot of damage, and had run off in a hurry. That was the last the storekeeper had seen of her and good riddance besides. Jamie had shared the tale with Chase, who was waiting with the horses on the streets of Denver while the sun set low in the evening sky beyond.

"How long ago was it?" Chase asked.

"He said about a week. It was early morning when they came in and he saw them take off out of town with Jenny in the back of the wagon. He said Miller was pretty mad at her."

"I can't imagine why."

Jamie had grinned up at his friend.

Oh, how Chase missed that grin—it always held so much life, so much promise. Jenny had the same grin, but when Jamie flashed it . . .

"I guess she hasn't been very easy to get along with," Jamie had replied.

Chase remembered Jenny flinging a mug at his head when he had crossed her in the orphanage; he could only imagine what she had been like to the men who were holding her prisoner. She had spirit. He hoped she still had it, that after all that had happened to her, Jamie's death hadn't taken that from her too.

"It's too late to track them tonight," Jamie had said. "How 'bout we get a real meal and maybe sleep in a real bed?"

"Sounds good to me."

Jamie checked them into the hotel, while Chase stayed in the background with both sets of saddlebags thrown over his shoulder, trying his best not to draw attention to himself. They both took baths and felt downright civilized as they headed over to the saloon for dinner.

The saloon was already gearing up for a busy night; most of the tables were full already as hands from the surrounding ranches gathered to enjoy their Saturday night. They found a small table in the corner and settled in, both sitting with their backs to the wall. A young barmaid approached with a sweet smile on her face that froze in place when Jamie turned slightly and she saw the scar going down the side of his face. She quickly regained her composure and took their order for steak and potatoes. She hurried on to another table after she served them, which suited them fine. It wasn't even dark yet and already the place was so noisy they could barely hear each other.

As the buckskin picked his way up over the ridge of the valley, Chase remembered the sights and sounds of their first night in a big city saloon. *Too bad we hadn't had Zane to show us the ropes*, he thought. Zane could walk into any establishment and own it with his quick charm and ready smile. Chase shook his head at their innocence at that time. They were just boys . . .

Jamie and Chase quietly absorbed the foreign atmosphere of the saloon. Neither had been exposed to such a place before and they watched the goings-on as they enjoyed their meal. They began to talk of Jenny as they became accustomed to the noise, and both felt great relief and hope that their search would soon be over. A haze settled over the tables as the place filled up, and they felt themselves relax for the first time in weeks as they became lost in the crowded room. They watched the card games and the ranch hands who were trying to get lucky with the fancy women who moved among the crowd serving drinks. There was one group, nosier than most, around a table. The girl who had served them was trying to dodge the large hands of the man who seemed to be the center of attention.

An old man, toothless and ragged, was wandering from one table to the next begging for drinks. He was shoved away repeatedly, stumbling into chairs and tables, only to be shoved again, sometimes right through the swinging door. Then he would hitch up his pants and come back in, his desire for a drink overcoming his pride and common sense. He finally made his way over to Jamie and Chase's dark corner and sat down.

"Can you boys spare a drink for an old man down on his luck?" The words were slurred and the smell emanating from him was overpowering.

"Sorry," Chase said, "I don't think you want what we're having." The old man grabbed at Chase's glass, which still contained a splash of the sarsaparilla they'd had with their dinner. He greedily drained it and then slammed the glass down in disgust.

"Are you playin' a trick on me?"

"No sir, I told you you wouldn't like it."

The man jumped up from the table, moving surprisingly fast for someone in his condition. His chair tipped over with a crash, quickly silencing the room as all eyes turned towards the corner.

"This stinkin' half-breed is tryin' to pull a fast one on ole Dan, boys."

Wind of the Wolf

The room suddenly turned mean as the word half-breed *circulated. The man who had been holding court at the loud table stood up.*

"Hey fellas, we got us a breed in here. Look at him sittin' over there in the corner all quiet like he's plannin' somethin'." Chase's eyes narrowed and his body tensed as Jamie moved his hand from the table to his gun. "You know what it means when you got a breed?" The man looked around the room, making sure that all eyes were on him and the great wisdom he was about to impart to the group. "It means that somewhere there was some whorin' going on. Now I don't know which is worse, a squaw whorin' with a white man"—he raised his eyebrows and licked his lips as if in sensuous pleasure—"or a white woman whorin' for some stinkin' Indian." Chase's chair hit the wall behind him as he leaped to his feet. "Which was it, boy, what kind of whore was your momma?" Jamie grabbed Chase's arm as Chase went for the knife at his side. The man stood up and his friends scattered away as he looked hard at Chase and Jamie.

"We don't want any trouble," Jamie said as he held onto Chase.

"Let go of me," Chase said, his voice low, his dark eyes shooting sparks.

"There are too many of them," Jamie said. "Now let's go."

"Let go of him, boy. Let's see what he's got." The man held his hands out as an invitation. "You gonna scalp me with that knife of yours, half-breed?"

Chase lunged and Jamie wrapped his arms around him,

swinging him around, causing Chase to kick the table over as he struggled against his friend. "I said we don't want any trouble and we're leaving." Jamie shoved Chase towards the door and backed out after him, holding his hands up where they could be seen. They heard the word yellow hissed behind them as the doors swung shut and the place erupted into laughter. Chase turned but Jamie caught him again and pushed him down the walk into the alley.

"Are you crazy? You can't take that guy; he'd shoot you down before you could make a move," Jamie yelled. Chase whirled away and punched the wall next to Jamie's head, the wood splintering under his fist.

"You don't know what it's like." Chase laid his head against the wall, his body still tensed in frustration.

"No, I don't, and I never will, but I am not going to let you get yourself killed over nothing."

"Nothing!" Chase turned to Jamie. "Didn't you hear what he said about my mother?"

"Chase, he doesn't know about you or your family. He's just a stupid drunk who's running his mouth, that's all, and he's not worth dying over."

Chase began to pace the alley, prowling the dark corridor in an attempt to dispel some of the tension coiled tight inside him. The constant prejudice was starting to wear on him, making him sensitive to the slightest look or word. He finally stopped and sighed. "Let's go get some sleep so we can get an early start," he said.

Jamie threw an arm over his friend's shoulder. As they came out of the alley, they saw the girl who had served them leaning against the rail. Tipping their hats, they were about to step out into the street to cross over to the hotel when a voice from behind stopped them.

"The boys and I decided we don't need no half-breeds hanging around town." It was the big man from the saloon with his cronies standing behind him.

"We're leaving first thing in the morning," Jamie said simply and evenly.

"No, you don't understand, boy. We want you and your friend gone now." The group drew themselves up as if summoning courage from their spokesman.

"Let's go, Chase," Jamie said and turned back towards the hotel. Chase glared at the group and then turned to follow Jamie.

"Yellow bastards." They both flinched at the words.

"Keep walking," Jamie whispered to Chase. Suddenly a bullet whizzed by, burying itself in the dirt beside Chase's boot. They heard laughter behind them. Chase stopped and turned.

"As you can see, I don't have a gun," Chase said to the group.

"Why don't you use your bow and arrow?" The big man snickered and the group joined with him in laughter.

"Why don't you leave them alone?" the barmaid asked from the railing.

"Mind your own business," the big man retorted. Chase stood in the street with his arms crossed, looking at the group like a king surveying disloyal subjects. His disdain was written plainly on his face.

"Why don't you fight me like a man, instead of hiding behind your friends?" Chase said.

157

"Oooh, did you hear that boys? This half-breed wants to fight me."

"No, I don't want to fight you, but I will if I have to." The big man walked up to Chase and did not stop until they were standing toe to toe.

"You know I could kill you, boy?"

"I know you could try."

"Go on and whip that stinkin' half-breed," one of the other men urged. The big man swung his fist, bringing it around with all his strength, hoping to finish Chase with just one punch. Chase ducked under the swing and butted the man in the stomach full force with his shoulder, knocking him on his backside in the dirt. The followers saw that their leader was down and advanced on the two who were now wrestling in the street. The big man tried to overpower Chase with brute strength but was unable to get a good hold on him. Chase was kneeling on his chest when a blow from one of the followers knocked him off. Jamie met the blow with one of his own and the entire group joined in. The barmaid went after the sheriff.

Three were on the ground and there was so much blood on the five that were standing that it was hard to tell who was who, but the sheriff and his deputies sorted them out, running off the group from the saloon until Jamie and Chase were the only ones left to face the music. They both were a bit unsteady on their feet as the sheriff looked them over.

"You two just passing through?"

"Yes sir," Jamie said through a swollen lip.

"You handled those boys pretty good."

"Yes sir."

"You know I'm going to have to arrest you for disturbing the peace."

"What?" Jamie began to protest. "They started it. We were just defending ourselves."

"Yep, but those boys come into town every Saturday night and spend lots of money. You two are just passing through."

"So let us pass," Chase said.

"You must be that breed they were talking about."

Chase sighed as he waited for the inevitable.

"We don't need your type coming in here and stirring up trouble. Now, the time for disturbing the peace is forty-eight hours, resisting arrest will add another twenty-four. So, what's it going to be?"

Jamie had groaned in frustration as the sheriff led them away. Chase had felt fury sweeping over him. Jenny had been so close.

It had all been so close—the perfect life, Chase, Jenny, Jamie, and Sarah living happily ever after within the safety of the ranch.

Chase reined in the buckskin and looked out over the snow-covered terrain that stretched out before him. "I know you're out there, Logan. You've left a sign, somewhere; it's just a matter of time."

The ride to town was a silent one for Ty and Cat; the usual sounds of nature were lost beneath the thick blanket of snow. The morose silence that surrounded the two of them made even the creak of saddle leather resound like a gunshot in the frigid air. Occasionally a bird would fly overhead, its sharp eyes searching for a meager tidbit in the frozen landscape, but except for that, the world was empty.

Cat wasn't sure if she was ready to deal with Sarah's grief. The blizzard that had arrived on the heels of Jamie's funeral had cocooned all of them in their sorrow, but now the snow had stopped and it was time for them all to get on with their lives. They were trying to pick up the pieces of their lives, except for Jenny, who had wrapped herself in her quilt and buried herself in the huge bed in her cabin. They were at wit's end trying to figure out what to do about her. She didn't respond to anyone or anything, it was almost as if she was lost in another world.

Now they were on their way to check on Sarah, widowed before she'd had a chance to be a wife, but at least she'd had one night with Jamie. *One wonderful night*, Cat thought. *Will I have that much?* Jamie's death had been a terrible blow to them all, but the thought that Ty could be next, that he could be here beside her one moment, and gone the next, was more than she could stand.

"I'm going with you." Cat announced.

Ty gave her a bemused look. "Of course you are." They were turning down the drive to Sarah's.

"When you go to North Carolina, I'm going with you."

Ty stopped his horse and looked at Cat in shocked silence. She kept riding, her heavy coat emphasizing the stubborn set of her shoulders. Ty didn't know if he should laugh or cry, shake some sense into her, or kiss her for being so sweet. Then he noticed that there was no smoke coming from the cabin's chimney.

"The place looks deserted," Cat said. Snow had drifted up over the front porch and there was no evidence of anyone going to or from the barn, which was a necessity for the animals no matter what the weather.

"I hope Roger didn't go off somewhere and get drunk and leave Sarah here by herself," Ty said as he dismounted. He tramped his way to the door with Cat behind him. There was no answer to his pounding so he tested the handle, only to find it locked. Ty leaned back and gave the door a swift kick and it swung inwards.

"You're getting rather good at that," Cat observed.

"I've had lots of practice lately."

A quick search of the three rooms found nothing. Everything that belonged to Sarah and her father was gone. "I guess they took off right after the funeral," Ty said as he ran his hand through his hair in exasperation. He was worried about how Jenny would react to the news, if she reacted at all.

"Sarah probably couldn't stand to be here, with all the memories . . ." Cat's voice trailed off as she ran her gloved hand over the tabletop. Sarah had memories, she had known passion, and she had confessed it to Cat the morning before the ceremony. Sarah had whispered that she couldn't wait for her wedding night, to be in Jamie's arms once again. Cat closed her eyes and imagined, as she did every night, what it would be like to spend the night in Ty's arms, to see his eyes go dark with desire, to see him take off, for a time, the heavy mantle of responsibility that he wore and just be, with her.

"Cat?"

"Hmm?"

"I said let's go into town and see if anybody knows what happened to them."

"We can get the mail too." Cat sighed. More letters from North Carolina, more newspaper articles about the strife in the South, more things to send Ty away from her. He had conveniently forgotten her earlier announcement. *I'll just let him stew on that for a while*, she decided as they mounted up. *We'll see who wins this war.*

Jason had aged more in the week since Jamie had died than in the entire time Grace had known him. The lines around his eyes had deepened, the set of his once proud shoulders had sagged, and there was a weakness about him now. Before Jamie's murder his frame had held strength and vitality, now it showed the years of hard work and recent disappointment. Grace hated to add to his burdens, but something needed to be done about Jenny.

"She won't eat; she doesn't even move when we come in. I'm at my wit's end about what to do for her. I don't even think she's shed a tear." Grace set the delicate china teacup down on the fine mahogany table as Jason stared into the fireplace. "How are you doing?" she asked when she realized his mind was elsewhere.

"I'm fine." Jason turned and saw the worry in

Grace's elegant features. "Really, Grace, I'm fine. It's just . . ."

"It's just that you worry about all of us," she finished for him.

"Yes." Jason rolled a log back into the fireplace with the toe of his boot. "It's funny how you don't really appreciate people until they are gone."

"Jamie knew how you felt about him,"

"Did he? I'm not even sure what it was I felt. I was so proud of that boy, of everything he did. I couldn't have been prouder of him if he had been my own son."

"He had a way of touching your heart."

"Yes, he did." The silence was comfortable as they both became lost in their memories of Jamie. "So what are we going to do about Jenny?"

"I'm ready to drag her out of the cabin and throw her in a snowbank."

"Remember when Jamie doused her in the trough?" Grace suppressed a smile as the memory filled her head. "They were ready to kill each other."

"She wouldn't back down," Jason added.

"Chase always said she should have had the red hair."

"Let's give her some more time, Grace. I believe she'll come around. She has a strong spirit."

"I hope it doesn't fail her."

Chapter Fourteen

Did killing become easier each time you did it? Did planning it out make it easier to do? Chase had imagined the feel of Logan beneath his knife at least a hundred times since he had left Jamie's side. He had visualized the look of fear in his eyes; his ears hungered for the sound of Logan begging, no, whimpering, for his life. Never before had he planned something like this. But now revenge occupied every waking moment. It wasn't as if he was new to this killing thing. He had done it before, mostly to stay alive, except for the one time, with Mason. He really did not remember actually cutting Randolph Mason's body. All he remembered was the black rage that consumed him when he had heard Jenny's cries, then the scream that came from the man as he separated his manhood from his body. He had awakened as if from a deep sleep with his knife in one hand and what was left of Mason's pride in his other. He had thrown that in the dirt and walked away, his mind and heart focused on Jenny.

He didn't want to think about Jenny now. He didn't want to wonder how she was doing. He didn't want to know how her heart was breaking. It hurt too much to think about her. He knew their friends would take care of her, that they would take better care of her than he had. He was the one who had let her brother get killed in broad daylight in the middle of a busy street on his wedding day.

Chase roared in frustration. The sudden outburst started the buckskin, causing him to jump sideways and toss his head. Chase settled the animal with a quick word and a gentling rub on his finely arched neck. The buckskin responded with a toss of his head, and settled while Chase rubbed his hand over his own neck and took out his canteen. *Concentrate on Logan*, he told himself as he washed the bitter taste from his throat. *You're going to miss the sign*. His hawklike eyes scanned the horizon. The country ahead was hard and cold, just like the weather. There was nothing before him but snow hiding the rough and rocky terrain of the badlands. He had headed into the Dakotas, toward the Sioux. It was a place where desperate men went to hide. A man could get lost there if he wanted to, unless someone very determined was looking for him. *Concentrate on Logan*, Chase reminded himself. He was going purely on instinct, yet he knew there would be a sign.

Jamie had learned in those first months on the trail to follow Chase's instincts. When they had left Denver after serving their time in jail, his instincts had saved their lives. They had been followed, Chase had felt it in his gut, and he knew there was more than one of them.

They were riding into the mountains, trying to make up the time they had lost while in Denver. "We could circle around and come up on that ridge to see if we can get a look at them," Chase had suggested to Jamie.

"We'd lose time that way," Jamie said and Chase knew he was afraid that Jenny was slipping away from them.

"I know, but at least we'd know who was behind us and maybe why."

"Let's keep going. Maybe it's just somebody going the same way."

Chase looked around at the mountains rising above them. "We don't have the luxury of hoping for the best. I'm going to climb up the ridge."

Sure enough, he had spotted four riders, a couple of hours back on the trail.

"Can you tell who it is?" Jamie asked.

"One of them is big. I'd say the guys from the saloon if I were guessing."

"Why would they be following us?"

"Because they hate us." Chase slid down from the ridge and dusted off his pants. Jamie shoved his hair back from his forehead and clamped his hat down.

"What should we do?"

"Be ready."

They had looked at each other then, each one taking the

Join the Historical Romance Book Club and GET 4 FREE* BOOKS NOW!

A $23.96 Value!

Yes! I want to subscribe to the Historical Romance Book Club.

Please send me my **4 FREE* BOOKS.** I have enclosed $2.00 for shipping/handling. Each month I'll receive the four newest Historical Romance selections to preview for 10 days. If I decide to keep them, I will pay the Special Members Only discounted price of just $4.24 each, a total of $16.96, plus $2.00 shipping/handling ($23.55 US in Canada). This is a **SAVINGS OF AT LEAST $5.00** off the bookstore price. There is no minimum number of books I must buy, and I may cancel the program at any time. In any case, the **4 FREE* BOOKS** are mine to keep.

*In Canada, add $5.00 shipping/handling per order for the first shipment. For all future shipments to Canada, the cost of membership is $23.55 US, which includes shipping and handling. (All payments must be made in US dollars.)

NAME: _____

ADDRESS: _____

CITY: _____ STATE: _____

COUNTRY: _____ ZIP: _____

TELEPHONE: _____

E-MAIL: _____

SIGNATURE: _____

If under 18, Parent or Guardian must sign. Terms, prices, and conditions subject to change. Subscription subject to acceptance. Dorchester Publishing reserves the right to reject any order or cancel any subscription.

full measure of the other, knowing that now their lives were at stake, taking stock of each other's weaknesses, each other's strengths. The time on the trail had changed Chase, or maybe Chase had just gone back to his element. He was completely at home in the wilderness and had summoned resources he hadn't known he had to keep them alive. The only time he was at a loss was when they went into town, and he let Jamie take the lead there. Their strengths complemented each other.

"We need to get you a gun," Jamie had finally said, flashing his grin.

Chase looked over the snow-covered badlands that stretched endlessly before him and his hand touched the gun that he had worn since that night. "I wish you had taught me to use it better."

Jenny restlessly kicked the blankets off and sat up on the edge of the bed. Her body ached from the long period of inactivity and her stomach growled with hunger. Her hair had long ago come loose from the chignon Grace had swept it into before the funeral, but a few pins were still hanging in the tangled mess. She pushed the stringy mass back from her forehead and stood up slowly, waiting for her legs to support her weight before she took a cautious step towards the wardrobe. She swung the door open and looked at herself in the mirror.

Her sapphire-blue eyes were sunk deep in her face and were surrounded by shadows, put there by dreams of her time with the Millers. Her skin was pale, the usual golden glow lost in the darkness that she had retreated to. Her cheeks were sunken, a reminder of the year of near starvation she had endured after she had escaped.

Thad had been right about the weather. As soon as they started into the mountains, the air had cooled down, making their hurried passage tolerable. Thad was determined to make it through the pass before the first snows came and had been pressing them hard every day. Jenny had been tied hand and foot in the back of the wagon since her escape attempt in Denver. Millie had not been much company for her either. The woman's condition made her feel every jolt of the wagon until all she could do was groan as the horses pulled them up the trail. Her time was approaching fast and they were all anxiously waiting for her labor to start.

It didn't take Jenny long to realize that Jamie would have no chance of catching up with them once they had gone over the mountains. California was a big place and there was no telling which way Thad would turn the wagon. She knew they were going to the gold fields, but their ultimate destination had never been mentioned at the mission the day she was taken. Jenny knew she had to make her move before the snows came; there was no way she could survive a winter in the mountains on her own. She desperately watched for an opportunity to escape

Some ten days out of Denver, Millie began to have labor pains. Thad pushed on until dark and they made camp as her pains came closer and closer together. Thad and Earl fixed her a bed in the back of the wagon and they waited, leaving Jenny tied to the wheel to listen to her screams.

"What we gonna do, Thad?" Earl asked after a piercing scream echoed through the darkness.

"*I wish you'd just kill me now,*" Millie moaned from the wagon.

Thad stopped his pacing around the fire and stopped in front of Jenny.

"*It's gettin' close. You need to get ready.*"

"*There's not a whole lot I can do tied up like this.*"

Thad pulled out his knife and cut the ropes around her wrists and ankles. "*I'll kill you if you try to escape. Do you hear me?*" His breath turned her stomach as he pulled her to her feet and hissed in her face. Jenny turned her head away and nodded as she rubbed her wrists. Earl handed her up into the back of the wagon, where Millie quickly grabbed her hand.

"*Jenny, make it go away,*" Mille cried, squeezing hard as another pain hit her. Jenny looked around the wagon, hoping a miracle would occur and give her some insight as to what to do. She had watched her father and Jamie deliver many a foal, but she knew nothing about babies. Common sense would have to guide her.

"*Earl, fetch some water from that spring and heat it up. Thad, we're going to need your knife, so pass it through the fire to clean it,*" Jenny barked from the back of the wagon as Millie screamed again.

"*I think it's coming,*" she wailed. Jenny lifted Millie's skirt up and saw the crowning of a small head in the dim light of the lantern.

"*Yes, it's coming. You're going to have to push.*" Thad was watching from the back of the wagon and Jenny noticed that he looked a little green. "*Thad, hold the lantern up so I can see what I'm doing.*" Jenny moved around to get between Millie's legs and noticed the rifle lying beside her.

She threw a blanket over it and moved so Thad was over her other shoulder. "Next time you feel a pain, push." Jenny noticed the lantern was shaking as Millie prepared herself for the push. "Earl, you'd better get over here," Jenny yelled as Millie began to bear down. Earl climbed up in the front and stuck his head in, his face shining white in the lantern's glow. "Get back here and take that lantern from Thad. Thad, you need to get in here and give her something to push against." Millie ended her push with a screech as the men changed places, both of them wishing they were somewhere else but each hastily obeying Jenny's commands. "Okay, Millie, you're going to have to try again. It's moving a little slow."

"Hey, like me, huh Millie?" Earl said.

"Shut up, Earl," Millie spat out as another pain hit her. She leaned back against Thad and began to push again, her ragged nails tearing into his arm as she bore down.

"The head is out, push again," Jenny announced. Millie had tears streaming down her face, but she nodded and gathered herself again. She screamed as she pushed and the shoulders came through, then the rest, landing safely in the blanket Jenny held out. "It's a girl!"

"Oh Thad, it's a girl." Thad did not look very happy as the baby began to cry. The wagon suddenly went dark as Jenny handed the baby girl into Millie's waiting arms. Jenny turned and saw the lantern lying on the ground next to Earl's prostrate form.

"We need the light, Thad. We need to cut the cord," Jenny instructed. He scrambled out of the wagon and held the lantern so Jenny could finish cleaning up Millie, who was cooing over the baby.

"Oh Thad, just look at her."

"Go ahead, Thad, look at your daughter," Jenny added, smiling encouragingly. Thad went back up to Millie's head and looked on in interest as she pulled the blanket down to reveal perfectly formed arms and legs and a wisp of brown hair. Jenny looked down at Earl, who was still laid out flat from the birth of his niece, and then she picked up the rifle. "I'm going to be leaving now," she announced as she leveled the rifle at Thad.

"Jenny, what are you doing?" Thad barked.

"I'm leaving and you have a choice. You can come after me, or you can take care of your wife and baby."

"Thad," Millie cried out. "She can't leave us here."

"Jenny, put the rifle down."

Jenny backed out of the wagon, carefully keeping the rifle leveled on Thad. She pulled Earl's gun out of his holster and stuck it in the waistband of her skirt.

"Jenny, come back here now." Thad came out of the wagon as she backed over to where the horses were tied. "I swear, Jenny, you put that rifle down, or so help me I'll kill you."

"I'd rather be dead than whore for you," Jenny said as she cocked the rifle. "Now what's it going to be?"

Thad advanced on her another step, then jumped as a bullet bit the dirt in front of his feet. "You can't shoot me; you haven't got it in you."

"I won't kill you but I sure will hurt you." Jenny shot again, and this time the bullet grazed his boot, making him fall over. Millie began to cry in the back of the wagon. Jenny untied the team and waved the horses off. Thad was on his feet again.

"*You won't get five miles out here on your own. You'll be crawling back by morning and I'll beat you but good then, I promise you.*"

Jenny swung up on Earl's horse, and leveled the rifle at Thad as he advanced on her again. "Take care of your wife, Thad. She needs you more than you need me," Jenny said and wheeled the horse around. She urged him back down the trail and dropped the rifle when she was out of sight of the fire. She knew they would need it to survive. She hoped that running off the other horses would give her enough time to escape. She gave the horse its head, letting him pick his way down the trail in the darkness . . .

Jenny realized she hadn't changed her clothes since the funeral. She ripped the nightgown over her head and violently flung it away. She ran her hands over her hollow stomach, examining the flat planes of it in the mirror. "I bet you need some food, little one." She turned sideways and patted her belly as she examined her figure. She wondered, again, what had happened to the Millers' baby. Chase had said that they had found the bodies of Thad, Millie, and Earl, along with a burned-out wagon, sometime after she had escaped. Somehow the little party had wandered onto a sacred burial ground and paid the ultimate price. There had been no sign of the baby but she hoped that the Millers' daughter was being loved by a Kiowa family somewhere. Chase had seemed to be certain of it.

"Let's see if we can find you something to eat," Jenny said and reached for her clothes.

* * *

Jenny wondered where the new dog had come from. He was a huge beast, and he was lying across the porch on Grace's cabin as if he owned it. He perused her with an almost understanding look as she stood before the stoop.

"Jenny?" Caleb came up behind her.

"Where did this dog come from?"

"He belongs to Cole. His name is Justice." Caleb swept her up in a hug, but Jenny pushed him away.

"Please Caleb, I stink. The only reason I'm not taking a bath right now is because I'm starving."

"Yeah, I noticed you haven't eaten much in the past few days." Caleb squeezed her shoulders despite her protests.

"I know you were the one carrying me food and keeping the fire up." Jenny blinked back tears as she looked into his warm brown eyes. "I appreciate it."

"I'm just glad you're back." Caleb took her arm and led her up to meet Justice, who sniffed her hand politely and thumped his huge tail on the boards of the porch. Jenny felt suddenly shy when Caleb opened the door and she saw the stranger sitting there with Jake.

"Jenny, this is Cole Larrimore," Caleb said, introducing them.

"*The* Cole Larrimore?" Jenny looked between Jake and Caleb in total confusion.

"Yes, ma'am."

Jenny's knees suddenly felt weak and Caleb caught her as she wobbled.

"I guess I wasn't ready for the walk over here." Jenny sighed as Jake dragged a chair over for her.

"You've been through a rough time from what I hear," Cole said. "I'll go get Grace; she's up at the house."

Jenny nodded in gratitude as he left, the dog following on his heels.

"He just showed up a few days ago," Jake explained when he was gone. "Jason hired him since we . . ."

"Since we're missing a few hands," Jenny finished for him.

"We'll go get the tub ready for you," Caleb volunteered. Jenny suddenly felt too weary to even think about bathing.

Grace arrived a few moments later, out of breath from her dash down the hill through the snow. She immediately began fussing as if Jenny were a long-lost child. She soon had her fed and soaking in the tub that Caleb and Jake had carried in and filled for her. She washed Jenny's hair for her and Jenny sat in front of the stove, wrapped up in a robe while Grace worked at the tangles that a week of neglect had wrought.

"Grace, do you ever think about the past?" Jenny asked while the fire cracked and popped companionably.

"What do you mean?"

"I've been remembering the time when I was taken away."

"I guess it would only make sense that you would think about that; after all, it was the first time . . ."

"That Jamie and I were apart."

"Yes."

"But then, I always had the hope of being with him

174

again." Jenny closed her eyes to summon her brother's face to mind. "Do you believe in dreams?"

"It depends. What kind of dreams are you talking about?"

"I had dreams about Logan, before he . . . I've been dreaming about Logan since Chase and I got married. Do you think that somehow I knew he was going to kill Jamie?"

"Oh honey, you would have no way of knowing something like that was going to happen."

"But Chase knew from his dreams that he would find me and we would be together."

"Have you had dreams about Chase since he left?"

"No, I've just dreamed about the time I was with the Millers and afterward."

"Afterward?"

"After I escaped from Thad, another man took me; I think he had been following us since we left Denver. We had seen him before, out on the trail, and then I ran right into him when I was running away from Thad in Denver."

"Well, what happened?"

"I was running Earl's horse hard down the trail . . ." Jenny began.

She had lost too much time in the darkness letting the horse have his head, relying on his instincts to get her down the trail in the black of the night. Now the sun was up and she had pushed him into a canter, wanting to put as much distance between herself and Thad as possible. Jenny knew someone was following her; the back of her neck had felt strange since the first light of day. She would rather die than go back to the Millers and the life they planned for her. The gelding was blowing hard now and she knew he needed a rest, but she pushed him on, urging him forward as the ground leveled out.

The next thing she knew she was flying through the air, and the hard ground was rushing up to meet her as the horse stumbled. She instinctively curled herself into a ball as she hit. The horse stumbled over her, his hoof striking her forehead as he struggled to regain his footing. Stars exploded in her head and she fell into unconsciousness.

Each step of the horse sent a jolt up through her stomach and into her head until she had to fight the urge to throw up. She was lying over her horse, her feet dangling on one side, her arms and head on the other. Her braid had been twisted around her neck to keep it from dragging on the ground. Jenny blinked, trying to get something to come into focus, and she finally decided that the grayness that she saw between the wild strands of her hair was the ground as it moved up and down with each clip-clop of the hooves. She tried to move, and groaned when she saw that her hands were tied together by a rope that passed under the horse's belly and attached to her ankles. Thad must have found her. There was going to be hell to pay, she thought miserably. Then she realized that they were going downhill instead of up, so she twisted her head around to get a look at who was leading her horse. All she could see was the back of a black suit coat under a black hat. Something about the man seemed familiar, but her head was still reeling.

"Hey," she said weakly, then cleared her throat to try again. "Hey!" The horses came to a stop and she heard the

sound of spurs clinking as the man in the dark coat came back to her. He lifted her head by her braid and Jenny's sapphire-blue eyes came up to focus on the man who had interrupted her bath at the pond, the same sharply dressed man she had crashed into on her mad flight in Denver. The teeth under his dark mustache gleamed white as he smiled at her.

"Pleased to make your acquaintance ma'am," he said in a deep Southern drawl.

"Could you get me down from here?" Jenny gasped as she felt her stomach roll. He pulled a small knife from his boot and cut the rope under the horse's belly. He pushed against her forehead and Jenny slid over the horse and landed in a heap on her backside.

"Thanks, I think," she said as she rubbed her posterior. The man pulled her to her feet and held on to her arms as she staggered, trying to regain her equilibrium.

"Wade Bishop at your service ma'am." He gave her a courtly bow.

Grace interrupted Jenny's story. "Did you say Wade Bishop?" They were seated at the table now, sipping coffee. Jenny had never talked about her missing years with anyone, just filling Jamie and Chase in when they asked, but never discussing the details.

"Yes, why?" Jenny asked. Grace's warm brown eyes were unreadable to Jenny.

"Nothing, just go on."

"Well, Bishop told me he'd found me unconscious on the trail," Jenny explained, remembering how she'd held her hands out to him, to be released. "I asked him why he'd tied my hands and he said he wanted to take every precaution possible to keep me from further injury." Jenny smiled ruefully." "He said he was a gentleman."

Grace snorted in disgust. Jenny recalled her own disgust at Bishop's next words.

"As a gentleman I have to protect you, so it would be best for everyone if you remain tied up at the present time."

Jenny had promptly swung her fists at him, hitting him in the jaw. The blow sent him staggering back against the horse and knocked his hat off, but he recovered quickly and backhanded her.

"Does everybody out here feel the need to hit me?" Jenny spat out with the blood from her lip.

"I was just returning the favor," Bishop drawled. "Now, do you want to ride on the back of your horse sitting up or should I return you to your previous position?"

"That depends on where we're going."

"Texas."

"Texas?" Jenny felt Jamie falling further and further away. Bishop offered her a hand, but she grabbed the horn of her saddle and swung up without his help. He grabbed her horse's reins and handed her his canteen for a drink before he mounted. He pulled her horse up close to his to keep an eye on her and they started back down the trail.

"Why are we going to Texas?" Jenny asked after they had been riding for a while.

"I know some people down there who would love to meet someone like you."

"Someone like me?"

"Why yes, someone with your natural beauty and grace." Bishop looked at her and smiled charmingly. "Why, I knew

the first time I saw you in all your glory back at that pond that you were destined for greater things than life with that big dummy."

"What makes you so sure that I wasn't happy with that big dummy?"

"You were running away from him when I saw you in Denver, weren't you?"

"Point taken." Jenny had to agree with him. "But what gives you the right to make such life decisions for me as taking me to Texas? Against my will, I might add."

"I was raised to be a gentleman and gentlemen always look out for women when they are in distress. I knew that you needed my assistance that day I saw you in Denver and I have followed you ever since so that I might lend you my aid."

"Thank you. Since you have gallantly rescued me, after I rescued myself, why don't you take me where I want to go instead of taking me to Texas? A real gentleman does consider a lady's feelings in such matters, does he not?"

"Well, where is it exactly that you want to go?"

"St. Jo. I have a brother there and I miss him."

"A brother?" The gray eyes flicked over her again. "St. Jo is no place for someone like you. It's a town full of farmers and such. No, I believe Texas would suit you much better, and I'm sure your brother only wants what's best for you."

"Why don't we go discuss it with him?" Jenny smiled sweetly to cover her growing frustration. She knew that Bishop was far more intelligent than all the Millers put together and she would really have to be on her toes to escape now. Winter was coming and Texas was in the opposite *direction from where she needed to be going. If Jamie was following her, there was no way he would know to look in Texas. Jenny felt a knot of panic start to grow inside her.* "How far is Texas?" *she finally asked as they rode on.*

"Far enough."

"Jenny." Grace took Jenny's hand in her own. "I know Wade Bishop."

"What?"

"He's the man who did this to me." Her other hand trailed down the scars on her cheeks which ran from the corners of her eyes to the corners of her mouth. "He took all my money and then he cut me with his knife. The knife that he keeps in his boot. However did you get away from him?"

"I climbed out a window," Jenny said.

The trip to Texas had gone on forever. Jenny felt as if she had spent her whole life on the back of Earl's horse, following Bishop in the freezing rain and sleet. She felt frozen to the bone. They found what shelter they could at night, but each morning they woke up to the same dreary skies and incessant rain. Bishop pushed them on relentlessly, taking her farther from any hope of rescue with each step. He had managed to avoid every town on the way south. Jenny had no way of knowing where she was or how to find her way back. He watched her every movement, not even giving her privacy when she had to relieve herself. She became fearful of what he had in store for her when they reached their destination in Texas, and she knew whatever it was, it wouldn't be good.

They finally came to the outskirts of a town and Jenny

could tell by the set of Bishop's shoulders that they had reached their destination. He rode around some buildings and took her down an alley to the back of what looked like a three-story hotel.

"Where are we?" Jenny asked as he pulled her down from the horse.

"Austin, Texas."

Jenny blinked against the bright light that filled her eyes as they went into the huge kitchen of the building. There was a black woman working at the sink and a younger black man lounging in a chair.

"Cyrus, take care of our horses," Bishop instructed the man, who immediately went out, pulling his collar up against the rain. Jenny stood in the middle of the floor with the water dripping off her and began to shiver.

"Don't just stand there, child, go stand by the fire and get warm." The woman pointed to a large potbelly stove and Jenny shuffled her feet, trying to get them going in the right direction. She managed to make it to the warmth and pulled off her dripping coat. "You trying to freeze this girl to death? Look at her; she ain't got no scarf, nor hat, or nothing to keep off all that cold rain falling out there."

"I'm sorry, Eunice, couturiers are sorely lacking on the trails north of here," Bishop responded to her scolding.

"Where you from, girl?"

"St. Joseph."

"St. Joseph! Lord, girl, you're half way across the country from St. Joseph. Did you bring her all the way here from there?"

"I picked her up outside of Denver."

Eunice came over and picked up Jenny's coat, then stuck

181

her finger under her chin to survey her face, which was partially hidden by Jenny's wet, unkempt hair. "She's pretty, all right, but a bit scrawny."

"That's why I brought her to you first, so you can fatten her up." Bishop shook out his coat and ran his fingers through his wet hair. "Where's Monette?"

"In her dressing room, getting ready for business."

"Eunice will take good care of you, Jenny, so mind your manners." Bishop left, leaving Jenny steaming beside the fire.

"How old are you, girl?"

"Fifteen last spring."

"Fifteen, why, you're just a baby." The woman began to shake her head. "I swear, I don't know what these folks is thinking, bringing a young girl like you in here to do their business."

"What kind of business?" Jenny sat down at the table and Eunice set a bowl of stew and a biscuit down before her.

"The romance business. Miss Monette has the best whorehouse west of the Mississippi and she doesn't let just anyone come in here and do her business for her. You must be special, girl."

Jenny looked at the woman. The experiences she had been through since leaving the orphanage had taught her to keep her emotions well hidden, but this woman had just called her a whore. "I have never been with a man in my life," Jenny stated calmly as she brought the spoon to her mouth.

Eunice dissolved into laughter. "Lord, girl, that's what makes you so special around here. There are men who will *pay a pretty penny to deflower a virgin, especially one that looks like you."*

"What is so special about the way I look?"

"Nothing right now, but when Miss Monette gets through with you, you'll be as beautiful as Venus herself."

Jenny rolled her eyes as the woman turned back to the sink. Miss Monette had a surprise coming to her. There was no way she was going to be made a whore for anyone. But the first thing she needed to do was finish the delicious meal that was in front of her. She couldn't remember the last time she had eaten anything that hadn't come off the trail, and besides she needed to keep her strength up if she was going to escape. Eunice fixed her a second helping, and then set a piece of apple pie down in front of her.

A finely dressed woman came sweeping into the kitchen with Bishop behind her. She had coal black hair piled high over a face that was painted up to look like a porcelain doll. She was wearing a low-cut beaded dress of deep maroon and her long tapered fingernails were painted to match. Her hands, ears, and neck flashed with expensive-looking jewelry. She immediately came over to Jenny and examined her face like a piece of merchandise.

"You were right, Wade, she has a lovely face and great hair, but I can't tell anything else until we get her clothes off." Jenny slapped away the hand that held her chin. "Oh, spirited too. That's good, honey, there are lots of men who like that."

"I am not a whore," Jenny spat out.

Bishop grabbed her hair and pulled her head back so she had to look up at him. "You will be soon enough and you'll learn to like it."

"Take her up to the third floor and lock her in," Miss Monette said. "I'll have a bath sent up for her. Eunice, make sure you get rid of those clothes."

"I'll throw them in the rag pile, ma'am, that's all they're good for."

Bishop jerked Jenny up from her chair and hauled her up two flights of stairs. She was pushed into a small room at the back of the building that held nothing but a cot, a chair, and a chest of drawers. Bishop taunted her with the key before he locked the door behind him. Jenny slammed her fists in fury against the portal as his footsteps faded down the hall.

She whirled around and went to the small, high window in the gable. It was unlocked and she pulled the chair over so she could see out. She figured she had about ten minutes at the most before Eunice appeared with her bath, so she had to move quickly. The drop was straight down, but the window was high enough in the gable that she could reach the roof if she went out backward. She pulled herself up on the sill, sitting with her face looking in. Then she reached up and grabbed the peak of the gable roof. The rain had stopped but the wood was still slippery and she cautiously pulled herself up until she was standing on the sill. She braced her arms and let her feet dangle out, and swung to the side, moving one hand to the ridge of the roof and pulling herself up. She was now straddling the gable, looking out over the alley. She bent over and shut the window, hoping to buy some time. The building towered a story over the other buildings around it and had a pitched roof, while the others were flat. The building to the left was butted up against the one she was sitting on, so she edged her way to the end of the whorehouse, then dropped to the roof below, rolling as she landed to break her fall. Jenny got up and ran to the other side of the roof. There was an alley between this building and the next, but there was also a long board lying on the roof top, so she laid it over the opening and walked across as if she were on a tightrope. She pulled the board over to the new rooftop when she was done and kept doing the same until she was at the end of the row. The last building had a porch and she dropped onto the roof and shimmered down the post to the ground. The streets were deserted. She calculated her flight had taken about ten minutes, they would probably be looking for her soon. The buildings in the street beyond looked like houses, so she crouched low and ran across the street, making her way through a hedge behind a brightly lit home. She watched as several nicely dressed people came up the walk. From the sound she decided that there was a party going on. A window in the second story was slightly ajar, so she climbed up the trellis and entered the darkened room.

Jenny huddled on the floor under the window as she let her eyes grow accustomed to the dim light from the fire in the hearth. She rubbed her chilled arms and crawled over to the fireplace. She heard voices and the sound of Christmas carols being played on a piano in the room below. "Eight months," she said to herself when she realized that it was December. "It's been eight months." A huge rocking horse sat in the corner and there was a shelf full of books next to the bed, so she assumed she was in a child's room. Then she saw a gun belt and knife lying on the desk and she thought perhaps the child had grown up some. She silently went to the wardrobe and found it full of pants and shirts. Perhaps *a young man close to her age was the occupant, she decided, as she held some items up for size.*

Jenny helped herself to some long johns, socks, pants, and a shirt. She found some boots, smaller than the rest, in the back of the wardrobe and after she added another pair of socks, they fit her fine. There was also an old coat hanging next to a newer one, so she took it. She bundled her old clothes around her shoes and shut the door to the wardrobe, catching her reflection in the mirror that was attached to the front. She looked closely and saw deep blue eyes, huge and haunted in a pale face that was lean from hunger. Beneath her shirt, her collarbone was jutting out beneath the skin and she realized that she could now count each rib. Her hair hung down to her thighs in a messy braid, with stray curls shooting out everywhere around her face. She reached up to shove her hair out of her eyes and almost cried when the gesture reminded her of Jamie.

"Everyone who looks at me wants to make me a whore," she mumbled to herself. She turned and picked up the knife she'd seen on the desk. She pulled the braid from the back of her head and neatly sliced the whole thing off. She pulled fists full of hair up and sawed away, cutting until there was nothing left but wisps close to her skull. She wiped away the tears that had gathered with her sleeve and pulled the hat down on her head, bringing it low over her face. She laid the knife down and her hand drifted across the gun belt. She pulled the revolver out, checked its load and let it dangle in her hand for a minute. Jenny looked across at the mirror and did not recognize the person reflected back. She returned the gun to its holster and put the gun belt on, tying it down on her thigh and testing her draw before

gathering up her belongings and making sure she didn't leave any stray strands of hair behind. She dropped the bundle to the ground and went back down the trellis to the tune of "Deck the Halls." She made her way back to the main part of town and noticed a stable. The forge was behind it and some coals were still glowing, so she pumped the bellows and threw her bundle inside, watching as her hair went up in smoke. She ran her hand over the back of her neck, marveling at how light her head felt. Her shoes wouldn't burn, so she dropped them in the rain barrel and made her way back through the alley to the building that Bishop had taken her to. She heard the sound of raised voices and saw Bishop stalk out the back door and mount his horse.

"Find her, Wade. She's worth a lot of money and there's a ship leaving next week," Monette called from the door.

"She can't get far on foot. I'll find her," Bishop promised.

"You said she couldn't have gotten outside without us knowing it too." Monette's painted face looked harsh in the lantern light. Bishop smirked, then took off at a gallop. Jenny watched as Monette went back into the kitchen. She made her way to the stable and found Earl's horse nodding contentedly in a stall. Jenny quickly saddled him, walked him out, and headed in the opposite direction from that Bishop had taken, riding slowly east as if she had all the time in the world.

"If I hadn't got away, I would have become a whore in Austin, Texas," Jenny said, finishing her story.

"You never would have stayed in Austin," Cole said. Grace and Jenny looked up in surprise. They had not heard him come in. "Monette sells women to slave traders in Galveston. From there they are taken all over the world, mostly to the Orient or the Middle East."

Jenny felt a shiver go down her spine and pulled the borrowed robe tight around her. "Then that's what she meant by the ship."

"We were never able to prove it." Cole's eyes were distant. "You were very lucky to escape. You don't know how many beautiful young girls have disappeared from that whorehouse in Austin, without a trace."

Grace dropped her face into her hands. "When he cut me, he said it was for my own good."

"Wade Bishop is the man who cut your face?" Cole asked in amazement. "When did it happen?"

"Fifteen years ago, in New Orleans." Grace dashed a tear from the corner of her eye. "Jenny, I can't believe that we both ran afoul of that bastard."

"Monette set up her establishment at about the same time. Her brother started supplying her with girls and the choice ones got sent on to Galveston to be sold off to rich sheiks and foreign princes. They're brother and sister, you know."

"I never knew that. I never knew what kind of man he was; I was so foolish then, and lonely. I just let his sweet talk go to my head. And I've been paying for it ever since." Grace's hands went to her face and covered her scars.

"Grace, it wasn't your fault. You're not responsible for his evil. You were just a victim of it," Jenny exclaimed. "Just like we were victims of Randolph Mason, and Father Clarence and Lo . . . ga . . ." Her voice broke and Grace began to reach for her. Jenny put her hand out to halt her and swallowed hard. "I am not going to be a victim anymore." Jenny rose from the table and went into Grace's room. She came out a few minutes later in her clothes and went out the door, leaving Grace and Cole staring after her in silence.

Chapter Fifteen

Chase knew in his gut that he was headed in the right direction, but he would feel better if there were a sign. It was as if he were the only person left on the earth. He had ridden the entire day and not seen anything living, besides the occasional bird. It was as if every living creature had gone into hibernation, leaving no one but Chase and the buckskin to wander the earth.

"Oh how I miss him," Chase allowed himself to say as he made camp that evening and remembered a night they had shared on the trail while searching for Jenny: the night that Jamie had learned how to kill.

The fire had flickered brightly against the dark sky, signaling warmth to any who cared to approach, and danger to the animals that called the area home. The bedrolls on either side were placed close enough to keep those sleeping within warmth, but far enough away that a stray spark wouldn't be of any danger. The horses were tethered close by, both of them dozing at the line, tired from their long day on the trail. Four men approached the campsite on foot, each one coming from a different direction. They froze in their tracks as the soft 'whoo' of an owl broke the silence, but went on when the sleeping forms did not move. Each man had a gun in his hand. One quieted the horses' soft whickers as he passed by them, leaving the black and the buckskin to prick their ears and look towards the fire with quiet interest. A large man approached the longer of the sleeping forms, grinning as he realized that he had accomplished his feat without waking either of the two, who were so exhausted from their travels and so inexperienced that they felt safe in the wild. He thought to himself as he prodded the form with his boot, grinning at his friends over the fire. One of them snickered to himself in anticipation of the fun they were about to have, and another quickly shushed him. The large man placed a toe in the side of the form and prodded again, rolling his eyes that anyone could sleep so deeply while out in the wilds.

In one rolling motion the blanket came off and a gun was pointed at the large man's head. "Tell your friends to drop their weapons or you're a dead man," Jamie said as he stood, the gun still pointed at the large man's head. Behind him he could hear the sound of weapons being cocked. The big man looked at him in surprise, then looked back at his friends. Jamie now stood beside him, facing the other three with his gun still aimed.

"Where's the breed?" the large man asked as the other three kicked at the empty blankets.

"He's around. Now drop the guns."

"You gonna take all four of us?"

"Yeah, he can't take all four."

"No, but I could take out one or two, so who's it going to be?" Jamie cocked the revolver that was still pressed against the big man's temple.

Chase settled back in his blankets as he recalled the men's troubled faces. Jamie had sounded so confident facing down the men around the fire, but Chase had known he was scared to death.

Someone was going to die that night, you could feel it in the air. Then one of the men flinched. Jamie dived and fired, rolling away from the flames as the shot rang out. At the same instant, Chase dropped from the tree above the three, landing on two of them. He knocked one to the ground and buried his knife in the man's back as the other man tried to bring his gun around. Chase grabbed the second man's arms and rolled back, flipping him over his head and into the fire. The big man rolled to his feet and turned on Jamie, bringing his gun up to shoot, but Jamie shot first and the man fell, his eyes widening in surprise as he looked down at the spreading blood on his shirt. Chase was still rolling on the ground with the one he had thrown into the fire, each one trying to get a hold on the bloody knife. The knife slipped out of Chase's grasp and they both dove for it. Chase wound up on the bottom as they both grabbed the knife, first one, then the other, trying to bury it in his opponent. Jamie shot again and the smoking man slumped over on top of Chase. He pushed the body off and staggered to his feet with his shoulder bleeding from a gash.

"Are you all right?" he asked Jamie, who appeared to be

in a daze. Jamie shoved his hair back and looked at the four bodies lying around them.

"I don't know, am I?"

"You're bleeding."

"I am?" Jamie looked down at his upper left arm. "I guess a bullet grazed me."

Chase took a look at the hole in Jamie's shirt. "Yeah, you were lucky."

"I was?"

"Jamie, listen to me." Chase took his friend by the shoulders and turned him so he could look into his wide blue eyes. "It was either them or us. Do you understand me? They came to kill us. That's the way it is out here. You've got to kill sometimes to survive."

Chase remembered how the innocence had left Jamie's eyes that night when they buried the four bodies off the trail. He remembered the resolve that had filled the huge body of his friend when he realized the responsibilities he now faced, the things he would have to do to survive and find his sister. "It was them or us," Chase said to himself, "Then it was me, Jenny, or Jamie. Now it's down to me or Logan." Chase curled up under his blanket and went to sleep.

Cole had asked Grace a hundred questions about Wade Bishop. He wanted to know where he came from, how Grace had met him, how long she had known him, every intimate detail of her life at that time. His gray eyes took on the look of chipped ice as he interrogated her about her relationship with a man that she would as soon forget.

"Why are you asking me all these questions?" she finally hurled at him when she had reached the limit of her patience. Listening to Jenny's story had been trying enough without the added pain of knowing that Wade Bishop had played a role in the girl's life. Cole's interest was downright intrusive.

"There are a lot of Rangers who have spent a lot of time trying to bust up Monette's little business. Isn't it funny that I should wind up in Wyoming with two women who know him?"

"Know him." Grace practically spit the words. "Believe me, knowing Wade Bishop is not something anyone should want."

"You have to admit it's a bit strange." Cole's tone was hostile.

"Did you come here looking for him? I was under the impression that you had quit the Texas Rangers." Grace was growing angry with his implications.

The look that Cole gave Grace sent a shiver down her spine. His clear gray eyes were haunted, lost, and full of menace. She realized that she had seen that look before on Chase's face, when he left Jamie's deathbed. "You want to kill him, don't you?" She was so afraid of the answer, she could barely whisper. "What did he do to you?"

Cole jumped to his feet, causing his chair to skid away from the table. "I have quit rangering." Was he trying to convince himself? He left the cabin with Justice on his heels.

* * *

Ty and Cat found no trace of Sarah or her father in town. The last time anyone had seen them was at the time of the funeral. Ty and Cat picked up the mail and started for home, but then Ty turned his horse aside and Cat followed without a word.

The snow had covered all the graves but there was a fresh mound over Jamie's that made it recognizable. There was no marker—they hadn't set one before the blizzard and probably wouldn't until the spring thaw. Ty stood beside the small hill of snow with his hat in his hands, and then lowered himself until he was crouching in the snow. Cat watched from her horse as he said his own private goodbye to his friend. He had been strong for the rest of them, she realized. Damn Chase for leaving Jenny when she needed him the most. Cat dashed aside the tears that had gathered and waited. It was all she could do now—wait for Ty to make up his mind. Wait for him to decide, or get him liquored up and seduce him. For a few minutes she actually considered the second option as she watched him kneeling in the snow, but she knew she didn't want him that way. As Jenny had said, she should love him for who he was and let him be true to himself. But that didn't mean he shouldn't have some sense knocked into him.

Cat felt a great sense of relief wash over her as Ty made his way back to the horses. He carried a great many burdens on his wide shoulders. He had taken on the responsibility of running the ranch. He was worried about his home; he was worried about Chase; and he was concerned about Jenny. He didn't need another burden. Cat reached out her hand to him when he was mounted beside her. "Hey," she said. "I love you." Ty squeezed her hand and held on to it until the gait of the horses made it impossible to hang on any longer.

The long winter days fell, one after another, like the snow that never seemed to let up. Everyone took on his or her own pattern, like the ice crystals that formed on the window panes. Cole filled the void left by Jamie and Chase with his work, but there was no joy in him, he was outside the circle of friendship that had been so much a part of their everyday lives. He just relieved some of the workload for the others. Grace and Cole danced around each other at meal times. They had declared an uneasy truce over the Wade Bishop discussion, but they were always watching each other. Both realized they had touched things better left untouched. The man was an enigma to all of them, but he did his share and he was pleasant company, indulging Zane's endless questions with good humor. Grace could feel him watching her as she went about the endless tasks of serving meals and doing laundry. Strangely enough, his looks did not bother her, but left her feeling flattered that she was worthy of his perusal. She became accustomed to looking up and seeing his intent gray eyes watching her, eyes that never missed anything.

Cat seemed content for the time; perhaps it was just a sign that she was finally growing up. She doted on her father, who never seemed to regain his spark after

Jamie's death. She savored every moment with Ty, providing him with peace that he didn't even know he needed. They didn't speak of the South, or the coming war; they just took time to enjoy the simple pleasures of everyday life on the ranch.

Jenny sought her peace in the barn among the breeding mares. She spent her days there, her injured soul searching for a last connection with her brother. She tended the mares, brushing them until their coats gleamed in the soft light of the winter days. She carefully combed each forelock and mane, and untangled tails that flicked in appreciation of her tender care. The great gray tabby became her constant companion, weaving his way around the delicate legs of the mares and rubbing against Jenny's boots as she worked. She spent the most time with Storm, her last living connection with her father, mother, and Jamie and the dream they'd shared. Ian had never tended the stallion as carefully as she did now; his great age made him all the more precious to Jenny, and she vowed not to take for granted the days that she had with him. The work served as a healing balm, keeping her from thinking of Chase. There was time enough for that at night, when she was all alone in their big bed. She kept herself going for the baby that grew inside her, the child that was her secret. Chase did not know about the babe, and no one else would know until he did. In the meantime, work filled her days and dreams of Chase filled her nights.

As the days passed, the ranch remained buried in snow, insulating all who lived there from the outside world. Laughing was too hard, crying was too painful. Being alive was enough. They worked together, they ate together, and they surrounded each other with silence. And when the day was over, each sought peace in his own way and then said a prayer for Chase and his safe return.

Jason had let Ty take on more and more of the responsibility of running the huge spread that had been his home for many long years. Since Jamie's death it had been harder for Jason to get moving in the mornings, harder for him to find a reason to see to the things that needed to be done. He felt as if his sixty-odd years of life had finally caught up with him, turning him into an old man since those tragic days at the first of the year. Ty made it a habit to come up to the big house at the end of the day and report on the day's activities. They would sit in the study in front of the fire while Cat served coffee, and talk about the ranch and the people who lived there. Cat would listen to the goings on, offering an opinion occasionally, but mostly just watching and waiting for her father to go up to bed so she could sit with Ty and watch the fire burn down to glowing embers.

One night Jason seemed inclined to stay up and talk, and Cat finally went off yawning to her bed. Ty had sensed that something was bothering the old rancher. Jason usually made it a policy to let the people in his employ work through their own problems; the only time he'd interfered was when he'd sent Jenny and Ty off to Denver together to buy the mares.

"Cat has grown up a bit since New Year's," Jason

said as his daughter left the room. Cat had taken to dressing up for their evenings together, giving them an illusion of elegance and refinement in the wilds of Wyoming.

"I think settled down is more the word for it," Ty answered. Jason laughed a bit, something he had gotten out of the habit of doing.

"What about you, Ty? Are you ready to settle down?"

"I think you already know the answer to that, sir. I've discussed it with Cat already. I think it's best if we wait until we see what's going to happen in the rest of the country."

"Do you love my daughter, Ty?"

"Yes."

"I loved a young woman once. I wasn't much older than you are now."

"I guess you aren't talking about Cat's mother," Ty interrupted.

"No." Jason smiled as he recalled that disastrous marriage. "I was fresh out of school, had just studied for the bar and was rather full of myself. I was sailing with some friends on the Chesapeake Bay and I met the most beautiful girl I had ever seen. She had golden blond hair and eyes the color of a summer sky. Her name was Jenny, and the funny thing is, she reminds me of our Jenny." Ty nodded as Jason continued with his story. "That summer was the best time of my life."

"What happened?"

"My parents didn't approve of her. Her father was a merchant and therefore not of our social class. They thought she was just a phase I was going through, my little rebellion before I settled down to practice law and make a proper marriage. I told them otherwise." Jason leaned forward in his chair to talk more earnestly to Ty. "I woke up the next morning on a ship bound for England. By the time I got back several months later, Jenny had married and disappeared. Her family had been killed in a flood, so there was no trace of her. That's when I came west. I know my father thought he was just doing what was best for me when he had me drugged and placed on that ship, but he didn't understand. Without Jenny, life meant nothing to me. There has not been a day since then that I haven't missed her, or wondered about where she is or if she is still alive."

"You said she got married soon after you left."

"Yes, I wondered about that also. You see, there was a chance that she could have been with child. With my child." Jason let the words sink in. "I wanted to marry her before we made love, I should have married her after, but I wanted to do it up right, present her to my parents, have a big wedding. I was trying to make everyone happy instead of doing what I knew was right. I was so worried about tomorrow that I lost the days that were right in front of me." Jason looked earnestly at Ty, who was gazing into the fire. "Don't lose what's in front of you, Ty. I know you have a vision of taking Cat home, of impressing her with your plantation so she'll know that you are worthy of her. I also know that doesn't mean a thing to her. You could be the spawn of Satan and she would still love you. Make these days precious and live every minute of them so that if you don't come back, she will at least have that to remember." Jason stood and placed a hand on Ty's shoulder. "After all, you never know when your time is going to run out."

"Like Jamie's did," Ty whispered into the fire.

"Yes, like Jamie." Jason walked slowly out of the study, leaving Ty to stare at the fire.

"Cat, wake up." Ty gently shook her shoulders. Cat blinked and rubbed her eyes in the soft light of the rising moon.

"What . . . what's wrong?" She sat up in the bed and pushed the curls out of her eyes. "Is something wrong? Is it Daddy?"

"No." Ty sat on the edge of her bed. Now that he had her attention, he didn't quite know what to do with it.

"Ty, what is it?" She sat up and crossed her arms around her knees.

Ty reached out and smoothed a curl back against her ear. "Let's get married," he said softly.

"Are you serious?"

"Yes. I've wasted enough time. I love you, Catherine Lynch. Will you marry me?" Cat squealed and threw her arms around Ty's neck. "I take it this means yes," Ty laughed against her hair.

"Yes! When? Right away, I hope." The words that had been held back for so long tumbled out one upon the other. "Oh Ty, what about Jenny? It's not too soon, is it?"

"I think she'll be very happy for us." Ty kissed the top of her head. "And I want to get married right away too."

"We can do it here, and keep it small. I don't think we should have a big wedding with everything that's going on."

"Well, considering the weather, I think that's a good idea, but we can do whatever you want. After all, this is the only wedding you're going to have, and I want you to be happy."

"Hey, as long as you're the groom, I don't care what else happens."

Jason watched quietly from the hall as Cat raised her lips to Ty's. The moon had risen and was hanging in the window behind them, illuminating the couple as they kissed, and catching the reflection of a tear that was sliding down his daughter's cheek. *Well done, son*, Jason thought. He was smiling as he went back to his room.

Jenny once again pondered the two dresses hanging in her wardrobe. The blue calico had been made for her last summer when she was still lean from her years of searching for Jamie. There was no way it would fit now with the slight rounding of her stomach. The deep red velvet wasn't much better, and furthermore, she had worn it the day Jamie died. Even though Grace had managed to wash the stains away, Jenny could still see the blood that had poured forth from her brother's chest, and the pattern it had left in the soft fabric. So what was she to wear to Cat and Ty's wedding? Her reflection in the wardrobe mirror held no answers.

"The real problem is that you don't want to go," Jenny said to the reflection. She sat down on the bed and flopped on her back, throwing an arm up over her eyes. How could she attend another wedding when her brother's had ended in his death and her own was still so fresh and new, except for the fact that her husband was still missing. Two months had passed and still there was no word from Chase. His silence could mean any number of things. The weather made travel near to impossible, and since the land to the north was still mostly wild and unsettled, there was little chance of Chase sending word by mail. Or he could be dead, but Jenny refused to consider that possibility. She would know it if he was, wouldn't she? Wasn't that all that was keeping her alive right now? Knowing that Chase was out there, that he was coming back to her and the little one sheltered inside her? Her hand rubbed across her stomach, which had flattened slightly with her position. She felt a slight fluttering in response, so light that she caught her breath in case she had imagined it. But she felt it again, a tiny little butterfly whose wings beat against her insides, announcing its presence to the world.

"I'm here," the babe whispered to her. "I'm a part of you, a part of him."

Jenny rolled on her side and curled herself around that burgeoning new life. "I'll take care of you," she promised. "I swear it." But could she? Hadn't her own parents promised the very same, night after night when they had said their goodnights and tucked her and Jamie in? Hadn't Chase sworn to protect her from harm? And he had tried his best to do so, but fate had stepped in and claimed the life of her brother with a bullet that could have taken her or Chase just as easily. How could she protect this small being inside her? She could only try her best.

Jenny rose from the bed and dressed in the dark red velvet. "Let's go to a wedding."

"Cat must have bought every candle in Laramie," Zane whispered to Caleb as they watched her descend the staircase, which was wrapped with greenery and ribbons. She was wearing her mother's wedding dress, a satin and lace confection that would have been more appropriate for a big church wedding than the small intimate ceremony that was about to take place in the parlor. It was late afternoon, but the light was dimmed by the heavy clouds that had gathered in the sky, promising more snow and no end to the long days of winter. The rooms sparkled with candlelight, however; candles on the mantle, on the tables, candles in huge silver candelabrum balanced on petite tables that were made to hold plants or lamps. The bride outshone all of them, the smile on her face enough to lift the hearts of all who were present. The minister was waiting in front of the fireplace with Ty, who was dressed in a new suit and a shiny pair of boots. His hair had been trimmed and lay neatly in place, and his blue eyes anxiously sought out Cat's own gold-green ones as she gracefully floated down the stairs to her father's waiting arm.

Cat's heart skipped a beat when she saw Ty standing in front of the fireplace with Caleb, Zane, and Jake lined up beside him. What had happened to the raw boy who had shown up a few years past and asked for a job in a strong Southern accent? When had this man replaced him? When had his shoulders gotten so wide? Had he always been so tall? Where had this air of confidence and strength come from? Had she not spent every waking moment watching him and every sleeping one dreaming of him? Had his eyes always looked at her with such intensity? Were they seeing her very soul deep inside her?

A shiver of anticipation ran down her spine as she walked with her father in the slow step that she had made him practice over and over again in the days before the wedding. Grace beamed as she played the piano. Grace's brown eyes looked misty as Cat floated by on the arm of her father. She caught a glimpse of Cole in the corner, and heard the soft rustling of Jenny tiptoeing in behind her. Then Ty's face filled her vision, his incredibly handsome face, his soft sexy smile, his steady blue eyes, and his golden brown hair that had been tipped blond by the past summer's sun.

She was beside him, her hand was in his and he wrapped it around his arm, placing his own on top of hers as they turned to face the minister. *Dreams can come true*, Cat thought as the vows were pronounced and the rings exchanged. Then Ty kissed her, gently

205

touching her lips with his own until Cat threw her arms around his neck and rocked him back on his heels with her own celebration. Ty grabbed her around her waist and sought steady footing.

"I'm sure you could find an empty room upstairs," Zane commented as the room burst into laughter. Cat broke away with a victorious grin on her heart-shaped face. Ty narrowed his eyes at her.

"Well, now I know which one hog-tied the other," Cole commented to himself, bringing a flash of a grin from Jenny.

"You don't know the half of it," she whispered in return. Grace hugged Cat and Ty while Jason popped the cork from a bottle of champagne. The candles lent a golden hue to the room, casting a glow about the group that had gathered around the happy couple. Jenny closed her eyes at the sight, imagining Jamie's copper head towering over the rest with the flash of a devilish grin in a scarred but still handsome face. The pain had not lessened; it was more as if it were a part of her now, like the scar over her breast. It would always be there.

And Chase. She tried so hard not to think about him during the day, saving the tender memories for nighttime when she dragged her bone-weary body into bed. She pushed herself hard during the day so she would fall asleep quickly. But sometimes he would still come unbidden into her thoughts, the same way he had haunted her dreams before she knew that she loved him. Before she knew that he was the one she had been searching. If she kept her eyes closed, she could see the cast of the candlelight in his rich dark hair. She could see the flash of silver in his eyes, the way they settled on her and drew her into his heart with just a look. Her palm ached to feel the beat of his heart beneath the smooth skin of his chest. She squeezed one hand over the other to remove the longing and bring herself back to the room where Cat was calling her name to join them in a toast. Jenny pulled her shawl around herself, letting the ends of it cover the small bulge of her belly. The smile she gave them didn't reach her eyes, but they all understood, and as long as no one mentioned his name, she could function. It was another step forward; perhaps it would get easier with time.

"I can't believe that I am finally Mrs. Tyler Ellis Kincaid." Cat held her hand up to admire the gold band that flashed on her finger.

"And what's so hard to believe about that?" Ty asked as he pulled his boots off. The festivities were over and the house was empty except for the two of them. Jason had packed a bag and headed for the bunkhouse so the newlyweds could honeymoon.

"Let's just say you weren't exactly cooperative when it came to discussing the matter." Cat pulled the pins from her hair as she stared into her dressing table mirror, watching Ty yank his shirt over his head. Wasn't it funny how after all these years of waiting for this moment, she was nervous?

"What was there to discuss?" Ty's smile was bold.

"You chased me until I caught you. That's all there was to it."

"Tyler Kincaid, don't you dare go around saying that." Cat brandished her brush at him.

"Or what?" Ty swaggered towards her. 'You've been talking mighty big for the last few years, Mrs. Kincaid. It's time to back it up."

"Whatever do you mean?"

Ty placed his hands on her shoulders and bent down to kiss her neck. "What I mean is it's time for you to hush and let me do the talking." Cat's breath caught in her throat as his mouth traveled the slim column of her neck. Her arm came up and she wrapped her fingers in his hair.

"Ty—"

"Hmm?"

"Oh, umm, just so you know . . ." His mouth hovered over her lips. "That part about where, whither, wha . . ."

"I thought I told you to hush."

It was hard to talk when he was kissing her. "Where you go, I go."

"And?"

"I'm going with you to North Caro . . ."

Ty scooped her up in his arms and hushed her with a kiss. "We'll talk about that later, wife."

"Wife." Cat sighed. She twined her arms around his neck as he carried her to the bed.

Chapter Sixteen

Chase had lost track of the days. Each one was the same as the last. He awoke each day with the dawn and sent the buckskin in a northeastern direction, his hawklike eyes searching for a sign, any sign of Logan. He let his instincts lead him; Logan could have gone in any direction after the blizzard struck, but Chase's gut kept him going towards the badlands. If he were Logan, that was where he would go, and so he stuck to his course and prayed for a sign. The small gathering of buildings barely visible in the evening light was not what he'd expected, but he was grateful for it nonetheless. He blinked as if awaking from a dream when he came upon the settlement in the valley. It had been so long since he had seen another person that the cluster before him was almost overwhelming. He urged the buckskin down the slope. He needed a

209

good meal and supplies, but most of all, he needed to know if Logan had passed this way.

It was a mining town, or at least was trying to be. There was one large building with a sign over the balcony that bragged of being a saloon, hotel, and a general store. A stable was next to it and then the rest were mostly just shacks thrown up around a mud hole where the snow had melted from the many feet going back and forth to the saloon. He led the buckskin into the small livery and gave his care over to a scrawny boy of about ten with a scarred face. Chase suppressed the flood of emotion that threatened to overcome him when he saw the scars, but the boy just looked at him sullenly and the feelings left as quickly as they had come.

The main floor of the big building was divided by a huge bar. One side was used to serve a variety of food and drink to its patrons, the other offered the rudiments of a store. A wide assortment of men filled the saloon side and all of them stopped their conversation to observe Chase as he walked to the bar. He felt their eyes on him; felt them branding him as a half-breed as they always did. His hat was pulled low over his eyes and his long dark hair spilled over the collar of his coat and down the middle of his back. A large woman who had been wiping the counter disappeared through a door as he approached the bar and Chase waited for whoever she had summoned. His dark eyes searched the mirror over the bar for danger, but he stopped when he caught his own reflection.

A lean, regal face looked back at him, the face of a

hunter, with eyes that flashed dangerously beneath the shadow of his hat brim. His high cheekbones had become more pronounced and his full lips were set in a grim line. Chase briefly wondered how long it had been since he'd smiled. When had he become this man who stared back at him with a scornfully superior air? No wonder everyone here was looking on him with fear or hatred. What had happened to the Chase who laughed and loved? Had it all been just a dream? Was this man in the mirror the man he was destined to be? Circumstances kept bringing this man to the forefront. Was this what his friends had seen when he had killed Randolph Mason? Jenny had not wanted him to see her after what had happened to her; perhaps it was best that she could not see him now.

A middle-aged man came through the door at the end of the bar with the woman behind him. He approached Chase rather nervously as the crowd beyond watched.

"What'll it be?" he asked timidly.

"A hot meal, a hot bath, and a warm bed." Chase wasn't sure if his voice would work after the days of silence, so he kept his answer short. The man inclined his head to the woman, who hurried back through the door.

"Ten dollars." The man became a bit braver. "If you don't like the price, you can take your business elsewhere." The crowd behind Chase tittered at the remark and waited as he dug a gold piece out of his pocket and dropped it on the bar. It satisfied the bartender and the tension seemed to lift from the room as he served his new customer. Chase took the drink over to an unused table and sat with his back to the wall as the crowd resumed its activities. The woman soon returned with a plate and even though the food was bland, it was filling and warmed his insides. She slapped a key on the table and gave him directions to the bathhouse, and then he was left alone to finish his meal in silence.

The steaming bath made him realize just how bone-weary he was. He sank into the tub and set his mind to not thinking about Jenny, to not thinking about what she was doing at this very minute. He concentrated on not wondering if she hated him for leaving her as Jamie lay dying. He swore to himself that he would not envision her body glistening from her own bath, that he would not remember how she felt in his arms, how smooth her skin was, how soft her hair. He would not close his eyes and see her sapphire-blue ones glowing as he took her in his arms. He would not feel her passion rising to meet his. The water cooled and defeated the urges of his body as he once again fought and lost the battle with his rebellious mind.

He found the bed that was waiting for him. It wasn't as clean as he would have wished for, but it was better than the cold hard ground and he gratefully pulled the worn blanket over his body, which was once again dressed and ready for travel with his gun and knife within reach as always, extensions of himself.

* * *

Laughing, Logan was laughing at him. Chase watched as the blood poured from Jamie's body, watched as the wide blue eyes turned on him in disbelief. He saw Jenny and she was laughing too, laughing with Logan, whose face was turning into that of a wolf with strange gold eyes. Chase fired his gun at him. Logan was so close, he couldn't miss, but nothing came out, not even the sound of the shots, just empty clicks. He looked in disbelief at Jenny, who was laughing at him. Why was she laughing?

Chase rolled from the bed in one fluid motion, bringing his gun up in one hand, his knife in the other. The laughter was still ringing in his ears and he shook his head to clear it, blinking in the dim light that filtered up from the saloon below. The laughter was near, a deep voice blending with that of a woman. Chase sheathed his knife and slowly opened the door to his room.

The hallway was empty and the laughter was fading into conversation as money was exchanged for services. Another light laugh came from the woman, flirtatious this time; a rumble followed. Chase knew that laugh; he had heard it many times before. He had heard it ringing in the halls of the mission orphanage, usually at the expense of some younger child. Jamie had always been quick to respond to that laugh, following it down the halls to save whatever victim Logan had in his sights. He had heard it again the day Jamie died, and it still rang in his ears. Logan had enjoyed his own sick joke at their expense, but the price of Jamie's life was too much to pay. Chase knew the voice too; he had imagined the sound of Logan praying for his life over and over again.

Chase pressed his ear to the door next to his own and listened to the sounds beyond. The couple was down to business now, soft murmurs and the rustle of clothing betraying the business of lust that was being conducted. He stood back, settled his gun in his hand and kicked at the jam, knocking the door back against the wall. Logan looked up in disbelief at the interruption and then pulled the half-dressed woman in front of him as a shield. He had been riding hard these past weeks; he was a bit leaner than the last time Chase had seen him and there was a hint of desperation in his eyes that hadn't been there before.

He held a gun to the woman's head and pulled her back towards the window. "Well, I'm glad to know I killed him." He sneered at Chase. "I'd have both of you on my tail if I hadn't."

"Let her go, Logan." Chase's voice held the promise of death. "Fight your battles like a man."

"Half-breed," Logan spat out. "I saw what you did to Mr. Randolph. Just like a stinking Indian." He kept easing his way towards the window.

"A fitting death for a coward like you," Chase assured him.

The woman whimpered; she looked as though she didn't know which man to fear more. Logan's back was to the window and he glanced quickly outside. Chase took a step and stopped when the gun cocked. "You want to be responsible for her death, too?" Logan sounded desperate.

"You're the one doing the killing, Logan. I'm here to make sure it stops."

Logan shoved the woman at Chase and jumped through the window. She immediately tangled herself around his neck, her body trembling. Chase pushed her away and she landed in a sobbing heap on the bed as he followed Logan through the window.

"There's a crazy Indian up there trying to kill me!" Logan screamed into the bar as he untied the reins of his horse. He shot at Chase, who was coming over the balcony rail. Chase returned fire as men began pouring out of the saloon. Logan mounted and fired again while wheeling his horse around. Chase straightened to fire back and then felt the impact of cold steel against his skull. He fell over the rail onto the porch roof and landed in the muddy street amid the miners who had come out to see the commotion. Chase struggled to his hands and knees and through the red haze that consumed his brain, he saw Logan tearing out of town. "Where's my gun?" he wondered out loud as he tried to bring his hand up to fire. He heard the grumbling of the miners as the darkness overcame him and he pitched face first into the street.

He must still be alive, or else his head wouldn't ache so. Chase wondered briefly if he was blind, but he managed to see the faint outline of his hand in front of his face and realized that it was dark. Very dark. Cold, damp, and dark. He was lying on a cot of some sort, so he took a moment to make sure all his parts were present and working.

When he was done with his inventory, he carefully sat up. The clinking sound alerted him that there was a chain somewhere. The reality of it hit home when his boot hit the floor with a clank in the solid dirt below. So he was chained to something in some sort of cave, and it was dark. Add to that problem the fact that he was a half-breed trying to kill a white man in a town full of white men. A half-breed covered in mud with a terrible headache and a very full bladder.

"At least I can take care of that problem," Chase mused to himself as he stood on legs that felt a bit wobbly. He flinched as his fingers found the goose egg on the back of his head. He stretched his leg to determine the length of the chain and found a bucket placed near the end of the cot. One problem was solved and he was ready to move on to the next one.

He reached out with his hands and found a rough rocky surface behind the cot. He followed the wall, groping in the darkness until he reached the end of the chain, then turned around and repeated the process in the opposite direction. He was able to determine that the chain around his ankle was attached to a ring in the wall. He was lucky to have the cot, a moldy blanket and the bucket, he decided.

There was nowhere to go and no answer to his shout, only echoes. His head throbbed with the silence that seemed to turn itself against him, driving him back to the cot and the dubious shelter of the blanket.

Where was he? Who had brought him here and why? His last vision had been of Logan riding hell-bent for leather into the night. His quarry had been so close but once again was totally out of his reach. Perhaps it was always to be like this, perhaps he would pursue the killer endlessly without ever finding him. Perhaps he had died that day instead of Jamie and this was his own personal hell: forever searching for a killer, forever apart from Jenny. It was justice, he supposed, for the things he had done, for the sins he had committed. He had prayed for forgiveness, hoped for heaven, had even lived it for a while on earth, but now . . . he just didn't know anymore. The darkness overwhelmed him until he couldn't even tell if his eyes were open or closed . . . except for the golden eyes of the wolf that glowed at him, but they had to be in his mind, didn't they?

A swift kick to his middle and the glow of a lantern brought Chase off the cot in a hurry. He quickly recognized a pair of men from the saloon as they beat a hasty retreat from the length of the chain when he gained his feet with the grace of a puma. Chase crossed his arms over his wide chest and looked down at the men who were contemplating him.

"Why am I chained here like an animal?" he asked the pair.

"We don't take kindly to anyone shootin' up our town," one of them replied.

"I wasn't the only one doing the shooting," Chase replied.

"Yeah, the other one ran out of town screamin' his head off. What were ya after him for anyway?"

"He killed my brother, murdered him in cold blood."

The man who had been doing the talking scratched his beard as he considered Chase. "Unlock that chain, Chet. I want to hear what this breed has to say."

The one called Chet cautiously unlocked the chain from Chase's ankle and then leveled a gun on him. "Don't be doin' nothin' foolish, breed. You ain't off the hook yet."

Chase raised his arms in supplication and gladly followed the lantern out of the cavern and towards the light of day. He could see the buildings of the small town down the rise and hoped that the buckskin and his rig were still safely stored there. The two men led him back to the saloon, where several of the men from the night before were gathered to hear his story. He gave it to them in briefly, skimming the history and bringing them quickly to the day of Jamie's murder, right after his wedding. The miners were jaded. They had all seen innocent people shot down, and Chase could sense that the verdict would go against him. He feared that his own death could be imminent, until a man from the back asked him a question.

"This Jamie that you're talking about, was he a big guy, red hair, could make a horse do anything?"

"Yes, he was at the fair in Laramie a few years back, showing off for the crowd."

"You two worked for a big spread round those parts?"

"Jason Lynch."

"That's enough for me, boys. If this feller works for

Jason Lynch, then he's a good man. Jason wouldn't have him if he wasn't. That other feller hightailed it out of here like a scalded cat, and he wouldn't of run if he was innocent. Let this man go. That other one deserves killin' and this one's got the right to do it." Several assents came from the crowd and the man holding a gun on Chase holstered it.

"Your stuff is still upstairs," the large woman at the bar offered. "You want another bath before you go?"

The buckskin was well rested, the weather was crisp and clear, and Logan had only a twelve-hour start on a horse that had not been cared for. Chase felt as if his luck were about to change. He had hastily written a note to Jenny and left it at the saloon with the hope that someone would carry it to Laramie for him when the weather broke. *I'm alive*, was all it said; it was all he could say for the moment. Whether he would be alive when it was all over with, he couldn't say. *Can you ever forgive me for letting Jamie die? For leaving you as he lay dying?* Those were the questions he wasn't ready to ask or hear the answers to. There was a clear set of tracks; not many were traveling this road. Chase recognized the distinctive print of Logan's horse and smiled. It was just a matter of time.

He was closer than he had ever been and if the weather held for a few more days, it would be over soon. Chase scattered the ashes from the fire that still held some warmth and mounted the buckskin. "Not much farther, I promise," he assured the animal as they left the rocky outcropping that had been Logan's campsite the night before. "Then you can rest."

At midday he dismounted and ran his hand over the tracks imprinted in the melting snow. Logan's horse was failing him. The animal was going lame. Chase rubbed the finely arched neck of the buckskin as he remounted. "We're down to the homestretch." The horse tossed his head and sidestepped as he swung up, sensing the anticipation that was coursing through Chase. "Let's go."

The sound of a rifle shot whining through the rocks brought Chase's head up and the buckskin to a stop. The report of answering gunfire sent the pair into a run. Logan, it had to be Logan. The long legs, stamina, and courage that had been bred into the buckskin reassured Chase as they ate up the rocky ground, great sprays of slush and show flinging out behind them as he leaned over the horse's neck with encouraging words. They came to a ridge and the buckskin reared as Chase pulled him to a sudden stop. There was a homestead below, a sod cabin, a corral with a shed, and a woman who was wrestling with a rifle. At her feet lay a man, and beyond was a horse that Chase recognized as Logan's. He urged the buckskin down. The woman shrieked when she saw him coming and turned the rifle on Chase, then doubled over as if she was in pain. It was then that he realized she was pregnant, enormously so, he decided as she straightened again. He raised his hands as he approached, using his knees to guide the buckskin.

"There's nothing left to take," she told him. "All we had was the one horse."

"I was chasing the man who took your horse," Chase said as he dismounted, "Is that your husband?" She looked down at the man at her feet and dissolved into tears. Chase quickly checked the man and found him bleeding from two bullet wounds, but breathing. "He's alive."

"He is?" The woman gasped and grabbed her stomach as another pain hit her.

"Is it your time?" Chase asked. She nodded through the pain. Chase looked at the man, at the woman who was dashing the tears away, and then he scanned the horizon towards the north. He couldn't leave them, so he gathered the man up in his arms and followed the woman to the house. "When did it start?"

"Out there, when Matthew got shot." The woman flung back the quilt from the bed and Chase lowered his burden to the mattress. "I swear whether he lives or dies, we're going back East. I will not raise this child in this wilderness where someone can just ride up to your home and shoot you for your horse." She stripped Matthew's shirt off and exposed two wounds in his chest.

At least they aren't close to his heart, Chase thought as he remembered the last bullet wound he had seen. The man murmured and moved his head. "I'll raise him up and you see if they passed through," Chase told the woman. Luckily, they had, but the raspy sound of Matthew's breathing gave evidence of an injured lung.

221

The woman began tearing strips into bandages and Chase helped her wrap her husband's chest after she had cleaned the wounds. She stopped every so often, as the pain of her labor caused her to grunt and pant for breath. Chase soon realized that she was going to be the more serious of the two patients he was stuck with. Would Logan's trail of terror never end? "What's your name?" he asked her when they had finished doctoring Matthew.

"Mindy Perry and this is Matthew, my husband." Matthew opened his eyes as she bathed his face. "We came out here last spring looking for gold, but all we found was trouble." She was pretty, Chase realized, even with her face creased in pain. They both looked younger than he felt, probably just barely out of their teens. "He promised me we'd go back after a year if we didn't find any and we haven't."

"No, you promised me." Matthew's voice was raspy and his breathing short but his eyes still held the magic of first love as he gently teased his wife. "This was all her idea, and don't let her tell you any different."

"Hush," Mindy chastised him. "You've been shot."

"Bashed on the head, too." Matthew wrinkled his forehead in pain. "Who are you?"

"Chase Duncan. I've been following the man who shot you."

"Well, I wish you'd caught him a day ago and saved me some trouble."

"Yeah, me too," Chase said with a nod.

Mindy grabbed the edge of the table as another pain

hit her. "I think this baby is in a hurry to get here," she said through gritted teeth.

"The baby's coming?" Matthew asked in astonishment. "But we have a few weeks yet."

"I think it wanted to join the fight," Mindy panted.

"I could have used the help. What kind of man steals your only horse out here in the middle of nowhere?"

"The kind who would have killed you for it. He's a cold-blooded murderer," Chase answered.

"Matthew just wouldn't quit," Mindy explained. "Even with two bullets in his chest, he kept on going. That man was on our horse and Matthew was hanging on for dear life. He finally hit Matthew in the head with his gun because he ran out of bullets." Mindy was proud of her husband, and the fight he had given the horse thief.

"His name is Logan."

"I'll help you write it on his tombstone." She was so feisty, Chase had to grin at her.

"Better cross that one off our list of boy's names." Matthew was struggling to sit up. Chase helped the younger man to a chair.

Chase realized it was going to be a long night as he watched Mindy strip the bloody sheet off the bed and lay out a gown. The husband was injured, the wife giving birth, and there was no one to care for them. He couldn't abandon them, so he decided to make good use of the remaining daylight. He bedded down the buckskin and Logan's exhausted horse, giving both animals the extra care they needed after weeks of hard travel. He was lucky enough to scare up a rabbit and made sure there was plenty of fuel for the fire. Mindy was in her gown when he got back and there was water boiling on the stove. Matthew was peeling potatoes and the two men managed to put together a good stew. Chase was satisfied that the couple would be able to survive for the next few days on their own, so he lay down on the floor to catch what rest he could before the baby came.

A wail of pain awakened him a few hours later. Matthew was trying to wipe the sweat from his wife's face but was having trouble because Mindy kept grabbing his hands. "Make it stop," she cried.

Chase watched as Matthew tenderly laid his forehead against hers. "I wish I could."

"Matthew, what are we going to do?" she sobbed.

Chase had never delivered a baby before. Childbirth had always been a secret part of the women's lives in the village he had been raised in, but he had helped many a calf and foal into the world and he hoped this wouldn't be much different. After all, women had been doing it on their own for thousands of years, hadn't they? "You'll be all right," he volunteered.

"See?" Matthew assured her.

"What does he know?" Mindy tossed her head. "Neither one of you know what this is like."

Matthew looked at Chase helplessly. "Have you ever delivered a baby?"

"Uh, no." Chase bit his lip. "But I work on a ranch."

"You work on a ranch!" Mindy screamed. "I'm not having a calf! Ohhhhh, maybe I am."

"It will be all right," Matthew tried to assure her.

"DO SOMETHING!"

"We need to see if it's showing yet," Chase suggested. Matthew nodded and Mindy helped him pull up the tail of her gown.

"I think I see something," he said.

Chase cautiously peeked around his shoulder. "It looks like the top of the head."

"That's good, isn't it?" Matthew asked.

"I think so."

"I am surrounded by idiots! Yes, that's good; it means it time for me to push." Mindy was panting as she gathered herself. "There's a blanket over there to catch it in. And pass your knife through the fire so we can cut the cord." She was barking out instructions as she waited for the next pain. Chase hurried to do as he was told while Matthew stationed himself on the bed. "It's coming. . . ." Mindy bore down and screamed.

"One more," Matthew encouraged. She rose up and screamed again.

"It's a girl," the proud father announced as the squalling baby landed in the waiting blanket. Chase handed him the knife as Mindy gave him instructions. Matthew gently laid the baby girl in Chase's arms and he timidly took her to the table to bathe. She howled the entire time he washed her, screaming her anger at coming into the cold dark world before she was ready. Chase wrapped her up in the blanket and placed her next to Mindy on the bed. She immediately calmed the squirming infant with the special touch that all mothers have, and the screams stopped. "Maggie?" Matthew asked his wife.

"Maggie," she replied. Chase gently shut the door behind him as he went out into the night.

It snowed again that night, a light dusting of an inch or so, not enough to really cover the tracks that the stolen horse had left in the soggy ground. Chase and Matthew talked late into the night, sharing their stories and their hopes for the future. It seemed a long way off to Chase. Jenny, the warm cabin they shared, the fellowship around Grace's table with the other hands, all were part of another life that someone else had lived a long time ago. His life now centered on the here and now, his only goal revenge, his prize Logan's death and the assurance that he would never hurt Jenny again. Chase promised Matthew he would return the horse if he were able, and the young man thanked him for his kindness and help. Mindy and the baby were still sleeping when he left that morning. Matthew was weak but able to move, so Chase went on, determined not to let Logan get any further ahead. It surprised him when Matthew told him what the date was. He had been gone for over two months; it seemed like a lifetime when he thought about it. He decided not to think at all, but to concentrate on what was before him.

Logan.

The badlands were aptly named, Chase decided. The landscape around him looked unreal, like a nightmare.

No wonder the Sioux had come to this land; no one else would have the strength of character to live here.

Logan was here. It was just a matter of finding him amid the canyons and rocks that had been swept clean of snow by the relentless wind that howled over the land incessantly. And what would he do when he did find him? The choices were before him now. Would he challenge Logan to a fight or would he shoot him down in cold blood as Logan had done to Jamie? There was always the option of taking him back to Laramie to stand trial for murder. After all, there had been plenty of witnesses. Chase decided he was too weary to think about it. He turned the buckskin up a canyon and started looking for signs among the rocks.

Logan found him instead. He was waiting for him in ambush; the rifle shot came from behind a rock slide. Chase dove for cover and sent the buckskin out of harm's way, knowing the horse would wait.

"Don't you ever give up?" Logan yelled.

"No, so why don't you?" Chase returned.

He heard a laugh and the words, "I hope he died slow and hard."

"He died well, but you won't."

Logan shot again.

"Keep it up," Chase said to the rock that was protecting him. "You'll run out eventually." Chase took inventory of his surroundings. He had shelter, but there was no fuel for a fire, and the skies above looked threatening. At least he had the satisfaction of knowing that Logan was going to be in the same miserable shape that he was in. Perhaps the weather could work to his advantage. Chase pulled his hat down low and hunkered down behind the rocks. It was going to be a long night, so he might as well get some rest. Logan wasn't going anywhere.

Funny how he had waited for this moment for so long, and now he didn't know what to do with it. When he had left Jamie's side, he had had no trouble visualizing the killing. He wanted to feel Logan squirming and begging beneath his knife. He wanted to see the moment of death, to savor the realization that it was over. He wanted Logan to know that his destiny was Hell and that Chase was sending him to it, that the flames were already licking at his flesh.

But now he wasn't so sure. Chase knew that Logan deserved to die but did he have the right to kill him? Was it part of a cycle that would never end? Jenny had killed Joe while Mason's men were trying to kill her and her brother. Logan had killed Jamie in retaliation for Joe's death. Chase could kill Logan in retaliation for Jamie's death. But would someone then come after him, or worse, after Jenny?

When would it end, or would it ever? The cycle of killing could go on and on; it could end up touching everyone he knew in some tragic way. Hadn't Jenny lost her parents for the same reason? When you got down to it, hadn't he lost his father and mother to vengeance, too? It had to end somewhere. Could it end here and now in a dead-end canyon in the badlands of the Dakotas?

Logan had shown him the evil in the world, but he had also seen the good on this trip, in the townspeople who had believed him and sent him on his way. And he felt as if he had tried to do good when he had the chance. He could have gone on instead of helping Matthew and Mindy. It was all a matter of choice. He had a choice to make now. Was the killing of Logan worth losing his soul?

The clouds were so thick that there was no way to tell when the sun set. The grayness of the day just faded into black. Chase sat and waited, his eyes scanning the shadows, his ears tuned to every sound of the night. A wolf howled in the distance, a sorrowful sound, a tragic, mournful wail of loneliness and despair. He fought the impulse to join with the wolf in a duet. He was sure he knew just how the animal felt. He hoped Logan was listening closely to the sounds of the wolf, and then maybe, just maybe he wouldn't hear him coming.

Chase moved silently through the night, becoming one with the stones that stood as silent sentinels guarding the gates to a land that no man wanted. The air was thick with the promise of more snow; he could smell it coming. Chase watched Logan as he tested the air, his body hunched over a meager fire that cast more light than warmth. Chase felt his fear, felt the trepidation that oozed from the huge body below him. Logan had seen his death coming, and it was not a pretty one. Yet after all this time and all these miles, he had made it so easy for Chase in the end.

"Drop your guns, Logan." Chase centered his rifle on Logan's head as he rose from the rocks above him. Logan jumped at the sound of his voice and finally settled on the silhouette he could just make out against the gray of the clouds. "Kick them away where I can see them."

"What are you going to do with me?" Logan's voice was shaky as he dropped the guns.

"I'm taking you back to Laramie to stand trial."

"You should kill me now, breed, or else I'll kill you before we get there."

"You're right, I should," Chase sighed. "It's a chance I'm willing to take." He jumped down from the rocks after Logan had kicked the guns away. It didn't take Chase long to tie Logan's hands and feet together. A whistle brought the buckskin searching for its master, and Chase made a quick camp around the fire that soon roared to warm life with the addition of some wood from a dead tree that had washed down from somewhere. It certainly was not from around these desolate parts.

Logan quietly watched it all with narrow eyes, waiting for his chance. Chase was determined not to give it to him. He stripped off his prisoner's boots and placed them under his saddle. Logan would have to kill him to get them and he wouldn't survive out here without them. Logan knew it and Chase knew it. Chase threw a blanket over Logan and sought his bed. He didn't think he would sleep, but at least he could rest now. It was enough.

The Perrys looked a lot better than the last time Chase had seen them. Matthew came to the door with his rifle in hand and then grinned when he recognized

Chase. Matthew gleefully placed a few kicks in Logan's midsection when they tied him up in the shed. Chase went to the house to share a meal and check on baby Maggie, who was sucking hungrily at her mother's breast when he came in.

"I see you haven't killed him yet," Mindy commented when he entered.

"I thought I'd rather see him swing for what he's done," Chase answered. "But he's tempted me to put a bullet in his head several times."

"You can go home now," Matthew added.

"Yes, I can." Chase's smile reached his eyes for the first time in a long time. "I'm going home."

Chapter Seventeen

Winter refused to let go. Occasionally there were a few mild days, bringing with them the hope of spring, but they turned out to be short reprieves before the wind and snow came back again to smother the earth. Jake made the mail run and returned full of news and letters. The Confederacy was calling for a hundred thousand volunteers, and they all knew it was just a matter of time before North Carolina joined the fray. The struggles of the South had been easy to dismiss before, but now bad news struck home, and it was a quiet group that watched Ty take his letter and leave the warm comfort of Grace's cabin. Cat let him go; she had known it would come sooner or later, and she was going with him, whether he liked it or not. Cole received a letter also, one written in a strange hand. He read it quickly, then crumpled it up and threw it at the stove. Grace saw the wave of pain wash over his face as he left the cabin with his dog at his heels. She picked the letter up from the floor where it had missed the flames, and the words caught her eye. She tossed her shawl over her shoulders and followed him out to the barn.

Cole was saddling his horse when she found him, using quick jerking motions to finish the job. Justice stood watching him with his tongue lolling, as anxious for the run as his master. Cole tossed a look at Grace over his shoulder as he worked. "Is there something you need?" he asked gruffly.

Grace placed a gentle hand on his arm. "You missed the fire." She showed him the wadded piece of paper. "I'm sorry about your sister."

"Do you make it a habit of reading other people's mail?" His steely gray eyes were shadowed, his voice bitter.

"I'm sorry, I was throwing it away and I just caught the words."

Cole looked down at her, his eyes boring into to hers. Grace returned his stare, openly sensing his loneliness. "Were you close to her?" It was a bold step. Cole had kept everyone at arm's length, especially Grace, since the day of his outburst about Wade Bishop.

He let out a heavy sigh, his body shifting as if he were readjusting a burden. His horse pawed at the straw and dropped his head to nibble at some missed feed. Grace touched Cole's arm again and the eyes that turned to her this time had softened. "We used to be, at one time." Justice sensed the change in his master and lay down, his head on his outstretched paws, his dark eyes watchful.

"Is that why you left Texas?" Grace asked, carefully picking her way into this unknown territory.

"Part of it."

"We all have our reasons for being here, Cole, mine is more obvious than others."

Cole gently laid a finger on Grace's cheek and traced the scar down one side of her face. "My reason for being here has a lot to do with yours."

"What did Wade do to you?" she asked in a shocked whisper.

"It's not what he did to me; it's what he did to my niece." Cole pulled a gold watch from his pocket and opened it, showing a miniature of two women on the inside. "This is my sister, Chloe." Grace admired the picture of the dark-haired woman. "And this is her daughter, Amanda." The girl was beautiful, with an abundance of dark hair and flashing gray eyes beneath dark lashes. "Wade Bishop took her off the streets of Laredo in broad daylight. Chloe sent for me when she disappeared and I tracked them to Monette's in Austin. From there Amanda was sent to Galveston and placed on a ship to God only knows where. I was too late. Bishop had disappeared and there was no proof that Amanda had ever been in Austin. It was if she had never existed. Warrants were served against Monette but there was no evidence. No one actually saw Amanda with Bishop, no one saw Amanda in Austin. She could be anywhere in the world right now and there's no way to find her. Chloe never forgave me for it."

"But it wasn't your fault," Grace exclaimed.

"I let her down and Amanda"—his voice broke on her name—"I can't stand to think about the hell she's living in now, and she doesn't even know that her mother is dead. That's what Chloe said—the not knowing would kill her. And it did."

"That's why you left Texas, because you thought you'd failed your family?

"I left Texas because I did fail my family. If I couldn't help the people I loved, how could I be of any use to anyone else?"

"It wasn't your fault, Cole. You had no way of knowing what was going to happen. You weren't even there. It's just like Jenny said, sometimes bad things happen to good people."

"Jenny doesn't know how lucky she was to get away from that man and his sister. This has been going on for years and the Rangers just now figured it out when Amanda disappeared. Monette is being watched now, but it's too late for Amanda and who knows how many other girls just like her."

"He said it was for my own good when he cut me like this." Grace's hands covered her cheeks.

Cole grabbed her elegant hands, hard from years of work, in his own strong ones. "Wade Bishop is the devil himself and he must be stopped."

"So why are you still here?"

Cole couldn't find an answer for Grace. He didn't have the answers himself at the present. Maybe he was hiding. He looked at the long delicate fingers that were gripped in his hands. He knew that her soft brown eyes were waiting for an answer. Her eyes had seemed to look right inside him the first time he saw her. He swallowed his pride. "Maybe I'm looking for a reason to stay." The steel gray of his eyes met the warm brown of hers.

Grace felt her stomach drop when Cole looked at her with eyes that were no longer guarded. His secret was out, his failure as a man there for her to see. Jenny had asked her last summer if she believed that there was one true love for everyone. Grace had answered that if there was, then she herself had missed hers. But maybe she hadn't, maybe it wasn't too late for her. Maybe the horrible things that had happened so long ago were destined to bring her to this place, this time, with this man who had his own mistakes to live with. He needed healing, just as she had when Jason had brought her here so many years ago.

"Am I a good enough reason?" She couldn't believe the words had come out of her mouth. What made her think that he would want her? Her fingers trembled as Cole raised them to his mouth and kissed the knuckles that were red from the hot dishwater and cold air. But when his mouth claimed hers, hesitantly, shyly, and her hands slipped around his neck, the doubts fell away from both of them. Cole pulled her against his length. Her shawl hit the ground as his arms wrapped around her. He needed to be strong for her and she wanted to be desirable for him. They saw the needs and want in each other and saw the answers there for themselves. His lips sought hers as a drowning man seeks air and Grace gave them willingly, her heart thrilling with the joy of the discovery.

"I hate to interrupt the latest adventures of Cole Larrimore," Zane said, grinning at them from over the stall door. "But Jason is looking for you."

Grace felt herself turn red but was amazed when Cole laughed. "Tell him I'll be along directly. And if you tell him anything else, I'll be writing stories about you and your sudden demise." Zane chuckled as he left the barn, a sound that Grace realized had been missing for a long while.

"I'll guess we'll be in for it at the dinner table tonight," she said to the smiling face above her.

"Let them have their fun. It's been a long time coming." He pulled her head against his chest. "I will go after Bishop when I'm ready."

"I know. I'm sorry about your sister, and Amanda."

"Thank you, Grace," Cole said softly as he kissed the top of her head.

Grace was greeted by a trio of smiling faces when she went back to her cabin. Zane, Jake, and Caleb all greeted her with broad grins went she went inside to start supper.

"How are things in the barn, Grace?" Zane couldn't resist asking.

"Just fine. Where's Jenny?"

"Don't change the subject, Grace," Zane lectured.

Grace picked up her broom and shook it at Zane. "I'm not changing the subject. I just realized that she wasn't in there, and she's not in here, so where is she?"

"I think she's taking a nap," Caleb volunteered. "I saw her go into her cabin after lunch. She's been doing that a lot lately."

"You know, you're right." Grace became thoughtful. "She hasn't been eating much for breakfast either."

"What's that got to do with anything?" Jake asked.

"It's got to do with Grace not wanting to talk about the barn, or Cole." Zane was determined to have some fun.

"I swear to goodness, Zane, one of these days I'm going to wring your neck." Grace swung the broom at his backside. "Now get out of here, all of you, so I can get some work done." The three stomped out and ran into Jenny, who was yawning as she stepped up on the porch. Grace threatened with her broom again when Jenny entered, thinking it was Zane coming back for another joke at her expense. She gave Jenny a careful perusal. "Why don't you take that coat off?" Grace asked. "It's nice and warm in here." Grace placed her hands on her hips as Jenny walked right by her. "Come to think of it, I haven't seen you without it all winter."

"I've been cold." Jenny wrapped her arms around herself as if she was still cold, and then began digging potatoes out of the bin. "I'll get these peeled for dinner."

"Jenny?" Grace laid a hand on her shoulder. The face that turned to her was pale and the sapphire-blue eyes were huge in her face. "Are you with child?"

Jenny's lip began to tremble as Grace stroked her hair. "It's okay, really it is."

"But Chase doesn't know yet."

"How far along are you?"

"Five months."

"It must have happened right away then."

"Yeah." It was more of a sob than an answer as Jenny wiped her nose with the sleeve of her coat. Grace pulled her into a hug as Jenny's shoulders began to tremble.

"Don't you realize how wonderful this is? Why didn't you tell anybody?"

"Because of Chase." Jenny pushed Grace away and rubbed her eyes. "He should be the first to know. But he wasn't, Jamie knew, he figured it out. He told me at Christmas that he knew, but I wouldn't let him say anything until I was sure everything was all right. And now he's gone, and Chase is gone, and I'm all alone."

"You're not alone. We're all here for you and you won't have to do this alone."

"Chase is coming back, you know." Jenny wiped her eyes and nose again. "I know you all think he's not coming back, but he is."

"Of course he is."

Jenny placed her hands over her heart. "I can feel him, Grace; I can feel him in here. He's still alive and he's coming back." The sapphire-blue eyes glowed with an inward light that Grace had never seen before. "He's coming back."

* * *

Would it ever quit snowing? It had been so long since Chase had seen anything green, since he had felt really warm, since he had slept in a real bed or had a real bath. The trip home seemed to last forever as they awoke each day to the same gray weather and the same dull white landscape. Logan threatened and complained every day as Chase heaved him into his saddle. He complained about the weather, he complained about the food, or the lack thereof. He complained about needing a shave, which was something Chase wouldn't know about. Chase managed to ignore him most of the time. He spent his days thinking about home and his nights dreaming about Jenny. Most of all he wondered if she would forgive him.

The route home was more direct that the one the blizzard had forced them to take back in January. At the Perrys' homestead, Chase returned their horse and picked up Logan's. Then he struck out in a south-westerly direction, crossing territory he had never seen before. Once again the weather made it seem as if they were the only creatures on earth. The winter had been hard everywhere. Occasionally they came upon the carcass of an elk or deer that had succumbed to the hard winter and then fallen victim to the carrion eaters, who were the only ones having a good season. Every night they heard the wolves, or the wolf—it seemed as if there were only one because his nightly calls were never answered. They just rang out in the night, going on forever. Chase was sure he saw the golden eyes in the distance beyond the glow of his fire every night, but the horses never spooked, and if Logan ever saw the creature, he never mentioned it.

They came out of the badlands and onto the rolling plains. Now there were trees and streams that were frozen over. But there was also more game, and under the snow some sweet grass that the horses managed to uncover. The buckskin was lean and Logan's horse was in even worse shape so their pace was slow; without the animals they didn't stand a chance.

"You're taking me right back to her, you know." Logan had remained mostly quiet the last few days. Chase figured he was watching for any sign of weakness, or else he had gotten as tired of his own complaints as Chase had. "She always thought she was too good for me, and then she wound up marrying a half-breed," Logan chuckled. "I guess you could call that justice if you wanted to." Chase ignored him. "After I kill you, I'm going to have my way with her." Chase's dark eyes flashed silver as they settled on Logan, who tilted his head quizzically. "Or maybe I'll let you watch. How would that be, breed, if I let you watch me pleasure your wife?" He laughed again. "And when I'm done, I'll cut your balls off and make her choke on them."

Chase's shoulder hit Logan in the midsection as he took him off his horse with a dive from the buckskin. They landed in the snow with Logan on his back and Chase on top. Logan's hands were tied behind his back and he began to buck with all his might as Chase landed a succession of blows around his head. He finally settled on wrapping his lean fingers around Logan's thick neck and began choking him. The face beneath him turned purple as Logan strained for air and his eyes began to bulge.

"You're not worth it," Chase gasped as sanity came back to him. He leaned back on his heels as Logan's face returned to its normal color. "Besides, why should I rob the others of the satisfaction of watching you swing?" He pulled Logan to his feet and shoved a bandana in his mouth. "I should have done this the first day," he said as he tied him to a tree. He heard the muffled curses coming from beneath the gag and recognized the threats as he walked away to cool his head.

Doubts began to plague him. Was he doing the right thing in taking Logan back? Would he be making Jenny relive Jamie's death by putting his murderer on trial? But what was the alternative? Murder Logan in cold blood and leave his body for the wolves? Would he be able to face everyone afterward, knowing that they were wondering what had happened out here? He remembered how they had looked at him after he'd killed Mason, the fear in their eyes, the doubt, and the bewilderment at his savagery. Could he stay on at the ranch knowing that they didn't quite trust him? Did he have the right to ask Jenny to accompany him without even knowing where they would go? Of course, he could always just let Logan go and live in fear of what would happen the next time he showed up.

Chase took off his hat and searched the sky. There was some blue showing behind the pile of clouds, a brilliant contrast to the dull gray that had hung over them for so long. Maybe tomorrow would be a better day. He ran his hand through his hair to push it off his face. How many times had he seen Jamie do the exact same thing? More than he could remember. Logan was still fuming against the gag when he got back. Chase shoved him back on his horse and turned toward home.

Chapter Eighteen

For the first time in months, Chase thought about spring. Maybe it was because he had awakened for once without shivering. The cold that was ever present seemed milder, the sun felt closer and cast definite warmth instead of hanging useless and pale in the sky. Perhaps they could even make good time today; the horses seemed to feel as change in the air. They were attacking the trail instead of just plodding along.

They made their way over ridges and down into valleys, Chase leading Logan, who was still gagged and tied. Chase was glad he wasn't a mind reader; he was sure Logan had killed him a hundred times over in his head.

One ridge they climbed looked over a valley full of elk. Chase stopped the buckskin to observe the huge creatures, which had taken shelter in the low ground where the snow wasn't as deep and the sweet grass below was easier to reach. The thought of a huge elk steak sizzling over a fire made his stomach growl and his mouth water. Logan's eyes bulged as he looked at Chase's rifle in its scabbard and the herd below. He was obviously thinking of the same thing. Chase urged the buckskin on; a hunt would take too much time and leave too much waste. He circled the ridge to bypass the valley and led the way into a forest of lodgepole pines.

The forest was alive with the almost imperceptible noises of the creatures who had taken shelter in the smaller growth of evergreens. Occasionally they heard the plop of melting snow that had been warmed on the branches above before sliding away and landing in the soft dirt below, where the canopy of branches had previously kept the snow from reaching the forest floor. The land rolled gently down and the going was easy for the horses. Chase hoped to make the other side of this valley by dusk. It would be nice to sleep on bare ground tonight instead of making a bed in the snow.

They came out of the forest into a snow-covered clearing in the floor of the valley just as twilight descended. Chase spied an outcropping of rocks in the distance beneath the trees and marked it in his mind as a suitable campsite for the night. Surely he would be able to scare up some game for a hot meal, and he loosened his rifle in its scabbard while he scanned the woods ahead of him for signs as he urged the buckskin onward. The horse tossed his head skittishly and took a step sideways, bunching his powerful muscles as if preparing for a jump. A sense of trepidation flashed in Chase's mind, matched by a chill running down his spine. There was a sharp crack, not unlike that of a rifle shot echoing on a cold winter day. The buckskin fought for footing as the snow gave way beneath his flailing hooves.

Chase felt the impact as Logan's horse crashed into the side of the buckskin, sending both of them into the frigid depths of a beaver pond that had until recently been frozen solid. The buckskin thrashed around the ice, searching for a foothold as Chase hung on to the side of the saddle. Logan, meanwhile, had managed to turn his horse and bolt back into the woods. Chase was half carried and half dragged by the buckskin to the other side, where he lay shivering with his legs still hanging in the water.

"Think." His lips were chattering. "*Move!*" He managed to crawl out of the water, a miracle in itself since he could no longer feel his legs. He used the stirrup to pull himself to his feet. He stomped the ground to get the circulation going and swung his arms, all the while cursing himself for a fool. The buckskin stood steaming beside him as Chase jumped around in the snow, looking for Logan. He had disappeared into the forest of pines, but Chase could still hear the crashing of his horse. Logan was gagged and tied and he didn't have a weapon. Chase was cold and wet and would die soon if he didn't find some warmth. Luckily the water was a barrier between them, but Chase knew it was only a matter of time before Logan freed himself and came looking for him.

Chase jogged into the forest, leading the buckskin behind him. He was shivering violently as his system fought the cold. He could barely make out the shadow of the rocks in the gloom of the forest and the deepening twilight. His limbs felt like lead, and a sheet of ice was already forming on his clothes. The day might have been warm but the lack of sunlight would drop the temperatures well below freezing again once night fell. If he couldn't get a fire going, he was done for. The toe of his boot caught in a burrow in the forest floor and he pitched forward on his face. The buckskin pulled against the reins, suffering his own agonies after the surprise dunking and then the mad flight into the woods. Chase rocked up on his hands and knees, fighting the cold, fighting the darkness, fighting his mind, which commanded him to lie down and die. He kept his eyes centered on the outcropping of rocks that had faded into the darkness. He staggered under the weight of his coat so he shrugged if off, dragging it behind him until he found his feet again. Finally he was there, a large outcropping of three huge boulders, silent reminders of the glaciers that had at one time covered the area.

His hands wouldn't stop shaking as he jerked at the girth of the saddle. His fingers refused to obey his commands. He finally wrenched the rig off the buckskin and with trembling fingers searched for his slicker in the saddle bags to throw over the back of the steaming horse. That was when he realized his rifle was missing, lost in the wild contortions of horse and rider as they went down. Chase looked back toward the clearing, now invisible in the darkness. Surely Logan could not have taken it; his hands were tied behind his back. It must be lost on the bottom of the pond, wet and useless. Chase dropped to his knees and dragged his hands around on the hard earth, pulling dried pine needles and miniscule twigs into a pile a few feet in front of a large stone with a curved side. He dragged the blade of his knife across the flint and prayed for a spark.

Nothing.

Again. And once again nothing. Chase sent a shivering prayer up through the tree tops to the patch of stars that twinkled through the branches. A spark this time and the tinder smoked. He blew gently as he fed the tiny flame with more needles and twigs. They caught, and he scrambled around the little bit of warmth searching for more fuel. He found a few dead branches about the length of his arm and dropped them onto the fire.

His clothes were covered with a crusting of ice that crumbled as he shed them. He turned his boots with the insides towards the fire and then shucked the layer of ice off his socks, pants, and shirt. He wrung out his long johns as he hopped around the fire to keep his circulation going. Luckily his head had not gone under, but the ends of his hair whipped against his back and chest tipped with icicles. He needed more wood. The tinder was so dry that it practically evaporated, and the branches wouldn't last long.

His toes ached as the circulation returned to them and the earth felt strangely warm against the soles of his feet as he moved in an ever-widening circle around the fire in search of wood. He knew the light of it would draw Logan and make him an easy target, but at the present time, he didn't have a choice. He was naked, shivering, and his weapons were back at the fire. He couldn't watch the forest floor and the woods around him at the same time. He just prayed that time would be on his side. He nearly tripped again as his frozen limbs refused to obey the commands his muddled brain was sending. He felt more than saw the darkness of a fallen treetop against the lighter gray of the earth. He wrestled the jagged end of the lodgepole pine into his arms and slowly dragged it back toward the beckoning warmth of the fire.

His blanket had only gone in halfway so he wrapped the dry end around his shoulders and let the fire steam out the wetness of the other side. The curved boulder was beginning to catch the heat and reflect it back towards the fire. Chase scraped around the circle of his fire with his foot to keep the flames from jumping to another pile of tinder and spreading. He broke off the branches of the dead tree and slowly fed them to the flames. He needed steady heat now, to dry his clothes and saddle. His own violent shivering had finally stopped, only to be replaced by a cold ache that he felt deep in his bones. He was vulnerable and he knew it. But Logan was weaponless. The blade of Chase's knife reflected the fire as he held it, ready in his hand.

* * *

Had he dozed off? The dancing light of the flame held him hypnotized. Chase felt as if he had been miraculously transported back to his own cabin. Hadn't he been sitting in one of the worn wingback chairs just minutes ago, running his hands through a braid of golden blond, separating the strands until they fell in waves around a perfect oval face? A pair of sapphire-blue eyes still held him in their grip; a set of soft full lips begged to be kissed. Jenny would make him warm again. His dark eyes blinked at the orange glow before him. The buckskin shifted his weight and nuzzled a small cut that the ice had made on the inside of his foreleg. Chase blinked again.

Something was out there. The hair on the back of his neck stood up as his eyes darted around the darkness. He tested the grip of his knife. *Easy, don't hold it too tightly, or he'll knock it out of your hand.* Chase bunched the muscles in his thighs and calves, holding himself in his crouch before the fire, ready to move if necessary, prepared to use the blanket as a decoy and strike with the knife. If only he didn't feel so vulnerable without his clothing, which was still drying before the fire. The night seemed to close in on him, shrinking around him oppressively as his eyes scanned the ring of light to see what was coming.

A pair of golden orbs glowed between the narrow trunks of the trees beyond the glow of the fire. The wolf was there. Surely the wolf had not followed him all this distance, all these many months. Chase squinted his eyes shut and opened them again. The eyes remained. He tested the weight of his knife again. The eyes were still there, silent and watchful as always; then they were gone.

Hunger and loneliness were miserable companions on a cold winter's night. But at least they kept him awake. He knew Logan was coming; it would just be a matter of time. Logan needed the supplies that Chase had wisely kept to himself. His clothes were finally dry enough to put on but still cold and damp enough to be a shock. At least he felt safer now, not so exposed. Chase stomped his foot into his boot and grimaced at the dampness against his toes. He checked his revolver—it seemed all right. He knew it could use a good cleaning but there wasn't time for that right now, not when he might need it at any second. Dawn would be here soon; he could hear the birds stirring in their roosts, chattering softly. There was no panicked flight that would indicate someone was coming. But Logan would come. And if he was successful he would go after Jenny.

Dawn arrived and with it light, but without the warmth of yesterday. It was going to be another gray, wintry day, a repeat of the ones that had come before. Maybe he had just imagined that brief hint of spring that had welcomed him the morning before. Chase swung up in the saddle and looked towards the clearing. He had to go back for his rifle. He had to know.

The hole in the ice left by his passing was now covered with a thin layer of ice. The opposite bank still held the signs of the mad scramble of the horses. There were so many signs, so many tracks. But it looked as if Logan had been back and left again. Surely the rifle had gone into the water; there was no way it could have landed, safe and dry, on the bank. Chase turned the buckskin back into the forest and the shelter it provided. His skin crawled with the sensation that he was being watched. He was a target and he knew it. His body prepared itself for the shot; his ears strained to hear the sound of a bullet sliding into a chamber; his hawklike eyes darted, side to side. He hoped against hope that he would see the attack coming, that he could move out of harm's way, that he wouldn't die out here in the forest with no one to mark his passing, nothing left but a carcass. Maybe that was why the wolf had been following him; he was waiting for him to fall. The creak of saddle leather was all he heard as the buckskin angled around the trees.

Logan had had time to circle around. It had been a clear night with a half moon, enough light for the murderer to find his way around the water and get in front of him. The forest seemed endless, but Chase knew better. It would soon give way to rolling plains with exposed ridges and valleys. Where was Logan? Was he ahead or was he behind?

How long could he go on like this? Was this how Logan had felt all these months, knowing that he was after him, never taking a breath without wondering if it was his last? The buckskin continued his slow canter through the trees, his breath gusting steam in the cold dry air. The woods began to thin; the trees were not as tall, the underbrush became thicker. Chase knew he was approaching the end of the forest and the end of his cover. Would Logan be waiting?

He felt the shot before he heard it. And feeling it wasn't as bad as the anticipation. There was a burning, the sensation of tissue tearing as the missile went through his body, leaving a tunnel from front to back. The back of his coat flew out and his hand went automatically to his abdomen. It felt like an eternity had passed, but it was only the space of a heartbeat. Chase hauled on the reins and threw his body against the neck of the buckskin. He had to go down, make Logan think he was dead, or he *would* be dead; the next shot would kill him. The snow would act as a cushion and protect the horse, maybe give him a bit of shelter. The buckskin rolled and Chase felt a rib snap as a hoof caught him in the side. He sank down in the snow and willed himself not to move, knowing that Logan would come. He would want to see him face to face. He would taunt him before he killed him, making promises of the horrors he would visit upon Jenny before he put a bullet in Chase's head. Logan would come.

Chase willed his heart to stop racing. He concentrated on regulating his breathing, which was painful with the broken rib. He felt the warm stickiness of his blood beneath his stomach and around the matching wound on his back. *Just like Jenny's.* Her wound was a present from Logan also, or maybe Joe. He couldn't remember which one had shot her. His cheek started throbbing from the cold of the snow; the skin was freezing, yet he could feel moisture from the melting snow in his ear. The gloved fingertips of his right hand touched the ground, waiting to feel the impact of hooves as Logan came for him. His other arm lay beneath him, his hand wrapped firmly around the hilt of his knife, waiting. Chase felt the presence of the buckskin. His horse pawed the ground with a foreleg, confused.

A bullet whizzed by his head, the echo of the shot hitting his ears at the same time the bullet buried itself in the ground some five feet beyond his head. The buckskin snorted and skittered away, trailing his reins in the snow. Logan was coming. Another bullet, closer this time, he felt it splitting the air above his ear.

Don't move.

He heard the chamber in the rifle opening as Logan cocked it; he felt the cartridge slide into place; this bullet had his name on it, spelled out his death. Chase tensed, then willed himself to relax as he heard the crunching of Logan's boots in the snow, as he felt the impact of his footsteps in the ground beneath his fingertips. His ears caught the heavy breathing, detected a faint snicker. The barrel of the rifle nudged the middle of his back, traced its way up his spine, tangled in his hair, flipped his hat off.

Don't move.

The toe of a boot found its way under his coat and nudged the broken rib. Chase's hand clenched his blade. He felt the foot tense, the calf muscle flex . . .

There was an explosion of flying snow as Chase rolled and pulled his knife. He swung with his right arm to knock the barrel of the rifle away and the shot flew into the grayness of the empty sky as he brought his knife around and sliced it toward Logan's thigh. Logan jumped back, minimizing the impact of the knife. Chase dove into his stomach, bringing his shoulder up into the bigger man's chest. Logan staggered back and swung the butt of the rifle around into the back of Chase's head. The blow dazed Chase but he managed to keep his arms wrapped around Logan's waist and dug his feet into the ground, finally toppling Logan over on his back. Logan swung the rifle again and hit it against Chase's temple. Blood gushed down the side of his head as Chase fell sideways, losing his hold on his knife. Logan scrambled away and brought the stock of the gun against his shoulder. Chase kicked at it, kicked it again, and finally knocked it out of Logan's hands. Logan roared and fell on Chase with his hands outstretched, wrapping them around his neck and squeezing, choking the breath from his body.

"How does it feel, breed?" Logan's breath was hot against his cheek. "How does it feel to know that when I'm done with you I'm going after your wife?" Chase bucked and clawed at the fingers that were cutting off his air. "Oh, we're going to have a good time, and when I'm tired of her, I'm going to kill her real slow." Chase's left hand searched the snow. It had to be there, it couldn't have gone far. Flashes of light danced before his eyes, and his lungs felt as if they were going to explode. There, something solid. His hand closed over the knife and he swung it around, burying it in Logan's back. Logan screamed and released his hold. Chase pushed him off as the air rushed back into his tortured lungs. Logan's eyes widened as Chase scrambled away from him. He'd caught a glimpse of the revolver that was still strapped to Chase's hip, and he lunged toward it.

Chase kicked at Logan and their hands collided as they both went after the gun. Logan pulled it out, Chase knocked it away, and they both went down into a whirling, snarling mass of hatred and death, rolling through the snow, both leaving trails of blood. The knife came out of Logan's back and was lost as they struggled for the revolver.

They crashed against a rock buried in the snow. Chase took the impact in his side and the breath was knocked from him again. Logan saw his weakness at once. He raised Chase's body and threw it against the rock again, then stood and gave him a well-placed kick. More ribs snapped, and Logan pulled back his leg for another kick. Chase managed to grab his other ankle and flipped him backwards into the snow. Logan landed with his arms sprawled and his fingertips brushed against the warm walnut of the revolver handle. They both stood at the same time and Logan brought the gun around and centered it on Chase's forehead.

"It seems like we've done this before." Logan laughed at the irony. "I wished Joe was around to share it. I'll make sure to tell Jenny all about it when I see her."

Chase sucked in the frigid air, feeling the burning in his lungs and the pain in his side. *Jenny.* A multitude of pictures flashed through his mind, but at the forefront of all of them was her face. Logan pulled the trigger.

Nothing.

Logan looked aghast as he tried to shoot again. Chase caught the gleam of his knife out of the corner of his eye. Logan roared his frustration and came after Chase with his head down, arms outspread, ready to try killing him again with his bare hands. Chase dove sideways and his hand found the knife. He turned with it ready in his hands. He came up, bringing the blade into Logan's lower abdomen. The impact stopped Logan in his tracks and he looked down in shock at Chase's hand, which had buried the knife to the hilt.

Chase felt the knife sink into Logan's stomach. He could see in his mind's eye the damage that it had done. Logan might die if it was left untreated, but he could live also. If only Jamie had been so lucky. Chase's mind replayed the scene on the street once again. He heard Logan's call; he saw the look of hatred and evil in his eyes. He felt the impact of Jamie knocking him to the ground as Logan fired. He saw the anguish and fear in Jenny's eyes when they rolled Jamie over in the street and saw the blood pouring from his body. He recalled the look in Jamie's eyes as he lay dying, he heard Sarah's heart-wrenching sobs and Jenny's stubborn insistence that Jamie could not die.

The rage consumed Chase, boiling up from his gut and swirling around him in a black cloud. It won't happen again. Their eyes connected, and Logan's went wide as Chase sliced across, opening Logan's belly and exposing his bowels. Logan's hands found the wound and he frantically tried to catch his entrails as they spilled out in the snow. He sunk to his knees, his mouth hanging open as his mind tried to understand what had just happened to him.

Chase backed away from the gory mess with the bloody knife in his hand.

"You bastard, you killed me," Logan sobbed.

"You're not dead yet." Chase was surprised at how flat his voice was. He turned and walked away from the blubbering form of Logan, who reached out after him with one hand while his other fought to stave off the death that would come, eventually.

Chase could not count how many steps he took before his legs gave out on him and he fell to his knees. The contents of his stomach heaved forth and he lost them in the snow. His stomach rebelled until he could no longer hold himself up and he pitched forward with his innards still cramping though there was nothing left inside. He felt the world swirling around him, but he could still see the blood on his knife and still heard the solitary death throes of Logan.

The cries were coming further apart now. It was funny how he didn't feel cold any more. Chase blinked against the crusting of snow that covered his eyelashes. He heard a soft, regular noise behind him, a gentle crunch like that of snow settling. He needed to move, but it felt too good just lying there. If only Logan would shut up.

Chase heard a crashing sound and realized the buckskin was still around. He sighed, which hurt his ribs, and looked at his knife. *You really should clean that before it rusts.* That was a task he should be able to handle. He flicked his wrist and buried the blade in the snow. Nope, it was crusty; he was going to have to rub it. He managed to gather his legs up beneath him and pushed himself up on all fours. The next step was to stand and he had to take a few minutes just to remember how. He finally made it up while holding one hand against his injured side. He rubbed the knife against his pants leg to remove the blood and returned it to its sheath.

The sun had come out from behind the gray wall of clouds. The brightness of it almost blinded him as it caught the reflection of ice crystals on top of the snow. Chase shielded his eyes with one hand as he pressed the other against his side. He was surprised when it felt sticky and he looked down at the blood that stained his coat and glove.

"Hat." That would help with the sun. "Guns." He would probably need them in order to make it home alive. "Home." His words made sense, but he just couldn't figure out how to get there. His hat and guns were back where Logan was. The cries were growing fainter but they were still audible. Ignoring them wouldn't make them go away. Chase began the difficult process of putting one leg in front of the other.

He found his hat where he had first fallen. Leaning over was agony but he managed to pick it up and dust the snow off before planting it on his head. Now he could see. He found his rifle, right beyond his hat, and haltingly made his way to the trampled bloody snow where he had fought with Logan. He found his revolver and returned it to its holster. He wondered briefly why it didn't fire when Logan had it leveled against him. And where was Logan?

A trail of blood and gore through broken snow answered his question. Chase followed the rambling trail down towards a small outcropping of rocks. He could hear Logan begging and crying. He came around the boulder and stopped dead in his tracks.

The wolf was there. The wolf with the golden eyes. He sat with his head tilted and his tongue lolling, watching Logan, who had backed himself up against the rocks with no escape.

"Shoot him," Logan begged. Chase turned. "Shoot me!" Chase walked away. "*Shoot me;* you know what he's going to do, please kill me!"

"I already have." The buckskin was waiting up ahead, his tail swishing, and his posture casual. Chase rode away from the place of death. He was going home.

Chapter Nineteen

"Hey Chase, wake up." Chase tried to open his eyes but they were so heavy he could not get the lids to move. He finally focused on a dim light and realized that it was the sky above him. Someone was talking but he could not see who it was. It hurt too much to turn his neck and he could not draw a deep breath. His horse was still with him. The buckskin was pushing his nose against his side, which hurt like hell. "Chase, can you hear me?"

"Yes." He did not recognize his own voice. It was hoarse and seemed to be coming from somewhere other than his sore throat and chapped lips.

"You need to get up, Chase. Jenny is waiting for you."

"Then help me," Chase said angrily. Whoever was talking to him should be able to tell that he was hurt and sick. Why wouldn't his rescuer just help him?

"I can't."

261

"Why?" Chase wondered why whoever it was wouldn't just leave him alone. He felt a shadow fall over his face and blinked his swollen eyelids again. A red fox was sitting on his chest. Now wasn't that strange? The fox wavered and turned misty, and then a face came into focus. "Jamie?" The vision became clearer. "Your face . . ."

"I know, it's perfect now. Just goes along with the rest of me. We all have perfect bodies here." The grin flashed. "You're having a vision. I guess it's from the fever."

"But you're dead . . ."

"Yep, and you missed the funeral."

"I had to go after Logan." Suddenly it was easy for him to talk and he didn't even feel his mouth move.

"You did it; you made sure Jenny will be safe." Jamie mused that over for a while. "But you know she won't care about being safe if you're not there, so you'd better get up, buddy."

Chase tried to move, tried to struggle to his feet but fell again, face down this time. "I can't," he groaned.

"Okay, I understand. I'll see if I can find someone to help you."

Winter had taken its toll on the herd. Ty dreaded the thought of the spring roundup. They were short-handed, especially without Chase, who knew all of the nooks and crannies where the cattle liked to hide. Ty surveyed the skies as he pondered the responsibilities before him. Snow was threatening again; the clouds were heavy with it. But there shouldn't be much accumulation and this would probably be the last snowfall. Then they would begin the process of bringing in what was left of the herd, rounding up the strays, branding the calves that had managed to survive the winter. And after that, he would be gone. The news of Fort Sumter had reached across the country in a hurry, along with the announcement of Virginia's secession. By the time he reached North Carolina his home would also be part of the Confederacy. His mother's letters had made that much clear.

It was funny how quickly he had become accustomed to the differences between the landscape in Wyoming and that of North Carolina. He had thought the deep woods and mountains back home were wild but that was before he had seen this untamed country. A vision came to mind of how the field he was now riding in looked with its soft spring grass gently blowing in the breeze. Then he recalled it covered in snow, not this sloppy crusty stuff that surrounded him now, but fresh light powder that flew around the horses when they ran.

Ty pulled his horse up on a small rise and let the memories wash over him. It might be a while before he could return to this place, if he ever did. The last time he had been here had been at dusk, after they had killed the wolves. They had come down out of the canyons beyond and taken time to observe the sun that was beginning to set in the western sky. Caleb had drawn it with his pencil, but Ty could still recall the vivid colors of that day, the way Jamie had taken off on his horse, bent low over his neck, one with the animal. The soft powdery snow sprayed up around them like fairy dust, causing them all to marvel at how man and horse could move so gracefully together.

His eyes traced the path that Jamie had taken that day, his mind seeing the russet head next to the black of the horse as rider communed with steed, urging him on. A red fox caught his eye, jumping over the mounds of snow. Ty watched it run towards a patch of color that showed dark against the dull gray of the melting snow. "Probably a dead cow," he thought to himself as he nudged his horse forward. He might as well go and check it out.

The form took shape as he approached and he realized it was the back of a horse showing above a small depression in the ground. It was a buckskin and its reins appeared to be tangled in something.

"Chase!" Ty was off his horse in a flash when he saw the movement beneath the buckskin's feet. Chase was on the ground, soaking wet in the snow and burning with fever, but his hands still tightly gripped the reins.

"Jamie?" His voice was nothing but a sharp rasp in his throat.

"No, it's Ty." Ty managed to get his arms under him, and pulled him up. "Chase, you've got to get in the saddle. Can you find the stirrup? Chase?"

Chase leaned heavily against the saddle. He could not breathe, but he managed to raise his foot and Ty pushed him from behind. The rest was automatic. His leg swung over and found the other stirrup, but he could not sit up. He fell forward over the buckskin's neck. His breath rattled in his throat and Ty grabbed the reins.

"Hold on, Chase, hold on."

The snow was upon them before they got back, clinging to their clothes and the horses until they were as white as the ground. Ty could hear Chase wheezing over his horse but there was nothing he could do for him except get him home. He saw smoke rising from the chimney of Jenny's cabin as he came over the rise and he screamed her name when he was in sight of the place.

Jenny came to the door with her quilt thrown over her shoulders, her eyes widening in surprise when she recognized the horse. She was down the stoop and beside the buckskin before it had a chance to stop. Chase toppled off and luckily Ty caught him before he hit the ground.

"Where did you find him?" Jenny asked as they carried Chase into the cabin.

"Up in the north pasture, lying in the snow. He's lucky he didn't freeze to death."

"Freeze? He's burning up." They laid him on the bed and Jenny ran her hand down the side of the pale, regal face as Ty pulled Chase's boots off. "His clothes are frozen solid." Jenny ripped at the shirt. "Ty, you'd better get Grace."

Ty bolted from the cabin as Jenny wrestled the clothes away. She stopped in shock when she saw the wound in his side. "Oh, Chase," she cried.

He could not answer. He could not breathe. His voice was stuck in his throat, but he knew she was there. Chase felt her cool hands and saw her face shimmering above him. Something about Jenny was different, but he couldn't tell what it was. He drifted away, knowing that he was home.

"Where do you think he's been?" Cat asked.

"To hell, by the looks of him." Zane's answer was the most accurate guess any of them could come up with. Chase had slipped into unconsciousness as soon as he had seen Jenny, and remained as still as death while Grace and Jenny bathed his feverish body.

"We should cut his hair." Jenny looked in shock at Grace, who had gathered the long strands together in her hand. "It's going to take every bit of what strength he has left to fight this fever." Jenny nodded and Grace took the mass off at the nape of his neck. "It will be easier for you to take care of now, too."

Jenny had a vision of her own long recovery last summer and of Chase gently brushing her hair after he had carried her to the swing. He had been so patient with her and so caring. "It will grow." She refused to believe any differently.

"This wound looks as if it's a few weeks old." Cole was examining the bullet hole that passed through from front to back. "It appears he has some broken ribs too." Dark bruises covered Chase's wide chest. They bandaged his wounds, cleaned the gash on his temple, and tucked him in with clean sheets and blankets. There was nothing to do now but wait, wonder, and hope. They were all there, the people who loved him, and though there was a sigh of relief at his return, there was concern for his condition. Jenny felt their presence, but for now her world began and ended with the man who was lying in the big bed. She wouldn't lose him now.

Did there come a point in your life when you were so weary that you could just lie down and die? Chase wondered if he was doomed to wander for eternity, never resting, never reaching his destination. He was so tired, but something kept him going. He didn't even know where he was, or what had happened to his horse, he just knew that he had to keep going and so he did.

There was a light up ahead and he made for it, realizing when he saw the light that he was in a tunnel. It didn't make sense, but nothing had lately, so he went on. The closer he came, the warmer it got, until he could feel his skin burning. The light turned out to be flames and over the snap and crackle of the fire he heard voices calling his name.

"Come join us, breed." It was Logan, and behind him, Randolph Mason. Beyond that were nameless faces, but he knew them. He had never forgotten the faces of the men he had killed. "After all, you're the one who sent us here." Chase shook his head in denial, but he could feel the flames searing his skin and the fire was drawing him in.

"No . . ."

Jenny wrung out the cloth that had dried almost instantly and placed on his forehead another one that she had dipped in snow. It was the only thing she could think of to cool the fever that ravaged his body.

"He's fighting it." Jason was watching with her. They were all taking turns helping her, out of concern for her health and the baby's, but she wouldn't leave her husband's side.

"Fight it, Chase. Come back to me, to us." She smoothed the ragged ends of his hair away from the face, which was so pale in the firelight. "Please come back."

"Hey Chase, come back!" Chase turned from the fire and saw Jamie motioning towards him, encouraging him to come down another tunnel where another light was glowing. "Where have you been?" Jamie flashed his grin.

"You found me."

"Yeah, I did. I got you help, too, just like I said I would."

"Where are we?" He looked around, but all he could see was a soft glow and some people in the distance.

The wide blue eyes twinkled and the grin flashed again. "It doesn't matter. You're not staying."

"But I'm so tired."

"I know, and Jenny's going to take care of you. Listen." The russet head tilted sideways to catch a sound. "Hear that? She's calling for you."

Chase turned his head towards the voice.

"Keep talking, Jenny, he can hear you," Jason urged.

"I love you, Chase." Jenny leaned over so she could whisper into his ear. "Please come back."

The dark eyes fluttered; his head turned toward her face. "Jenny . . ." It was more a breath than a word, but she heard it. Then he was still.

"Chase?" Jenny threw back the blanket and placed her hand on the wide, smooth plain of his chest. She held her breath until she felt the soft thump of his heart against her hand.

"He's resting," Jason assured her. She let out her

breath with a sigh and nodded. "You need to rest, too, for the baby."

"I can't leave him."

"You can stay here; just let us take care of him, and you." Jason recognized the stubborn set of her chin and placed a hand on her shoulder. "Please, Jenny. I couldn't stand it if something happened to you."

"You really miss him, don't you?" Jenny squeezed Jason's hand as he brought the other one up to stroke her hair.

"Yes, I do." It was still too hard to say Jamie's name, so they didn't.

The shaking of his body woke him. He was so cold, his teeth were chattering violently, making it harder than ever to draw a breath. He felt like he was suffocating, like someone was sitting on his chest, but there was nothing there but a blanket.

"Jenny?" His voice rattled in his throat, but she heard him. She was there. "I'm so cold." She was wearing a long gown with the quilt thrown around her shoulders. She put the quilt over his blanket and then pulled the gown over her head. He saw her silhouette against the glow of the fire and saw the soft rounding of her belly before she slid under the blankets. Jenny stretched out against Chase, her skin touching his, the warmth of her body caressing the chill from his flesh. She wrapped her arms around his neck and pulled his head to her breast. He felt a movement against him, a little kick that protested his intrusion. His hands were shaking as he placed them over her stomach. "When?" It was painfully whispered.

"The first time." Jenny kissed the top of his head and smoothed her hand through his hair. His chills subsided and he rested then as Jenny stayed with him, holding his body tight against hers for the rest of the night.

Chapter Twenty

The last burst of winter had followed Chase home and then the snow melted away, leaving behind fresh green grass that reached joyfully for the sun. Chase was better, but weak, barely able to walk from the bed to the wingback chair in front of the fire where he would sit for hours, just staring at the flames. Grace trimmed his hair, which brought a smile from Jenny. It looked the same as it had when she had first met him seven years earlier. His face had matured, however, since that time, no longer softened by the innocence of youth, and his eyes . . . they had seemed haunted then, full of pain from the untimely deaths of his mother and fathers, but now . . . Jenny wasn't sure if she wanted to know the secrets that were hiding in his dark eyes. Chase didn't comment on his missing hair, he didn't say much of anything. It seemed to take all

271

of his strength just to wake up in the mornings. Jenny patiently took care of him, and they never mentioned Jamie's name or the months when Chase had been gone. They really didn't talk of anything except for the most mundane aspects of everyday life. He didn't ask about the baby and didn't reach out to touch her. He was present in body only and Jenny worried more for his spirit than his health.

Eventually Chase was able to go outside for a while to sit on the stoop soaking up the weak spring sun. His color returned and he began to take small walks down to the corral to watch the work that was being done after the roundup. The boys whooped and hollered at him but he didn't respond beyond a polite wave and a slight smile. Jamie's absence was too obvious to be filled by the noise. Jenny went about her chores as before, taking care of Storm and the mares during the day and sewing clothes for the baby at night.

One day she as she came out of the barn she saw Chase running slowly across the ridge above the cabin. Last summer he had told her that he had run to recover from his broken leg back in the orphanage, and it lifted her heart to see him doing it now.

The running exhausted Chase and he fell asleep before dinner. The baby was restless and Jenny felt lonely, so she wandered down to Grace's to help with dinner. Zane met her sheepishly at the door with a letter. It turned out to be the one Chase had sent from the mining town several months past.

"Well, at least it got here." Jenny smiled ruefully as she scanned the letter.

"At least yours was good news," Zane replied.

"What's wrong?"

"North Carolina finally seceded," Zane explained. "Ty's packing to leave. Caleb and Jake are going with him."

"Idiots." Grace slammed the door of the stove shut. "They're rushing off to get themselves killed for no good reason."

"Ty and Caleb I can understand, but why is Jake going?"

"You know how much Jake loves a good fight."

"He thinks killing Yankees will get rid of all that hate he carries around for his father." Grace had worked herself up into some righteous anger. "Or else he just wants to die so his father will feel guilty about all the abuse he heaped on him when he was growing up. Either way he's a fool, just like the rest of them."

"Where's Cat?"

"She's packing too." Zane grinned at that. "She told Ty she was going with him and the only way he could stop her was to shoot her. It wasn't a pretty sight, believe me."

"Does Jason know about any of this?"

"I'm sure he does now. I'm sure that the cows out in the north pasture know, the way they were hollering at each other. I'm surprised you missed it."

"What are we going to do now?" Jenny sat down at the table. "Half of the ranch is going to be gone."

"Shouldn't be a problem, since we lost half of the

stock over the winter." Zane poured himself a cup of coffee and joined Jenny at the table.

"That many? I guess I really wasn't paying attention."

"You've had other things on your mind." Grace decided to sit down as well. "We'll be okay. Jason thinks the army is going to need a lot of beef, which will drive the price up. He'll hire some hands for the drive this fall."

"The drive." Jenny studied her hands, which were clasped on the table. "So much has happened since last year's drive."

Grace placed a hand over Jenny's. "Yes it has, but it wasn't all bad, you know." Grace looked into the sapphire-blue eyes that held so much pain. "What happened to you was horrible, but you're all right now. And losing Jamie was the most terrible thing that could have happened to any of us. We all loved him, you know that. A person couldn't help loving him." Zane nodded in agreement. "But some good things have happened too. You got married, you're having a baby, Cat and Ty got married . . ."

"Finally," Zane interrupted. "And don't forget about Cole. We know how happy you are about that."

"Shut up, Zane," Grace continued. "But most important, Chase is alive and he's here."

"Yes, he's here. But I don't know how long he'll stay."

"Oh Jenny, he's not going anywhere." Zane was eternally optimistic.

"I don't know, Zane. Sometimes I get the feeling

he's just biding his time until he's healthy again so he can leave. He hasn't said a word about what happened out there. I don't even know for sure if he killed Logan. He just won't talk about it. He won't talk about anything."

"But he has to be excited about the baby," Grace said.

"He won't even mention it." Grace looked shocked. "When his fever broke he asked me when it happened, but after that . . . nothing."

"He's only been back a few weeks; you'll just have to give him time."

"Just like he gave me last fall." It all seemed so long ago.

"Exactly."

"Cat, you are not going with me." Ty pitched his hat in the chair as Cat stubbornly continued her packing.

"I think I'll have Daddy ship my trunks out so we can travel faster." She held a summery dress up and perused her reflection in the mirror. "I guess it's a lot warmer there than it is here, isn't it?"

Ty tossed the dress back in the wardrobe and grabbed Cat by the shoulders. "I need you to stay here."

"And I need to go with you."

"Cat, don't you see, I need to know that you're here waiting for me."

"And I need to be able to get to you in case you're hurt."

"I'm not going to get hurt."

Cat kicked him in the shin and stomped her foot in frustration. "Grace is right; you're all a bunch of idiots. You think you're invincible or something just because you say it's not going to happen. It's a war, Ty. people get killed everyday, men just like you who have wives that desperately love them. And I am not going to be halfway across the country waiting for word from you."

Ty uttered an oath and rubbed his leg during her tirade. "But I won't be able to protect you." His gallantry only angered her more and she considered giving him another kick.

"Protect me from what? Yankees?" Cat picked up a newspaper clipping that her mother-in-law had sent and waved it under his nose. "From what this says, the South is going to beat the Yankees in record time and send them all packing." Ty pulled the clipping from her hand. "I'll stay with your mother; surely the North is not going to make war on the mothers and wives of the Confederacy."

"Cat, life is different there. I'm not sure if you're ready to handle it."

"What you mean is you're afraid I'm going to be a disappointment to your mother and brother."

"Actually, I'm afraid you'll haul off and shoot my brother's wife because she bores you to tears."

"Have you ever considered a career in politics?" Cat laughed as Ty pulled her into his arms. "Ty, I spent a season on the continent when I was sixteen years old. I spent every winter in New York with my aunt until you showed up. I think I can handle some silly Southern belle."

"Please stay here so I don't have to worry about you. I already feel responsible for Caleb and Jake going."

"You will feel responsible for every soldier you run across. Somebody has got to be responsible for you. You can either take me with you, or wait for me to show up, but I'm going."

"Am I ever going to win with you?" Ty kissed the top of her head.

"What do you mean win? You got first prize." The slanted green eyes tilted into a smile.

"I did?" he teased.

"Yes, you got me, didn't you?"

"Cat, promise me one thing." Ty was suddenly serious again.

Cat traced her finger down the front of his shirt and stuck her lip out in a mock pout. "That depends on what it is."

Ty stooped to look into the green eyes flecked with gold. "If things get bad there, you'll leave. And I'm the one who decides."

"I'll agree on one condition."

"Which is?"

"Don't be a hero. You've got to keep yourself safe and come back home with me." She flung her arms around his neck and he pulled her petite body close.

"All I can promise is that I will do my best."

"Then that's good enough for me."

* * *

Chase showed up at Grace's looking for supper just as she was clearing the table. Grace fixed him a plate, then herded Jenny out to the swing, leaving Cole to get acquainted with him. Chase took the time to make friends with Justice, who was polite as usual before taking his place again beside the stove.

"It's good to see you up and moving around," Cole began.

"I should be back at work in no time."

"I don't think anybody's worried about that. Everyone here has been worried about you and it's a relief to them to see that you're better."

Chase's dark eyes looked up from his plate in surprise. "They were?"

"Yes, they were. When I came here last January this place was like a ghost town. Nobody smiled, nobody laughed, and they were barely eating."

"Everyone loved Jamie."

"Yes, and they loved you too." Chase looked down at his plate in embarrassment. Cole continued. "Lord knows I'm the last one who should be telling you something like this, but I've found out a few things about myself since I've been here." Chase looked at Cole and saw the wisdom the years had etched on his face. "What a man leaves behind says a lot about him when he's out doing what he has to do to protect the ones he loves. There wasn't a day that went by when somebody wasn't worrying about you or praying for you. That's a good thing to have waiting at home. I never realized what was missing from my life until I showed up here and saw it. And the Lord willing, I'm going to have someone to care about me from now on."

"Grace?"

"Yes. She's one hell of a woman, and as soon as I get some things straightened out, I'm going to make her my wife if she'll have me." Cole warmed up his coffee. "You've got a good life here, Chase. Don't take it for granted. I can see you got a lot of demons in you. It's time to put them to rest and come back to your life."

"I don't know if I can. I don't know if I deserve this life."

"That's something only you can answer." Cole slid his plate away. "Now I'm going out on the porch to enjoy a beautiful spring evening with two beautiful ladies."

Chase finished his meal in silence.

Caleb stepped up on the porch of Grace's cabin with his sketch book under his arm. The two women slid apart and made room for him on the swing. Caleb perused Jenny's stomach with a doubtful look, but then slid in between the two women with a grateful smile.

"Do you have something new to show us?" Grace asked.

"No, not really. You've seen the picture of Cole and Justice, and I haven't drawn much of anything else since Christmas." The words trailed off as Caleb immediately regretted what he'd said. Nothing left to do now but forge on ahead. "Jenny, I want you to keep my sketchbook for me."

"Why? You're not taking it with you?"

"No, I'm afraid something might happen to it, and besides, it belongs here."

"Caleb, you don't have to go, you know," she said. Caleb had always been the silent one but suddenly Jenny realized just how much she was going to miss his quiet strength and calming ways. "No one would think less of you if you decided to stay."

"I know."

"I thought you had no family left in the South anyway." Grace hoped to talk all of them out of leaving.

"All I had was my dad. That's why I have to go, for him. We had a little store down in the mountains of Georgia. It wasn't much, but it was a good business. Dad was always ready to help someone out when they needed it, and folks would pay him when they could. But that made it hard for Dad to pay his bills. One day a banker showed up and said he had paid off all the notes on the store. We were thrown out on the street without a second thought. It was winter and we had no place to go. Dad got sick. Before he died, he told me to make sure that no one ever had the same power over me that the banker had had over him. No one has the right to come in and tell you how to live your life. That's why I have to go. The North is telling the South how to live and it's not right."

"But Caleb, the South is doing the same thing with the slaves," Grace exclaimed.

"We never owned a slave, so I don't know anything

about that. I just know what that banker did to my dad, and it wasn't right."

"Caleb, you've got to do what you feel is right," Jenny said. "I'd be honored to take care of your book. But you have to promise to come back for it."

Caleb smiled his gentle smile. "I promise." Grace jumped out of the swing and took off towards the barn. "I guess she's pretty mad at all of us," Caleb said as they watched her go.

"She's worried about you, all of you."

"Jenny, if it's our time to die, then there's nothing we can do about it."

"Do you really believe that?"

"Yes, I do."

"But by going to fight, it seems you're almost looking for death."

"Lots of men go through wars without ever getting hit," he pointed out.

"And some men get killed in cold blood walking down the street on their wedding day," she replied.

Caleb took Jenny's hand in his and squeezed it gently. "Some men meet their deaths bravely. That's all we can hope for, that when the time comes, we face it with dignity, knowing we've done our best. I just hope that when my time comes, I can die as bravely as Jamie did. He gave up his life for you, for this baby, for Chase, and for Sarah. His death counted for something and his life counted for something. I will never forget him as long as I live." Jenny forced back the lump in her throat. "My only regret is that I won't be here to see this little one come into the world."

281

"You'll see him soon, Caleb."

"I will." He sounded so sure of it. Jenny threw her arms around his neck and swallowed the tears. She hadn't cried yet and she wouldn't cry now.

Luckily Cole came out just then, which was enough of a distraction to keep the tears at bay. "She took off for the barn," Jenny answered before he could ask where Grace had gone.

"I guess she's still mad at all of you."

"You could say that." Caleb laughed. "Poor Zane will be catching a lot of grief from her after we're gone. He won't have anyone to share it with."

"From what I've seen, Zane calls it down on himself pretty good, but maybe I can distract her enough to make his life easier." Cole sauntered off the porch and headed towards the barn with Justice behind him.

Chase made his appearance a few minutes later as Jenny and Caleb sat in companionable silence in the swing. "Is there something going on?" he asked.

"We're leaving tomorrow," Caleb answered.

"Leaving?"

"For the war." Chase looked at Caleb in surprise.

"He doesn't know, Caleb. We haven't talked about it."

"Me, Ty, and Jake are going to fight for the South."

"And from what I hear Cat's going, too," Jenny added.

A smile flitted across Chase's face. "Bet that was interesting." Jenny felt a pleasant warming deep in her stomach. He almost sounded like himself again. "Guess I'd better go find Ty."

"He's up at the big house arguing with Cat," Caleb offered.

Chase held out his hand to Caleb. "Take care of yourself."

"I'll try." The handshake was warm but brief, almost as if the contact was too much for Chase, who quickly left for Jason's house without a word to Jenny. "He'll be all right, Jenny."

"I hope so, Caleb." Jenny patted the mound of her stomach. "There are a lot of us who are counting on it."

Jason wasn't sure how much actual packing had been accomplished in his daughter's room. He had heard the arguing as the couple came up the hill, had heard it resounding up the stairs and then heard the muffled voices behind the slammed door of Cat's room. He had heard the stomping of feet, heard Ty's exclamation of pain, and rolled his eyes at the ceiling. It had been blessedly quiet since then and he waited patiently for the outcome. Jason knew Cat was going; he had even encouraged her to go and made provisions for the trip. The bottom of her small trunk contained enough gold pieces and treasury bills to insure against any contingency, including the ransom of all of them if they were taken prisoner. It was all he could think of to do to insure their safety and he hoped it would be enough.

Once again the events of New Year's Day ran through Jason's mind. Was there anything any of them could have done to avoid the disaster on that day? Logan had been determined to kill someone and the courage he'd found in a whiskey bottle made it impossible to reason with him. Would the pain have been any different if it had been Chase or Jenny? Jason once again wished it had been he who'd taken the bullet instead of Jamie. Had Jamie realized what he was doing? Had it been his intention to sacrifice his life or was he just trying to get his family out of harm's way? There were no answers to the never-ending questions, just a hollow feeling in his heart whenever he thought of Jamie.

Thank God Chase has returned, Jason mused to himself as he watched Chase come up the hill. Chase had always been a mystery to him, more reserved than the other hands, but fiercely loyal to all who lived at the ranch. Jason had always felt that Chase was out of place in this time. He should have been a prince or a warrior in some time or place of old that was mentioned in the story books Jamie always liked to read. But here he was, a half-Kiowa ranch hand married to a beautiful woman and until January seemingly content with his lot in life. Would they ever know what had happened to him in those months he had been gone? He hadn't mentioned anything, not even whether Logan lived or died, but one look into his dark hawklike eyes and everyone knew that he had visited his own personal hell.

Jason's mind wandered back to the night after they had rescued Jenny from Randolph Mason, and the things Chase had done to the man before he died. He had not apologized for his act of violence or even explained it except to say it was part of who he was. Jason briefly wondered what kind of death Logan had found at Chase's hands. *He deserved it.* The intensity of his feelings surprised him. Jason poured himself a drink as Chase entered the room.

"It's good to see you up and around," Jason commented.

"I'll be going back to work tomorrow."

"Don't push it, son. We'll be all right until you're able." Chase declined when Jason offered him a drink. "I guess you heard about the mass exodus to the South?"

"Yes sir, I wanted to talk to Ty before he left."

"You're not the only one."

Chase arched an eyebrow. "Sir?"

"Cat had several things to say to him when he announced he was going."

"So I heard." Chase offered a grin which brought an answering smile from Jason.

"I guess things will be fairly quiet around here this summer," Jason said. "In comparison to last, that is."

Chase let his mind drift to the past year. Jenny had shown up just a year ago and then there had had been the frustration of watching Ty court her, watching Jenny and Jamie fight, the fear of losing her, then the joy of discovering that she'd loved him all along. The long hot days of late summer had been spent together, building their relationship, only to have it shattered by Randolph Mason and his never-ending hatred for the Duncan family. But they had made it, in spite of everything that had happened, they had made it. He had been patient with her while she sorted through the pain of what had happened to her. Would she do the same for him? Hope sprang forth within Chase, opening him to the possibility as the earth was now warming towards the sun. Maybe, just maybe she could forgive him, and then maybe he could forgive himself.

"I'm planning on hiring some new hands before the drive." Chase realized his mind has been elsewhere when he really should have been paying attention to Jason. After all, it was just he and Zane now, and Cole, who seemed to be all right and very attached to Grace. "We're going to be all right, even with the harsh winter."

"I hope so."

The opening of a door sounded in the hall above and soon they heard the noise of boots on the stairs as Ty came down. "Chase, it's good to see you out and about," Ty commented.

"Just in time from what I hear." Chase swallowed hard. *One step at a time*, he told himself. "I wanted to talk to you before you left."

"I'll go see if Cat has any last-minute instructions for me on running the ranch." Jason excused himself with a slight smile and then the two men shared an awkward moment of silence.

"I never got a chance to say thank you for finding me that day," Chase began and then smiled ruefully. "Another couple of days and there wouldn't have been anything left but my carcass."

"Yeah, you were in pretty bad shape. If I recall correctly, you had a death grip on your horse's reins."

"Maybe I should have let go. He would have shown up at the barn and—"

"And Jenny would have had all our hides until we found you," Ty laughed.

"Yeah." It wasn't hard to imagine Jenny's reaction to the buckskin showing up without him.

"I really can't take credit for finding you that day," Ty began. "It was the strangest thing, I was thinking about Jamie and the day when we came down out of the canyons after killing the wolves . . ."

"The way he rode, and the sunset . . ." Chase remembered the day well. It had been glorious, perfect, a tribute to their camaraderie and friendship. Their lives had intermingled as they worked together for one purpose, to make their little corner of the world better for all who lived there.

"Yes." The memory was still fresh and pure. "Then I saw a red fox running across the snow and it just led me to where you were. I don't recall ever seeing a fox out there before."

Chase's eyes went wide as he listened to Ty. "It was Jamie."

"What?"

"Jamie said he would find me some help and he did." Chase dropped into the thick cushioned chair in front of the fireplace and scrubbed his face with his hands.

"What are you talking about?"

"I saw Jamie that day. He woke me up and told me to move and I couldn't. Then he said he would find me some help. I thought I was hallucinating because of the fever."

"You were."

"No, it was Jamie." Chase was certain of it, which made Ty briefly question his sanity. "I know it was, because before I saw Jamie, I saw a red fox."

"That doesn't mean anything."

"But it does. I'm not going to argue with you about what I believe and what you believe, but I will tell you about a vision that Jamie and I had before we started looking for Jenny."

"A vision?"

"It was in a Sioux camp—one of the men there was a friend of Jamie's father and he wanted to provide us with visions to aid our quest. Our visions were separate, but pretty much the same, except for one thing. Mine had wolves and Jamie's had a fox."

"You fought the wolf last winter."

"That was the first time."

"You saw him again?"

"I saw him many times over. And Jenny had dreams about wolves before all this happened, and they terrified her."

"So she had a vision too."

"More like a premonition." Chase rose from the chair and walked over to the window and the view of the small valley below that held his home, his family, all he held dear. "When Jamie was dying, he said he understood his vision. You see, he had found Jenny, but then he went on to a peaceful meadow where a fox was playing. It didn't make sense at the time but when he died, it did. He moved on and left us behind."

"Have you had any visions or premonitions about me, or Caleb and Jake?" Ty was amazed at the story and did not doubt it.

"No, and I don't want to. Even when you have a vision, there's nothing you can do about it."

"Caleb says when it's your turn to die, it's your turn and that's the end of it."

"Jenny's father said only the good die young."

"I guess that was true in Jamie's case," Ty observed.

"And their father's," Chase added.

"So I guess that means I'll be safe." Ty shook his head and laughed, but stopped when he saw the serious look in Chase's dark eyes.

"Take care of yourself, Ty."

Ty extended his hand. "You do the same. And take care of this place, because I'm coming back."

"We'll be fine." Chase took Ty's hand.

"Chase, the ranch needs you." Ty placed his other hand on Chase's shoulder. "And the people here need you." Steady blue eyes met dark ones. "I need to know that you will be here taking care of things."

"I will." Chase had said it, he had made the commitment. It was enough for Ty. The handshakes they exchanged were strong, the respect mutual. "I owe you my life."

"Here's hoping I won't need you to return the favor." Ty grinned.

"North Carolina is a bit further than the north pasture."

"Well, if my horse shows up, you'll know where to start looking."

"I'll be there; you can count on it," Chase assured him. Ty didn't doubt it for a minute.

Early morning found Ty, Cat, Caleb, and Jake loaded into the wagon and ready to leave. Cole and Jason would drive them into town, and Grace alternated between crying and scolding as she packed a hamper of food for them to take on the stage. Hugs and handshakes were exchanged along with promises to write. Cat became tearful when she hugged Jenny.

"I wish I could be here for the birth," she cried as she stood on tiptoe to wrap her arms around Jenny's neck.

"Just try to make it back before you have one," Jenny replied as she hugged Cat's slim frame.

"Oh, I hope so." Cat smiled through her tears. "As long as I can bring the father back with me." She squeezed Jenny's hand and Jenny in return said a silent prayer that they would be spared the pain of losing another loved one. Cat's eyes sought Ty's face as she returned to her own litany of prayers.

Caleb and Jake both hugged Jenny in farewell, to be followed by Ty, who gently kissed her forehead. "Take care of yourself."

"I will, and anyone else who happens to come along," she promised. Behind Ty, she saw Chase silently fading away from the group. He had said his good-byes. Ty's eyes followed Jenny's, watching as Chase disappeared into the barn.

"He'll make his way back, Jenny, just be patient with him."

"I'm not going anywhere, Ty. He knows where to find me when he's ready." She gave him a glorious smile. "I'll be right here waiting for all of you."

"That's good to know, Jenny." Ty swung up on the wagon. "Take care of the place, Zane," he hollered as they moved out.

"Don't worry, I will," Zane hollered back. He stood between Jenny and Grace with an arm around each of them. Grace broke down into sobs and buried her face in his chest as he patted her back comfortingly. Jenny waved until the wagon disappeared over the ridge and then the quiet that settled over them became more than she could stand. She made her way back to her cabin as Grace wiped her eyes with her apron.

Chapter Twenty-one

Chase was able to work again, although he had not recovered his full stamina yet. He would come home from his days weary, barely able to eat before he fell asleep in the big bed, leaving Jenny alone once again to sew clothes for the coming baby. Her loneliness was unbearable; the wall Chase put up around himself was impenetrable. Sometimes she would catch him watching her with a look of longing in his eyes but then the wall would come up again, and she knew he was the only one who could bring it down.

Jenny had put Caleb's sketch book aside in the confusion of the departure and forgotten about it until one rainy night, as she was sewing at the table, she noticed it lying on one of the chairs. The rain had made her irritable and restless and the aches and pains in her back and neck left her downright frustrated. She put aside the delicate stitches of the little gown and opened the book on the table.

It was easy to recognize the people in the book; Caleb had an amazing talent. She flipped back and forth at random. There were Cat and Jason on horseback, looking out over the acres of ranch land. Grace was sitting on her porch shelling beans into a pot. Jake looked stern as usual, it was too bad he didn't smile more. A sketch of Zane made her smile; you just couldn't help loving him, even when he was stirring up trouble. Caleb had captured Cole and Justice to perfection, creating better likenesses than the illustrations in the dime novels they had all read. Page after page recorded the ordinary moments of their lives that they all took for granted. But Caleb had seen the wonder in them and had captured it all on paper.

She knew it was inevitable. The next picture tore at her heart. It was Jamie, on horseback, tearing across the pasture with snow flying around him and a glorious sunset behind. The horse and rider seemed to be moving as one creature, moving freely as if there were no tomorrow. For Jamie, there hadn't been. The next sketch was of Jamie and Chase, leaning casually against a fence, their heads together in silent communication. Chase's wry smile had been captured; it had been so long since she had seen it. Jenny flipped through the pages and found her place in the book, a ragged page where the picture of her bathing in the spring had been ripped out, then a drawing of her sleeping in Jamie's bunk with her braid dangling down. It had been drawn the day that she was reunited with Jamie. Tears sprang unbidden to her eyes and slid down her cheeks as she flipped the pages. On one page Jamie was teasing her and she was smacking his arm. One was a view of their backs with his arm hung casually over her shoulder. Then she was with Chase, the two of them looking into each other's eyes, smiling secrets at each other. It was amazing—Caleb had caught every moment of their lives since they'd arrived and recorded it in his book. The last page stopped her cold, bringing a sob to her throat. It was Christmas time, and Jamie was reading, with Sarah perched on the chair beside him. Her head was tilted and there was a look of wonder on her face as she listened to the rich timbre of his voice. Jenny closed the book and laid her head on the table as her body was overtaken by a sob that tore up from the depths of her soul. She wrapped her arms around her stomach to cradle her infant against the grief that was pouring out of her.

She was lost and alone, cast adrift on a sea of tears. There was no hope and no end to the pain that she had kept at bay for so long. She felt as if she would drown in the grief.

Strong arms wrapped around her and she leaned against a solid chest. Her hands sought a purchase against it, searching for a lifeline to hold on to as her body convulsed with racking sobs. "I'm so sorry, Jenny, I'm so sorry," Chase murmured against her hair. She couldn't stop. For the life of her, she couldn't stop, so he carried her to the bed and wrapped the quilt around her before he pulled her into his arms again.

Finally she was too exhausted to continue, too exhausted to move. She kept her head against Chase's chest and when her own body relaxed she was able to hear the gentle thump of his heart. Her hand crept out from the quilt and she laid it across his bare chest with her palm pressed tightly against the smooth skin as if she were holding his heart in her hand. She felt him swallow, felt his sigh, raised her head, and saw his heart in his eyes. Time stopped for an instant as their eyes connected, as Jenny saw all his fears laid before her in the split second between the beats of his heart. *Save me*, his eyes said and Jenny brought her mouth to his with lips that were still salty from her tears. His arms crushed her body to his as their lips touched and the months of separation fell away as their bodies rediscovered each other. He pulled the gown from her shoulders, his mouth tracing a path that he had known so well. His lips touched the scar and his hands found the new fullness of her breasts and the curve of her stomach where their babe kicked against him in protest. He kissed the swelling and Jenny pushed him over on his back and straddled his body.

"The baby?" Chase whispered as she mounted him.

"He'll be fine." Jenny closed her eyes and threw her head back as he filled her. His hands sought her breasts as she moved against him, slowly, wanting time to stand still again, wanting nothing more than to be with Chase and to have him love her again. He grabbed her hips with his hands, helping her to move, not wanting to hurt the baby inside, but not wanting her to stop. His eyes darkened and she watched his face change with a look of shocked surprise. Then she felt her own call to join him.

Chase laid his hands across Jenny's stomach and watched, amazed, at the contortions that were going on within. He brought the lamp over from the bedside table so he could see her skin stretch where a fist, or knee, or foot was sticking out. "When will he be here?"

"He?" Jenny stretched in contentment. "Late July, early August, I think."

Chase laughed as his hand was bumped by the baby. Jenny tilted her head and looked at him quizzically. "What is it?"

"I haven't heard anyone laugh since . . ." Jenny started.

"Since Jamie died?"

The sound of his name tore through her like a knife and she sat up, wrapping her arms around her knees. "Did you kill Logan?" she asked.

Chase got out of bed and found his pants. He pulled them on and then ran his hands through his hair as he searched for the right thing to say.

"Yes, I killed him and I hope I never kill anyone again." Chase went to the fireplace and leaned against the mantle with his arms outstretched before him as he looked down at the hearth. "I hated what I became and I became that way because of hate. I abandoned you and I abandoned our child all because I hated Logan more than I loved you." His voice broke on the words.

"I don't believe that, Chase."

"I do, I was consumed by it." He turned to face her. "I was bringing him back. I was going to bring him back to Laramie and have him stand trial for murder but I killed him instead." Chase raised his hands up and looked at them as if he had never seen them before. "All I could think about was killing him, and I enjoyed every minute of it." His eyes turned inward again. "And I'm terrified of it happening again," he whispered.

"We won't let it." Jenny wrapped the quilt around her body as she went to him. He turned away from her, so she took his face in her hands. "Logan was a threat to us, so you killed him; it was that simple."

"But you don't know how I killed him." His dark eyes were haunted again. "I should have brought him back."

"Chase, you barely made it here yourself. You can't tell me that Logan didn't fight back. You were shot, you almost died. It had to have been self-defense."

"Part of it was, but then the hate took over."

"You killed him because he took something precious from us. Before we were married, Jamie told me that if I turned away from you because of what Mason did to me, then Mason had won. Chase, if you go away from me, and I don't mean physically, I mean your spirit, if your spirit leaves me because of Logan, then he wins. He will have destroyed all of us, and that's what he wanted. I'm not justifying what you did, I'm just telling you that he was a destroyer. He was always seeking ways to make people unhappy because he was unhappy. Jamie died because he wanted us to live. Please don't make his death meaningless."

The picture on the mantle still faced the chimney. Chase picked it up and turned it around. Three faces looked at him from behind the glass. Caleb had placed Jenny in the middle with her shoulder against Chase's chest. They were both smiling at Jamie who was grinning back as he always did. Chase put the picture in its rightful place, where everyone could see it upon entering the cabin. Jenny came into his arms and he pulled her tightly against him, the baby, for once, not protesting.

Laramie looked much the same as the last time he had seen it, but apparently he didn't. It was the first time in a long time that Chase could remember riding through a town and not getting suspicious looks. The dark hair that had fallen nearly to his waist was missing now. He had worn it long in tribute to his father and his heritage, but it had always drawn the hatred of those who judged a man by how he looked instead of who he was inside. If given a choice, most of those who used to stare him down would have preferred Logan over him, just because he was white. Chase's hand brushed the back of his neck which still felt bare. One of these days he was going to have it out with Jenny for letting Grace cut his hair off.

He guided the buckskin through the busy thoroughfare, trying not to remember the last time he had seen these streets. Jenny had not been back since Jamie's murder; as a matter of fact she seemed determined never to leave the confines of the Lynch spread again. Chase couldn't really blame her and knew that she would venture forth again when she was ready. He should have been there for her when they put her brother in the ground, but like his missing hair, there was nothing he could do about it now. He soon came to the small cemetery on the outskirts of town and threw the buckskin's reins over the freshly white-washed picket fence that surrounded the grouping of monuments to loved ones who had gone on.

It only took him a moment to find the stone that Jason had commissioned. It held three lines. "James Ian Duncan. Jamie. Forever in our hearts."

"*And in our minds,*" Chase murmured, kneeling beside the earth that had settled under the heavy snows of the past winter. He caressed the smooth marble that Jason had imported from St. Louis to mark the last resting place of the one they had all loved so dearly. *It's not enough.*

Chase looked beyond the stone and out across the plains that rolled east, where at this very moment his friends were on their way to fight for the principles they believed in. *What do you believe in?* Chase asked himself. Six months ago the answers would have been easy, because they were right in front of him. Jenny, Jamie, and the life they had made for themselves. He believed in the bond that he and Jamie had shared, stronger than blood, forged out of friendship and their love for Jenny.

Chase looked down again at the stone. A name carved into marble would mean nothing to the people who would pass this way in time. The stone would outlast all those who knew and loved Jamie Duncan. There was nothing here that would tell how wonderful he had been, how he could ride like the wind, how he could light up a room with one of his foolish grins. Where would it be written that Jamie could work magic with horses, how his voice could transport listeners to another time and place? It wasn't enough.

"You don't belong here." There was no answer from the firmly packed earth, which was pale and green from sweet new grass that had taken root. "You belong out there with the wind and the land and the clouds. That's where I want to be when I go." How close that had come to being a reality, Chase realized as the words fell onto the earth. He could have died in the snow and never been found, his body left to the wolves. There would have been no monument to mark his passing.

But perhaps there was. A child grew inside Jenny, a child conceived in the first days of their marriage. It was a part of him and a part of her. *Let it be the best part.* Jamie would live in the child also. "I will tell him about you," Chase promised the earth. "He will know you as I knew you, and loved . . ." Chase squeezed his eyes with his hand, but a tear escaped and trickled down his lean cheek, falling amidst the tender blades that covered the grave. He stood and blinked against the sun that was suddenly too bright in the sky. "You don't belong here," he said as a goodbye and went to where the buckskin was waiting, patient as usual.

Chapter Twenty-two

Sleeping with a beautiful wife whom you dearly loved was one thing. Sleeping with the same woman going into her eighth month of pregnancy was something else entirely. The bed that at one time had seemed so huge was now small in comparison. Especially when you were sharing it with a set of long, strong legs that kicked at the covers and then sprawled in every direction. Or when you had pressing in your back a huge round belly containing a multi-limbed creature that poked and kicked every chance it had. The snoring part was cute, though, Chase had to admit, as he sat up in exasperation and watched Jenny, who was now on her back with her legs folded up at the knees. He laid his hand across the mound of her belly and felt the gentle movement of the babe.

Fatherhood was not something he had given a lot

of thought to. Sure, he had wanted to make babies with Jenny, but his mind had been more on the making part than the actual results. His thoughts wandered back to his own father and the loving home they had shared, in spite of the difficulties facing his family. Even though they lived in a village, his childhood had been solitary, but the hours his father spent with him had been filled with joy. Chase wondered if he could do as well.

From what he had heard of Ian, Jenny's father, it would be nearly impossible to fill his shoes. He must have been a special man to raise such special children. The values he had instilled in them had stayed with them, even after they had been orphaned. Jenny had admitted that she was becoming more like her mother, Faith, whose carved angel box now resided on the bedside table. Becoming a mother had gentled her in a way that she'd never expected.

But they still had half the summer to get through before the child was due to arrive. Jenny was already feeling the heat. The sheet was scrunched around her ankles and the blanket had all but disappeared. Chase felt the baby roll beneath his hand, and he leaned close to Jenny's stomach to murmur words she had never heard before.

"What does that mean?" Jenny whispered above his head. Chase turned and saw her eyes glistening in the moonlight.

"Child of my heart."

Jenny ran her fingers through the short ends of his hair. His eyes flashed as he bent to kiss her, his lips gently touching, caressing, as if he was afraid she would break. A sudden shift in her stomach bounced his hand and Jenny groaned. "I don't think this child is ever going to sleep."

Chase chuckled in her ear and pulled her around until he was spooned against her. He wrapped his arm around her belly and tucked her head under his chin. "I guess we'll just have to start teaching him now."

"What makes you so sure it's a him?"

"What makes you so sure it's not?"

"What makes you think you can teach whatever it is anything at all?"

"Shh, go to sleep, some of us have to work in the morning."

Jenny opened her mouth to argue but then decided the pressure of his body against her back felt good. And the large circles Chase was massaging on her stomach did seem to have a calming effect on the babe inside. She nestled up against the wide chest of her husband.

"Chase?" she said as she felt her body relax.

"Hmmm?"

"I'm cold."

Chase rolled his eyes above her head and felt for the quilt with his foot. With one quick motion he flipped it up over their bodies. Jenny grabbed a corner of it and pulled it under her chin.

"You're getting good at that, you know." Her voice was lost in the pillow.

"I've had lots of practice."

* * *

Two new hands were hired, Dan and Randy. Dan was tall and slim, with curly dark hair and blue eyes. He spent most of his free time reading, to Zane's complete chagrin. Randy was shorter, with blond hair and brown eyes, and had a very easygoing personality. Nothing seemed to bother Randy at all, which tremendously annoyed Zane, who had enjoyed getting a rise out of Jake, Ty, and Jamie with his constant teasing. Zane was still too much in awe of Cole to bother him and since Dan ignored him and Randy just laughed, he was quickly running out of targets. Until one morning, as he stepped out onto the porch after breakfast, he saw Jenny waddling across the valley. She had taken to wearing Jamie's clothes when she outgrew her own, something she had done all her life, but even those were getting too small for her belly, which seemed to have doubled in size overnight. She was well into her eighth month and feeling every bit of it. Sleep was almost impossible with the heat and the constant activity of the baby. Her feet were swollen, her eyes had huge circles beneath them, and she didn't have the patience to braid her hair. Jenny was miserable, but Zane was bored, and as she labored up the steps to Grace's cabin, he couldn't help himself.

He mooed.

Jenny stopped in her tracks and looked at Zane, who returned her look with a gleeful smirk. She didn't hesitate. A mop and bucket were sitting by the door and Jenny took the mop in her hand and swung the wet mass at Zane, striking him squarely in the jaw. She lost her balance as she spun on her heel and crashed into Dan, who was coming through the door. He managed to catch her without too much trouble and looked up to see Zane teetering on the edge of the porch with a mop tangled in his arms. Jenny straightened up and went for the bucket, which was still filled with dirty water from Grace's earlier cleaning. Dan grabbed it instead and pitched the contents at Zane, who was still trying to regain his balance. He handed the empty pail to Jenny as they stood on the edge of the porch and watched Zane untangle himself from the mop.

"Dang it, Jenny, I was just teasing," he exclaimed. Jenny threw the bucket at him and went on into the cabin. "She's as bad as her brother," Zane muttered as he pulled the wet fabric of his shirt away from his chest. Randy had joined Dan on the porch and they both laughed. "What are you looking at?" Zane griped as he came to his feet and dusted himself off.

Grace had watched the entire incident from her window and greeted Jenny with a saucy smile when she came in. Jenny's wide blue eyes sparkled with merriment as the sound of Dan and Randy's laughter drifted in.

"What did he do?" Cole had to ask.

"He mooed," Jenny said as she settled heavily into a chair. Chase and Cole exchanged glances, then burst into laughter. Jenny stuck her tongue out at both of them as she reached for a biscuit. "The next time he does it, I'm going to change him from a bull into a steer."

"You mean finish up what you started last summer?"

Chase was happy to see some of the tension ease from Jenny.

"Exactly." Jenny grinned around the biscuit.

"What did you start last summer?" Cole was anxious for the story, especially if it involved Zane, and soon the four of them were laughing hysterically as Jenny told them about Zane trying to get romantic with her in the tack room and how he had limped painfully afterwards. Unfortunately, the laughter along with the weight of the baby put too much pressure on her bladder and Jenny had to make a mad dash for the outhouse. Chase, Cole, and Grace managed to restrain their laughter at that until she was safely out of earshot.

"Oh, it's so good to laugh again," Grace finally said as she wiped the corner of her eyes.

"Yes, it is." Cole grabbed her hand and squeezed it gently.

"Do you think you can spare me for the day?" Chase asked.

"It's not up to me; you're the top man around here now that Ty's gone," Cole replied.

"I was thinking about taking Jenny out to the lake before the baby comes."

"That's a great idea." Grace jumped to her feet. "I'll fix you a lunch."

An hour later found Chase and Jenny in the buggy slowly making their way to the lake where Chase had taken her the summer before. It was the place where they had learned about each other and made their plans for the future. There wasn't much of a trail to the place, which made passage difficult in the buggy, but luckily the terrain was fairly flat and rolling. Jenny had not been away from her small valley since the day of Jamie's funeral, and she soaked up the sights and sounds gratefully from beneath the cover that Chase had raised to keep the sun off her. It wasn't much help, however, and by the time they arrived, Jenny was miserable again, although she tried not to show it.

I am a cow, she thought as she lumbered down from the buggy with Chase's help. She pulled the damp fabric of her shirt away from her sides. At least her hair was out of her way. Grace had braided it for her and pinned it up off her neck. Chase spread the quilt and helped her down. "I might not be able to get up again," she huffed as she tried to find a comfortable spot.

Chase returned to the buggy and came back with the hamper and a pillow. The pillow helped, but Jenny still looked miserable. Chase sat back on his heels and cocked his head to the side as he looked at her.

"What?"

"Exactly. What am I going to do with you?"

"This is all your fault, you know." Jenny squirmed against a rock that was gouging her backside. Chase patiently flipped the quilt up and tossed the offensive stone towards the water.

"I don't remember you protesting too much," he said as the rock hit the water with a distinctive plink. "As a matter of fact, I remember a time last summer when I was the one saying no." Chase unlaced the short boots that Jenny had taken to wearing when she could no longer pull her usual ones on. "And if I re-call, it happened right here." He pulled off her boots and then her socks.

Jenny settled back on the pillow to enjoy the feel of the cool grass against her swollen toes. "That wasn't my fault," she said, closing her eyelids. "You were tempting me." The bright sunlight disappeared from her view as he leaned over her. She opened one eye to find his face inches from her own.

"As you tempt me." He planted a kiss on her sur-prised lips.

"Liar," she laughed as she shoved him away.

"You are beautiful, Jenny. How could you not be?"

"I'm fat and swollen and my hair is a mess."

"You're carrying my child and you're beautiful." He kissed her hand and brought it up to his cheek. "I think I know what you need." Chase reached for a button on her shirt.

"Chase, no," Jenny groaned.

"Shh, trust me."

Jenny pushed his hand away.

"You're supposed to love, honor, and obey, remem-ber."

"Where's that mop I used on Zane?"

Chase laughed as he unbuttoned her shirt and pulled it off. The pants were easier since they were tied together with a piece of rope. He pulled them down and tossed them aside, along with her under-garments.

"Just hurry up, it's too hot for this."

"I know." Chase quickly stripped off his own

clothes, a sight that Jenny didn't mind watching. He had finally put back the weight he had lost last winter and regained his strength and more. He was now doing the work of two men. The scar on his tightly sculpted abdomen stood out starkly white against the tanned bronze of his skin. Another scar marred his back, a wound that matched her own, which was now stretched beyond recognition. Chase made a show of flexing for her, which brought a giggle, followed by a laugh as he scooped his arms beneath her and carried her down to the lake.

The water was chilly against her warm skin and Jenny finally felt herself relax for the first time in weeks as she was taken into its cool embrace. She floated on her back, lightly supported by Chase's sturdy arms, and sighed as the tension eased in her back and sides.

"Better?"

"Yes." It was heavenly, she realized. She suddenly felt serene in the quiet of the lapping waves. Chase dropped his arms from beneath her as she found her balance and floated on top of the water. She felt the gentle rolling inside her as the baby shifted position. "This is what's it like."

"What?"

"For the baby, he's inside floating like this."

Chase scooped some water up between his hands and let it drip over her protruding belly. "And here I thought he was wrestling cows the whole time." He scooped up another handful of water and let it sluice over her stomach, watching her face as the lines of anxiety dissipated. The past year had been hard on her, but except for an occasional complaint about the heat, she had born it with grace and dignity. He wished he could say the same about himself. He continued pouring water on Jenny's belly, enjoying the sight of the drops trickling down and pooling between her breasts where her silver locket nestled, before they found their way back home. He made it into a game, quickly bringing another handful up before the last trickled away. But when he looked up and found himself drawn into the azure pool of her eyes, his playfulness faded away. And he suddenly felt very warm.

Jenny found the soft bottom of the lake with her feet and stood. She took Chase's hand and pulled him out to where the water was deeper and her stomach disappeared beneath the surface. "There is one difference between this summer and last." Her voice was husky as her arms came around his neck.

"What's that?" His mouth found the ticklish spot on her neck.

"We are married now."

Chase felt the familiar tightening in his loins as Jenny wrapped her legs around his waist. Dare he, with the child so close to coming? Her hand trailed down his cheek as she leaned back in the water. He gripped her hips with his hands as she tightened her long muscular legs around him. "Jenny," he groaned.

"Yes." Her eyes were fathomless, wide and deeply blue against the gray of the lake. "Please," she whispered against the water. He had carefully held himself in check since the last time, afraid he would hurt her or the babe. He felt his manhood surge against her opening as if it had a mind of its own, which was usually the case where Jenny was concerned. He eased in, gently, carefully and then cocked an eyebrow at Jenny who suddenly had a fit of the giggles. "Afraid you'll run into somebody?" she laughed.

"Let's just say I'm not in the mood for company right now." The water surged around them as he tightened his hold on her waist. Jenny suddenly became serious and Chase found that it did not take him long to follow her lead. His legs buckled beneath him as they climaxed, and they both went under. Jenny was delirious with laughter by the time Chase half dragged, half carried her back to the quilt.

The sun warmed them as they shared the lunch Grace had packed and they talked of little everyday things such as expanding the cabin to fit their growing family, and their worries about their missing friends, who had only sent a note to say they had made it to St. Louis. Then the subject turned to names for the baby.

"I was thinking Hannah, after your mother, if it's a girl," Jenny said.

"That would be nice, Hannah Faith?"

"I like that," Jenny dreaded the next question.

"What if it's a boy?"

"I can't name him Jamie; I can't stand the thought of putting another face with that name." The words tumbled out with her fear.

"I agree," Chase said soothing her. "That's why I brought this." He dug in the hamper and pulled out

Jenny's family Bible. "This is a good place to look for names."

"Oh really?"

"Yes. Just about every name in the Bible is listed right here in First Chronicles."

"I don't think I've ever read Chronicles."

"That's because it's mostly just a list of begats, along with names of places that are hard to pronounce."

Jenny settled down on the quilt with the pillow. "I'm ready, inspire me with some names."

"Adam, Seth, Enosh," Chase began.

"Enosh?"

"Shh. Kenan, Mahalaleel . . ." Jenny giggled at his pronunciation. "Lamech, Noah, Shem, Ham, and Japheth."

"That one would work when I'm calling him in for dinner," Jenny observed.

"Better than calling him Ham."

"Zane would love that one, for sure."

Chase continued with the names, which soon had Jenny yawning. The next time he looked up, she was sound asleep, something she desperately needed. Chase smoothed back a few of the damp tendrils of golden blond hair that had escaped her braid, and continued with the names. Most of them were impossible to pronounce but he kept on, hoping something would make an impression on his mind. When he came to the fourth chapter, verse nine, he stopped.

"And Jabez was more honourable than his brethren: and his mother called his name Jabez, saying, Because I bare him with sorrow." Chase hoped this child would not be

born in sorrow; he hoped this child would bring joy.
His hand stroked Jenny's stomach.

Verse ten was a continuation of the story. *"And Jabez called on the God of Israel, saying, Oh that thou wouldest bless me indeed, and enlarge my coast, and that thine
hand might be with me, and that thou wouldest keep me
from evil, that it may not grieve me! And God granted
him that which he requested."* Verse eleven picked up
with the names again. Chase read it again in amazement. What was it about Jabez that caused the writer
to stop and mention him among all the names as
someone special? Was it because he was more honorable? But the Bible was full of honorable men.
Could it be that simple, that all he had to do was ask
for God's blessing? Was it a chance he himself dared
to take?

It was the most peaceful moment he could remember in a long time. He reveled in it. The worry over
Ty, Caleb, and Jake was still there, the fear over the
coming birth, the responsibilities of impending fatherhood were still present, but for the moment it was
enough just to be. To be Chase lying next to Jenny in
the place that he loved the best. There was sorrow,
there was sadness, but there was also hope and happiness. *"I am blessed."* It wasn't a revelation. He decided to take a chance at everything he had always
wanted. *"Oh bless me indeed."* He had always known
that he was blessed from the moment Jenny had told
him she loved him; he had just never accepted it.
"Thank you God."

A movement on the far shore of the lake caught his

eye and he rose up on his hip. The tall grass parted and he saw the large gray head of a wolf. The wolf moved into the clearing beside the bank, followed by a pair of cubs, who tumbled around his hind legs. The female brought up the rear with another cub. The male sat and watched as his family drank at the lake's edge. Dark, hawklike eyes connected with glowing gold as the males took the measure of each other. *Be at peace, my brother.* Chase did not want to fight him anymore. The cubs nipped at the fur around the male's neck as he patiently watched Chase, who had placed a protective arm around his still-sleeping wife. With a soft yip from the female, the pups followed her back into the shelter of the grass. The wolf cocked his head as he looked at Chase and then he was gone also, as silently as he had come.

"I've been thinking about the name thing, Chase," Jenny said later that afternoon when they were on their way home.

"And what did you come up with?"

"Your father had a vision when he named you. You will do the same."

"I will?"

"Yes, it will come to you and when it does, you will know it."

Chase thought about the revelations that had come to him that day while Jenny had been sleeping. It was funny how she had figured it out in her slumber while he had to think it through. *I took a chance with her last summer as she's taken a chance with me now. Between the two of us, we have a chance to make it.* He put his arm around Jenny and pulled her close. "You're right, I will."

Chapter Twenty-three

On a hot morning toward the end of July, Jenny's water broke, soaking the straw beneath her, and scaring the tabby who had been weaving his way through her ankles. He beat a hasty retreat to the loft to lick his injured pride, leaving Jenny to waddle to the door and call for Grace. It was a relief for her when it happened. She had not slept at all the night before and wondered if she had the strength to make it through another day, much less give birth. She had sworn that her size rivaled the mares and on more than one occasion she'd wondered if she was having twins. Grace came running, along with Randy, who quickly jumped on his horse and took off to find Chase and the others somewhere out on the range. Grace tried to get Jenny into her cabin, which was closer, but Jenny insisted on having the baby in her own bed so they made their way haltingly across the valley with Jenny squeezing Grace's hand every time a contraction hit. By the time Chase arrived with the others in tow, Grace had Jenny in her gown and on the bed and was alternating between wiping the sweat from her forehead and fanning her. Jenny was in the middle of a contraction when Chase flew into the cabin, and she greeted him with clenched teeth and whistling breath as she grunted her way through it.

"This could last all day and all night, you know," Grace said as she wrung out the towel into a bowl. Jenny rolled her eyes at that bit of information and prepared for the next wave of pain that washed over her.

"Maybe we should send for the doctor?" Jason suggested.

"This is women's work," Grace replied. "And all of you should leave." There was a shuffling of feet as Jason, Zane, and Cole joined Dan and Randy on the stoop, but at Jenny's next groan they were all back inside.

"I helped deliver a baby," Chase said, deciding Jenny needed a distraction from the long hours of labor still ahead of her.

"When?" Jenny panted.

"Last spring, somewhere up in the Dakotas. It was a girl and her name is Maggie Perry." Chase shared the story and they all listened in amazement, it was the first time he had spoken to any of them of the time he had spent hunting Logan.

The day seemed to drag, along with the contractions. Cole finally herded the men over to Grace's to find some dinner and they returned as soon as they were done. Jenny was suffering without accomplishing anything, so they all took turns walking her, hoping that exercise would bring the baby faster. She was tired of their constant attention, tired of the heat, and tired of the pain. She dissolved into tears. Chase scooped her up and with one look cleared the cabin of everyone, including Grace.

"Jenny, listen to me."

"I can't."

Chase laid her on the bed and took her face firmly in his hands. "You are going to have this baby."

"I can't, make it stop."

Mindy had said the exact same thing to Matthew. Was there any more helpless feeling than the one he was having right now? "I would if I could. I would do it for you if I could. But there's a reason why women have the babies."

"There is?" He felt her body tense as she looked at him with eyes full of tears.

"Yes, you're the stronger ones." She gripped his hands as another pain took her. "Look at me, Jenny. You're stronger than I am. You could survive without me, but I'm nothing with you."

"No, not without you." The words were lost in the tide she was riding. "Don't leave me."

"I will never leave you. I love you and I love this baby. And now you have to get him here."

"Him?" She collapsed against the pillows.

"Yes, him."

"You're sure?"

"Let's say I'm half sure." Jenny smiled and then squeezed his hand again as another wave overcame her. "Grace!" The time was getting close.

Grace had been waiting by the door and was through it in a second with the men timidly following behind. Jenny had gathered her reserves and gave Grace an encouraging nod when she came in. Finally, after the lamps had been lit, it came time for her to push. The men refused to leave; even after Grace had run them out, they turned around and came back in when they heard Jenny scream. Chase stationed himself behind her on the bed and helped her up, bracing her back against his chest so she could get leverage with her legs.

"Chase," Jenny panted out between contractions. "What if it's twins?"

Chase bent his dark head over her blond one. "Then we'll love them both."

Jenny bore down again, screaming as Grace shouted encouragement. Jason and Zane crept up on the bed, anxiously peering around Grace's shoulders. A dark head slipped out, a lusty cry was heard, and then the baby boy slid into Grace's waiting arms.

"Look at that!" Zane elbowed Jason as Grace took the baby to the basin to be washed. Angry wails filled the cabin. Chase gently laid a kiss on Jenny's lips.

"You have a son," Grace announced as she placed the baby in Jenny's waiting arms. Chase pulled the blanket away so they could count fingers and toes. His skin was dark, his hair dark and silky, and his eyes, when he finally unclenched them to take a look around, were startlingly blue beneath his dark lashes and eyebrows.

"What are you going to call him?" Jason asked Jenny as he admired the baby.

"His father will name him, as his own father did." Jenny looked up at Chase.

Chase took the baby from her arms and held him against his chest. "His name is Chance. Chance Duncan."

"Chance," Jenny repeated.

"He's our chance, we took a chance with each other, and we took a chance at happiness. This is what it brought us." Chase placed Chance back into Jenny's arms and kissed his forehead before he brought his lips to Jenny's. "Chance Duncan, I am happy you are here."

"Finally," Jenny couldn't help adding, much to everyone's amusement.

Jason came to the cabin bright and early the next morning, anxious to see Chance again. The baby had been on his mind all night long, bringing a feeling of contentment that had been missing from his life for quite a while. Jenny was feeding him when he came in, propped up in the bed with the quilt thrown over her shoulders for modesty's sake. Chase came in behind him, carrying breakfast over from Grace's for Jenny. He sat down on one side of the bed as Jason shyly approached from the other. Chance finished his nursing, lying back lazily against Jenny's arm and taking the opportunity to look around. Jason laid a long finger in his palm and the baby gripped it tightly, rolling his eyes around as if to focus on the adult's face. Jenny laughed at him, a silvery laugh full of joy, and Jason said a prayer of thanksgiving for the blessing that had been bestowed upon them.

"Jason, I was wondering if you would do something for me," Jenny asked, bringing his attention back to the present. "Would you write Chance's name in the Bible for me? My handwriting is not that good. Jamie was always better at it than I."

"That's because he had more patience than you," Chase pointed out.

"Guess who gets to be patient now," Jenny retorted.

Jason smiled at their gentle teasing. "It would be an honor." The Bible was lying on the bedside table and Jason picked it up while Chase went to search for a pen and ink. Jason turned to the first pages and stopped, unable to believe what he was seeing as he looked at the words written in a familiar hand. The same hand had written letters to him, letters that were tied with a faded blue ribbon and carefully stored in a box in his study.

The whole story was laid out cleary with just a few names and dates: Jenny McSwaim married to Malcolm Taylor," and a date in 1817, a date that was close to a month after he had been drugged by his own father and placed on a boat to England; Faith Taylor born on a date that was five months after the wedding, but nine months after a Sunday afternoon picnic that ended in lovemaking on a blue double-wedding-ring quilt.

"Jason, are you all right?" Chase grabbed the older man's arm to keep him from falling. Jason's eyes focused on Jenny and his knees faltered. Chase turned him so he landed sitting on the bed, the Bible still clutched in his hands.

"Jenny," he began hoarsely and had to stop to clear his throat. "The Bible, where did you get it?'

"It was my mother's. It belonged to her mother. She died when my mother was fifteen."

"And her father?"

"She said she didn't know who he was, just that the man she'd always thought was her father wasn't. Why? What's wrong?"

Jason smoothed his hand across the surface of the quilt, a quilt that he remembered well. Its pattern had become familiar some forty years ago when he lost his heart to a woman named Jenny. His Jenny, who looked so much like this Jenny. His Jenny, whom he loved more than life but whom his parents would not accept because she was the daughter of a merchant.

"I am your mother's father."

Jenny stared at Jason, then at Chase, who looked just as surprised as she felt. Jason opened the Bible to the page of names. "Jenny McSwaim was the love of my life, but I lost her. You look a lot like her." Jason fingered the corner of the quilt. "One of these corners has her initials on it, and a date. April 3, 1817. She had just finished it and was so proud of it. We took the quilt on a picnic and that's where your mother was conceived. Only I didn't know." He put his head in his hands. "I didn't know."

Jenny reached out a hand to Jason's shoulder and Chance protested the interruption. Chase took him from Jenny as she sought to comfort the man who was her grandfather. She knew the initials and dates were there. She had asked about them many times as a child, but her mother had not known anything beyond the fact that the initials were her mother's.

Jason stood and scrubbed his face with his hands. He walked to the fireplace and stared at the picture on the mantle. "He was my grandson and I didn't even know it." A tear slid down his weathered cheek as he looked at Jamie's grinning face.

Chase was behind him with Chance still in his arms. "I think you felt it. There was always something between you, a spark that none of the rest of us had."

Jason wearily nodded his head in agreement. He had felt it; he'd never understood it, but he'd felt it. Chase looked at Jenny, who nodded in agreement. "Take your great-grandson." He held Chance out to him. It had been a long time since Jason had held a baby, but he reached out his arms and took Chance, cradling his head in one hand, his behind in the other. He gingerly lowered himself into one of the wingback chairs and gazed into the wide blue eyes of his great-grandson.

A letter arrived a few days later from Cat. They had arrived in North Carolina with a hero's welcome. Apparently Ty's family felt that he, along with Jake and

Caleb, was single-handedly going to whip all the Yankees and send them packing. The letter was full of anecdotes about their trip, along with a few snide remarks about Lucy Ann, Ty's sister-in-law. There was also a quick sketch of the manor house, which had been added by Caleb. Despite her humorous tone, Cat's worry for Ty was obvious. She also begged for news about the baby.

As he took his pen in hand, Jason hoped that Cat would be happy to find out that Jenny was her niece. He had never told his daughter about his first love. Ty had been the only one to hear that story. He had never loved another, not even Cat's mother. Theirs had been a marriage of convenience: she wanted all the riches he had to offer and he wanted an heir. He had got the best of the bargain. She had died shortly after Cat was born, having spent all her time and effort making the big house the showplace of the territory. Cat's only memories of her mother came from her aunt in New York. Jason hoped that she would accept Jenny now as a member of their family, along with the baby, Chance.

Chance. In just a few days he had already proven himself to be feisty and stubborn, attacking Jenny's breast with ferocity whenever she offered it. His demands were endless and the valley rang with his cries until he was satisfied. Jenny had explained that she had been the same way, according to her mother. Jason had wanted to hear every detail of Faith's life, about Jenny and Jamie's childhood, and about Ian, the man who had married his daughter. It was easy to visualize him. Just think of Jamie, Jenny had said. Ian had been a strong man who had fought against all odds for the hand of Faith, and won. Would he have turned her poor but ardent suitor away had he been a father to Faith? He hoped not. He thought himself the kind of man who judged others by their character. Hadn't he done that with Chase, and Jamie, and Ty, and the others who had shown up with nothing more than the clothes on their back, and the desire to work? Ian sounded like the kind of man he would have respected. The kind of man he would have wanted his daughter to marry. Just as Ty was.

Jason had seen the homestead that Ian had built. He had walked the rooms where his own daughter had been murdered. He remembered well the sight of Randolph Mason tied to the fence, his dying breath a curse against Jenny and Jamie. He had been shocked at what Chase had done to the man with his knife, but he was shocked no longer. He wished he had done it himself.

The thoughts tumbled through his mind as he took pen in hand to write Cat the news. He hoped Ty would be around when she read it. The letter would be a shock, but he hoped she would be happy to learn its contents. *My dearest Catherine* . . . he began.

Chapter Twenty-four

Summer, like the winter before it, seemed to hang on forever. Preparations were underway for the drive east, a profitable year guaranteed by the army's need for beef for its soldiers. They were still waiting to hear back from Cat on the news about Jenny. Jason checked the mail constantly, always taking time to visit Jamie's grave. One day he came back from town and went immediately to the ridge opposite the house, which overlooked the valley on one side and the range beyond. Jenny and Grace watched him from the porch of Grace's cabin as he walked the ridge, scuffing at the grass with his foot as he measured the distance with his stride.

"Do you think he's all right?" Jenny asked.

"I hope so. It's hard to tell what he's thinking." Grace had been concerned about Jason. He had been unusually quiet lately. She hoped it was just worry over Cat and the boys and nothing else. She had enough to worry about without adding Jason to the list. Zane, Dan, and Randy waved as they rode by, on their way to town for some Saturday-night fun. "It sure didn't take Zane long to corrupt those two."

Jenny shifted Chance to her other arm. "They're young men, Grace. I'm sure they went willingly wherever ever he led."

"Listen to you—they're young men. They're the same age as you." Grace stood with her hands on her hips, looking at Jenny, who had settled in the swing with her squirming son. Chance butted at her breast with an open mouth.

"Yes, they are, and look at what they're missing," Jenny cooed at the sweet face of her son. His wide blue eyes looked at her in complete rapture as he nursed greedily.

Chase and Cole came out of the barn, both of them grinning widely. Justice danced around Cole's feet with his tail wagging like a flag.

"Where's Jason?" Chase asked as he stepped up on the porch. Grace pointed to the ridge, where Jason was standing with his back to them, surveying the land beyond.

"I'll get him." Cole took off towards the ridge.

"What's going on?" Jenny asked.

Chase caressed the dark swirl of hair on his son's head. "We've got a surprise for you."

Jenny looked at her husband quizzically. "What is it?"

"Just tell the bottomless pit here to hurry up so we can show you."

"Oh no, you're not going to torture me like this. What is it?"

Chase just grinned at her and shook his head. Jenny stuck her finger in Chance's mouth to break his suction on her breast and he blinked at her in surprise. "You're just going to have to wait, young man." She handed him to Chase and buttoned her shirt as Chase put Chance up to his shoulder, where he promptly belched his satisfaction with his snack.

"Come on, it's in the barn." Chase took Jenny's hand and led her off the porch. Grace stood undecided for a moment, and then saw that Cole and Jason were coming down the ridge and went to meet them.

The barn felt dark and cool after the late afternoon heat of early August. Chase led Jenny down the row of stalls and then stopped before one with a flourish. Jenny looked over the door and saw, to her delight, a light gray foal standing on wobbly legs beside its mother. His coat was still damp from the cleaning the mare had given him, and his dark tail stood up like a flag as he nursed.

"It looks like Storm!" she exclaimed as she opened the door to the stall.

"*He* looks like Storm," Chase corrected her.

"It's a colt." Jenny wanted to scream, she was so excited, but instead spoke in loud whispers as she sank to her knees in the straw. "In all the years of breeding, we never got one that looked like Storm." She gently touched the dappled gray of the foal. The mare looked at her with soft eyes and recognized that this human was no threat to the newborn who was still nursing away. Jenny ran her hands over the colt's flanks and down the long legs that already showed promise of attaining the length and strength of his sire's.

Jason, Cole, and Grace joined them, Jason chuckling as he saw the foal. "Life goes on," he said with a smile, shaking his head. Jenny looked up and saw them all grinning at her like fools, except for Chance, who was sucking on his fist, for once patiently waiting to finish his interrupted meal.

"Yes, it does." Jenny reached for her son.

Dan and Randy showed up for lunch on Sunday afternoon grinning like fools.

"What's got you two in such a good mood?" Cole asked around a mouthful of food. "Besides the fact that you spent last night at the whorehouse?"

"I would never do such a thing," Dan retorted, filling his plate. "My momma raised me better than that."

Grace poured him a cup of coffee. "She probably taught you not to lie, too, but here you sit doing it."

Randy's easy laugh came forth. "We got Zane good last night." Dan nodded in agreement.

"Oh really?" Grace pulled up a chair as Jenny, Chase, and Cole all leaned in for the story. "Tell us, please."

"Well, you know how he gets around all the ladies—"

"Yes I do," Chase interrupted before details could be divulged.

Cindy Holby

"He was bragging all the way to town about how there wasn't a one of them who would turn him down, and the only reason why he had to pay for it was so they wouldn't get into trouble with Maybelle."

"Maybelle?" Jenny asked.

"The madam."

"Oh." Jenny blushed.

"Well, Dan bet him money that there was one who would turn him down for sure." Dan grinned at them. "Well, you know Zane. He said it had yet to happen and so on." Randy started laughing. "So this morning we put a dress on old Bud, who had passed out in the alley, and snuck him into bed with Zane."

Dan picked up the story. "Zane rolled over and put his arm around Bud and started nibbling on his ear. Then he got a whiff of him and got tangled up in the sheets trying to get away from him."

"He hit the floor so hard that it rattled the chandeliers. Folks came running out of their rooms to see what the commotion was." Randy had to take over for Dan, he was laughing so hard. "And there was Zane, naked as the day he was born, pulling on his boots and trying to climb out the window with the sheet wrapped around his waist . . ."

"And Bud was just lying there all frilly in his dress and still snoring away."

The peals of laughter woke Chance, who had been sleeping in a basket on the floor. Jenny tried to shush his cries but couldn't stop her own giggles at Zane's comeuppance. She carried her son into Grace's room to change his diaper.

Grace wiped the corners of her eyes with her apron. "I wish I could have seen it."

"Oh, the next part is going to be much funnier." Zane was standing in the door, his face red from rage or embarrassment, they couldn't tell which. Dan and Randy took one look at him and then both set off, bowling him over as they tried to squeeze through the door at the same time. They jumped on their horses and rode off in opposite directions. Zane reached for his gun and then decided that he couldn't follow both of them so he headed for the barn instead to bed his horse down and then sleep off the night he had just suffered through.

"If those boys are smart, they'll keep one eye open while they're sleeping," Cole commented as they watched Zane's wobbling progress to the barn.

"Chances are you won't be getting much rest until Zane takes his revenge," Chase laughed.

"Maybe I should find someplace else to sleep." Cole grabbed at Grace's waist as she carried a pile of dishes to the sink.

"I hear the barn is comfortable," she replied saucily. Cole narrowed his eyes at her and gave her a devilish smile. Grace responded by firmly shutting the door against the cool breeze that had sprung up overnight.

"I'd offer you a bed at our place, but it's a bit crowded now," Chase added. Jenny smiled at him over the dark head of their son and handed him to Cole, who took him eagerly.

They all sat back down to laugh some more at Zane's expense and enjoy the coffee and apple pie that

Grace had made for dessert. They all looked up in surprise at the sound of a knock at the door. No one ever knocked at Grace's door; people just came on in, unless it was late at night. Grace answered the summons with some trepidation.

Roger Nelson stood in the doorway with a bundle in his arms that seemed to be moving. He spied Jenny right away and carried the bundle to her. "Sarah asked me to bring him to you," he said with a sigh of relief as he deposited the blanket and its contents in her arms.

Jenny drew back the blanket and saw a shock of red hair falling over wide blue eyes and an open mouth that immediately began butting at her breast.

"Poor thing is near starving. I ran out of milk for him a while back and he just plum run out of energy to cry," Roger explained.

Jenny dropped in a chair and unbuttoned her shirt. The baby latched on to her nipple with a vengeance. "Where is Sarah?" she asked as she watched the baby nurse greedily. Chase laid his hand on the russet head.

"She died birthing him two days ago. If you ask me, she died the day his daddy died. She just stayed around long enough to give this little one life."

"He's Jamie's for sure. Look at him go," Chase said as contented little gulps were heard.

"She named him Jamie, too, and told me to bring him to you. She said you'd take him, so here he is."

"But what about you—don't you want him?" Jenny was still in shock over this turn of events, but the gentle tugging at her breast made the baby feel very real.

"No, I done lost everyone I ever loved and I don't want to hurt no more. I'll just be better off alone." He walked out without another word, leaving the four of them sitting there in open-mouthed amazement.

Chance squirmed in Cole's lap and smacked at his fist. "Hope you got enough for two," Chase said as he picked his son up and handed him to Jenny. Little Jamie had gotten his fill and let go of Jenny's nipple with a resounding pop. They traded babies and she put Chance to her other breast.

Chase held Little Jamie up. His diaper was falling off him and there was a sleepy look of contentment on his face. A loud burp escaped from the sweet face and his mouth widened into what could only be described as a grin. Chase laughed and pulled the baby against him, dirty diaper and all. "You are Jamie all over again," he laughed against the shock of red hair. "Look at him, Jenny; he's grinning like a fox."

Later that evening Jason sat in the swing with a baby in each arm. Excited words drifted to him from the barn. Another new foal had come, another sired by Storm, and Jenny was ecstatic. Once again the Duncan magic was at work; Ian Duncan's dream of breeding horses was being carried on by his daughter with the help of his champion, Storm. Chase had said Ian must have been a strong spirit, since Jamie resembled him so. And now this little one, whom Chase had christened Fox, embodied his spirit again. Two sets of wide blue eyes looked up at him as he gently moved the swing back and forth, lulling the babies into a state of contentment. Jason knew this wouldn't last long, since Chance was already sucking greedily on his fingers. "Faith and Ian." Saying their names helped him to know them better. "Look at what you started."

The trip to town had not been as hard as Jenny had thought it would be. Of course, this trip had not ended as tragically as the last one, nine months ago. This one had been for the christening of her two sons, Chance Jason Duncan and James Ian Duncan, Junior. The entire service had almost been comical when she thought about it. Jenny and Chase had served their roles of proud parents well; Jason had beamed with pride at having two great-grandsons. But the well-meaning honorary uncles had caused nothing but problems as they all gathered around the font of the church, jostling against each other for position. It was a miracle that they made it through the service without Chance screaming the church down. Luckily Fox had behaved; he was as easygoing as his father had been.

Jenny patted the back of her son as she gently pushed the swing, hoping the gentle swaying would put him to sleep. She felt a bit sleepy herself after the feast they had all enjoyed at the big house. The demands of two babies were catching up with her, but she didn't mind. The joy of having both of them outweighed any problems they caused. It was a good kind of tired, a contented one. Jenny happily mused over the letter from Cat that Jason had read to them; it was full of excitement over the news of Chance, and Jenny's relationship to them. Of course, Cat expressed her worry about Ty, Caleb, and Jake, but there was nothing they could do about that but pray. Jenny couldn't wait to hear about Cat's reaction to the news of Fox's arrival.

She looked up on the ridge where she could see a shock of copper hair against the strong shoulder of her handsome husband. Chase knelt before the marble headstone that had been placed over the newly dug grave that now lay on the ridge. Jenny watched as he rearranged Fox in his arms, bringing him down on his lap and facing him toward the stone. He reached out a hand to touch the letters that were carved in the monument and even though she couldn't hear him, she knew what he was saying.

"Fox, this was your father, Jamie."

CHASE THE WIND
CINDY HOLBY

From the moment he sets eyes on Faith, Ian Duncan knows she is the only girl for him. But her unbreakable betrothal to his employer's vicious son forces him to steal his love away on the very eve of her marriage. Faith and Ian are married clandestinely, their only possessions a magnificent horse, a family Bible, a wedding-ring quilt and their unshakable belief in each other. While their homestead waits to be carved out of the Iowa wilderness, Faith presents Ian with the most precious gift of all: a son and a daughter, born of the winter snows into the spring of their lives. The golden years are still ahead, their dream is coming true, but this is just the beginning. . . .

SAVAGE LOVE
CASSIE EDWARDS

Monster bones are the stuff of Indian legend, which warns that they must not be disturbed. But Dayanara and her father are on a mission to uncover the bones. Not even her father's untimely death or a disapproving Indian chief can prevent Dayanara from proving her worth as an archaeologist.

Any relationship between a Cree chief and a white woman is prohibited by both their peoples, but the golden woman of Quick Fox's dreams is more glorious than the setting sun. Not even her interest in the sacred burial grounds of his people can prevent him from discovering the delights they will know together and proving his savage love.

Cassie Edwards — Savage Moon

Night after night she sees a warrior in her dreams, his body golden bronze, his hair raven black. And she knows he is the one destined to make her a woman. As a child, Misshi Bradley watched as one by one her family died on the trail west, until she herself was stolen by renegade Indians. But now she is ready to start a family of her own, and Soaring Hawk is searching for a wife. In his eyes, she reads promises of a passion that will never end, but can she trust him when his own father is the renegade who destroyed her life once before? As Soaring Hawk holds her to his heart, Misshi vows the tragedies of the past will not come between them, or keep her from finding fulfillment beneath the savage moon.

White Dove

Susan Edwards

White Dove was raised to know that she must marry a powerful warrior. The daughter of the great Golden Eagle is required to wed one of her own kind, a man who will bring honor to her people and strength to her tribe. But the young Irishman who returns to seek her hand makes her question herself, and makes her question what makes a man.

Jeremy Jones returns to be trained as a warrior, to take the tests of manhood and prove himself in battle. Watching him, White Dove sees a bravery she's never known, and suddenly she realizes her young suitor is not just a man, he is the only one she'll ever love.

___4890-6 $5.99 US/$6.99 CAN

Dorchester Publishing Co., Inc.
P.O. Box 6640
Wayne, PA 19087-8640

Please add $2.50 for shipping and handling for the first book and $.75 for each book thereafter. NY, NYC, and PA residents, please add appropriate sales tax. No cash, stamps, or C.O.D.s. All orders shipped within 6 weeks via postal service book rate. Canadian orders require $2.50 extra postage and must be paid in U.S. dollars through a U.S. banking facility.

Name_____
Address_____
City_____ State_____ Zip_____
I have enclosed $ _____ in payment for the checked book(s).
Payment **must** accompany all orders.☐ Please send a free catalog.
   CHECK OUT OUR WEBSITE! www.dorchesterpub.com

WHITE DREAMS
SUSAN EDWARDS

Why has the Great Spirit given Star Dreamer the sight, an ability to see things that can't be changed? She has no answer. Then one night she is filled with visions of a different sort: pale hands caressing her flesh, soft lips touching her soul. She sees the flash of a uniform, and the handsome soldier who wears it. The man makes her ache in a way that she has forgotten, in a way that she has repressed. And when Colonel Grady O'Brien at last rides into her camp, she learns that the virile officer is everything she's dreamed of and more. Suddenly, Star Dreamer sees the reason for her gift. In her visions lie the key to this man's happiness—and in this man's arms lie the key to her own.

Also includes the twelfth installment of Lair of the Wolf, a serialized romance set in medieval Wales. Be sure to look for other chapters of this exciting story featured in Leisure books and written by the industry's top authors.

Half-Moon Ranch

Somewhere in the lush grasslands of the Texas hill country is a place where the sun once shone on love and prosperity, while the night hid murder and mistrust. There, three brothers and a sister fight to hold their family together, struggle to keep their ranch solvent, while they await the return of the one person who can shed light on the secrets of the past.

From the bestselling authors
who brought you the *Secret Fires* series comes . . .